The Demise of a Texas King

By: Ronald Long

EDITION II

Dolly,
It was nice meeting you
& hope you enjoy the read!

**A Detective Robert Lee James Series
Crime Novel**

1

LEGAL AND ACKNOWLEDGEMENTS

Some stories in this book are similar to true situations experienced by this author, while working as a police officer and criminal investigator. In these scenarios, all names and locations, along with specifics about each incident, were changed to protect those involved. Not all situations in this book are based upon true events. Therefore; any similarities to specific individuals or events could be merely coincidental, and are not reflective of facts known to this author.

The hard work and input from the following individuals helped make this project become a reality:

- Editor (Edition II) – Kristin Williamson

- Technical assistance - Dr. Bill Rickman, Diane Rickman, Jim, Renate and Rena.

I also wish to give a special thanks to my family, who encouraged me throughout this venture.

INTRODUCTION

The time was late spring in Texas, 1985. The recession from the oil bust was now just an image in the rearview mirror. Texans were once again showing their resilience. Technological advances, corporate incentives and the absence of an individual income tax aided the state in a rapid economic rebound. The state's financial troubles of the early 1980s were practically gone. Again, Texas was leading the country in economic opportunity.

Of course, money attracts many things, including the lust of some for the illicit pleasures of life. A new evil which recently raised its ugly head in California, was now working its way into Texas. A type of speed was recently created which replaced the pills referred to as Black Beauties or Yellow Jackets. This speed was a powder much more potent than its predecessors. Law enforcement was not prepared for this revolutionary drug. Methamphetamine had made its grand entry into the powerful and corrupt drug world.

Crime statistics in Texas began to increase to historical numbers. Individuals murdered as well as police officer deaths lead the nation. The Texas penal institutions could no longer contain the criminals who needed to be incarcerated. This rise in crime was attributed mostly to the repercussions of the drug industry in the state. Cocaine and heroin were arriving over the border from Mexico and Central America. Methamphetamine labs were springing up all over Texas. Then, there was a new drug called, "Ecstasy."

During this time-period Robert James, a young rookie detective, evolved into one of the top law enforcement agents in his field. However, Robert exhibits professional immaturity as well as a zest for women, which hinders his ability to recognize his own skills and accomplishments. This novel follows Detective James' journey through an exciting and exhilarating career, and observes as Robert is forced to transcend from a basic boy-scout into a true professional, which became necessary for what is forthcoming.

For the past eleven years the FBI and other law enforcement agencies engaged in the frustrating pursuit of Drug Lord, Gene King. The cops finally begin to realize that Gene is one of the most intelligent and elusive criminals they have ever encountered, and their frustrations become more apparent as they are forced to deal with the trail of dead bodies that his organization leaves behind. A criminal who seems to be untouchable and a junior detective who is unsure of his capabilities are destined to meet. Unknown to each, for the past five years their paths have crossed several times. Therefore, a collision course is inevitable. The question becomes "can the fox survive the wolf?"

This novel will captivate readers with suspense and intrigue as Detective James enters into the world of drugs, the sex industry and murder. Will this junior detective be able to dethrone Gene King? The exciting journey and stunning conclusion will leave all readers begging for the next Detective James novel.

MEMORIAL DONATION FUND

On the night of June 04, 2009, Coach Don Nelson's life was tragically taken by a suspected drunk driver. Don was a father, brother, school teacher and coach, along with a friend to many throughout the State of Missouri.

For the multitudes who knew Don, memories of unselfish acts and giving, along with his incredible sense of humor, will never be forgotten. Only second to his family, Don's love for school children and his desire to see each one excel was his life's priority. To assure that Coach Nelson's endeavors and dreams are not forgotten, a scholarship fund was initiated. We would ask that each of our readers consider donating to the Don Nelson Memorial Scholarship Fund, to help keep Coach Nelson's dream alive. In addition, a portion of the profits derived from this book purchase will be donated to the Don Nelson Memorial Scholarship.

Donations can be mailed to:

"**The Don Nelson Memorial Scholarship**," In Care of Security Bank of Pulaski County, Post Office Drawer S, Waynesville, Missouri 65583"

DEDICATION

This book is dedicated to the men and women who serve and protect their citizens as law enforcement officers. A special recognition is due to those individuals who work in an undercover capacity, and the sacrifices they make on a daily basis to fulfill the obligations of their assignment. "Taking a journey to the dark side of society," is a unique task that few of their peers will ever experience. The overtime hours each investigator works, along with the dangerous situations they endure, are appreciated by this author. Hopefully my book will enable fellow officers and citizens to better understand and appreciate the efforts of these special law enforcement officers. May God bless and protect their journey.

During my tenure as an undercover law enforcement officer, I had the opportunity to work with exceptional detectives and supervisors who were inspirational to my life and career. To these eternal friends I express my gratitude for the guidance, protection, and memories while serving by your side. Without you, the Detective Robert Lee James series would not have been a possibility.

A special recognition also goes out to the soldiers of the United States Military Forces, who help make the world a safer place.

"Semper Fi, Kristin Paige!"

CHAPTER 1

Summer-1983

Summers in the Ozarks were hot as hell. No breezes existed —just thick, hot air. The heat of Texas or Arizona would have been more welcomed.

The best part of summer to Robert James was that the hot weather seemed to bring out the liberal personalities of the young women in his city. Short shorts, mini-skirts and tank tops — it didn't get much better.

Women draped in scanty summer attire always made working patrol a worthwhile project during the warm months. This summer would be different. Recently, Robert was promoted to the rank of detective, so the benefit of working patrol was gone.

Robert's five-day work week always seemed to interfere with playtime. Working property crimes and fraud cases became routine, to the point that this junior detective longed for the one, "Big" exciting case to come along. Robert's statistics reflected that he had become one of the better detectives in the department. Detective James' clearance rates were exceptional, and his arrest statistics were second to none. This meant little to the detective, who attributed his success mostly to luck. Despite his doubts, Robert was ready for the big case, which was soon to come.

Several months later, the summer heat was beginning to fade as the fall weather forced its way in, making cooler temperatures in the Ozarks. In September, Robert received the news that serial killer Luke Henry was coming to town. Luke was arrested several months earlier for committing a murder in Chicago. Since it was now 1983, an investigative tool, DNA testing, was becoming the new crime crusher in the law enforcement arena.

After his arrest, Luke Henry was linked to numerous other crimes. Once he discovered that his murderous road was ending, Luke entered into a plea bargain with a Federal Prosecutor. In exchange for his life being spared, Luke agreed to assist authorities in solving other related murder cases, several of which were committed in southern Missouri.

Luke Henry's murderous past included taking the life of numerous men, women and teenagers, of whom many were young boys. Thus, Luke could not be placed with the jail's general population and special accommodations had to be made. In the detective's office at Springdale P.D., a lone holding cell became the temporary home of Luke Henry. Instructions were given by FBI agents that Mr. Henry would be under constant surveillance by police officers, twenty-four, seven. The twenty-four hour a day vigil soon began.

Detective James' first assignment with Luke happened to be the midnight shift on Saturday night.

"Go figure," thought, Robert. *"I was hoping to add another number to my little black-book tonight."*

"Damn the bad luck." This thought was followed with a heartfelt chuckle.

Babysitting Luke Henry was one of the few jobs that Robert did not mind interfering with his social life. Still, a free-spirited detective bachelor did not often have a date with a serial killer.

As Detective James entered the police station, it seemed peculiarly quiet. He had not worked a night shift for over a year. As Robert proceeded to the second floor, he made his normal stop at the vending machine, put in seventy-five cents and pressed A-5. Down came a small bag of chocolate chip cookies. After purchasing a diet cola to wash down his favorite food, Robert made his way to the detective division.

"About time," exclaimed Detective Gus Ross, who was attentive to the eleven minutes that Robert was late.

"What the hell can be so exciting for an old fart like you to get home to anyway? The three kids and wife?"

"Hell, boy, its Saturday night. Momma has a date with her daddy!"

"The city is fortunate tonight. If I were not here in this dump, the riot squad would be responding to my house to help me fight off all the women. Better yet, Gus, you stay here and I will go home and take care of Momma for you. She probably would appreciate a little excitement in her life!"

"Crazy ass rookie! Over there is your date for the night," Gus replied, pointing toward the holding tank as he exited.

For a moment, Robert forgot his purpose for working on this Saturday night. The thought of Gus going home to his wife of twenty-two years was intriguing. A woman usually could not keep Robert's attention for more than three or four dates. Now here is his friend Gus, going home to someone that he has slept with hundreds, or possibly thousands of times.

"Absolutely mind-boggling, thought Robert. *Absolutely mind-boggling."*

Before Luke Henry's arrival, the FBI had briefed Springdale's finest about the do's and don'ts regarding this investigation. As of this date, Luke had possibly cleared over twenty homicide cases. To one investigator, Luke alleged that he had committed over eighty-five murders throughout his life. Some claims were obviously bullshit; others probable, but only a few were confirmed at this point.

The motive was to keep Luke Henry so content that he wanted to cooperate. Contentment would include feeding the man whatever he wanted, and whenever he wanted. In other words, if Mr. Henry wanted a steak at three a.m., it was the duty of the watch detective to find a steak. This duty might even require calling the finest streak house in town to open the door and grill one up. Of course, the top priority was to keep this monster behind bars, while confessions and solving cases ran a close second.

The FBI agents who gave the briefings warned the detectives to exercise extreme caution when interviewing Mr. Henry. At the drop of a dime, this mild-mannered man, who stood five-feet, eight-inches from the floor, and weighed in at a whopping one-hundred and sixty-five pounds, could turn into a lethal killing machine without warning.

The agents that were leading this investigation were members of an elite bureau. The two primary agents were referred as Doctor, not Special Agent like most of the other FBI guys working the case. Each man had obtained PhDs in Psychology and received some of the most extensive training from Criminalists around the world. Detective James recognized one as being a familiar face that had been seen on television. Their vast experiences included assisting agencies such as Scotland Yard and Interpol. Without a doubt, these were two of the world's best in dealing with criminal behavioral science. They had indeed seen some of the most demented minds one could imagine. Therefore, their requests and orders would be complied with devoid of the slightest deviation.

The assisting detectives were also given explicit instructions not to interview the prisoner unless you were a team member assigned to interrogate him. The primary reason was that whomever Luke gave a confession to was required to investigate the crime and possibly testify in court about the facts. The case agents were given details about the other crimes so being able to recognize the familiarities was important in distinguishing the difference between fact and fiction.

Secondly, Mr. Henry was a master interrogator himself. He possessed a demented mind, capable of committing crimes that were unimaginable to most. Luke also had the unique, untrained ability to turn the tables and begin extracting facts about the crimes from detectives, without them recognizing what was occurring. Those capable of conducting an interrogation with this type of person were few. By chance, Springdale had one of the finest homicide investigators in the state, but as of this date success was not achieved. Monday, he would have the opportunity again, to put his abilities to the test. Hopefully, the results would be more favorable during the second attempt.

When Robert entered the station, despite being close to midnight, there were still a dozen or more TV news' crews in the parking lot. They were obviously praying they would be the first to catch an exclusive story about another one of Luke Henry's murderous confessions. This made Robert snicker as he walked past them. If only the press knew that Mr. Henry would be spending the evening with a twenty-six-year-old Property Crimes' detective, they probably would

14

be at their hotel bar right now. KTTA, the local TV station, was nowhere in sight.

"Obviously, they received word that I would be guarding Mr. Henry tonight, Robert thought. *I am not a detective on this date - just a glorified babysitter."*

Luke Henry's holding cell was a ten-by-ten-foot room, composed of steel-reinforced concrete, with a two-inch thick bulletproof glass on the front. The door was the typical metal jail cell door, with a small opening that was just large enough to slide a plate of food. This was certainly not the local Hilton Hotel. As much as the Feds were kissing Luke's ass, Robert was surprised they did not rent him a Penthouse Suite.

As Detective James devoured the last bite of his cookie, he got his first glimpse of the man who sent the local press into a feeding frenzy.

Standing next to the jail cell window with his back to the room, was the infamous Luke Henry. To Robert, who stood six feet tall and weighed a muscular one-hundred and ninety-five pounds, Mr. Henry looked somewhat meek. He resembled nothing of a man who purportedly tortured and killed over eighty-five people with a knife or similar weapon in hand. In Detective James' mind, this man would have needed a forty-four Magnum to do the job. It was now time to meet the monster man.

Luke Henry did not move or acknowledge the young detective's presence as the detective silently approached. The closer Robert got, the more apprehensive he became. There was no physical intimidation, not even a word spoken, but a certain aura filled the air. Robert was certain that Luke knew instinctively that he was closing in, maybe similar to that of a creature in the wild.

Now twenty feet and closing, Robert almost approached the criminal, when suddenly Luke turned around to face him. The room was only partially lit, which cast a slight shadow on the killer's face. From what Robert could see, the man classified as a monster looked more like a pussycat. His face appeared to be older than his age. His facial skin was wrinkled and drooping, with little to no muscle tone. Luke's body was not much different. For certain, Luke had never seen a day in the gym or ever stepped onto a construction site. Physical labor was obviously not part of his daily routine; nevertheless, that uncomfortable aura was there.

Detective James' footsteps slowed from a brisk walk to a cautious, silent shuffle-seemingly to avoid Mr. Henry hearing his approach.

Luke Henry watched every step Robert took, as if he were evaluating his prey.

Three feet from the glass window, Detective James stopped. Initially no words were spoken. The first interaction was from Mr. Henry, which consisted of a slight smile. His eyes did most of the speaking. This man of small stature was not transparent. Without a mistake, he was the monster, the notorious "Luke Henry."

Mr. Henry's appearance added up now-the aura, the smile and the evil eyes were definitely those of a killer. Detective James had met very few true killers, but Luke was unmistakably a killer. It did not take a trained detective to make that conclusion. Robert had to commend the Feds. Maybe they were right this time. Luke Henry's crime spree was too big for most law enforcement officers to handle. At this point, Robert fully recognized his role as being that of nothing more than an insignificant babysitter.

The young detective spoke the first words.

"I am Detective James and I will be your babysitter for the evening, Mr. Henry."

"Nice to meet you, Robert," replied Luke, revealing a slight smirk on his face.

It was obvious that Robert was seasoned in this game and knew not to let the cat know that the mouse was out of the bag.

"You know the rules. I must keep this brief. So, what can I get you to eat, Mr. Henry?"

"How about some chocolate chip cookies and a diet cola?" Again, Luke smiled with his reply.

"Coming right up."

Robert turned his back to Mr. Henry, knowing the criminal was proud of the fact that he took the detective by surprise. He knew that right about now Robert was trying to figure out two things. The first, how the hell did he know my first name and second, what about the chocolate chip cookies?

Little did he know that Gus had told Mr. Henry that Robert James would be the detective relieving him. Gus also made a comment to Luke after he heard someone at the vending machine. Knowing that Robert was a chocolate chip cookie fanatic, the sounds from the machine were very predictable.

Luke Henry was pleased that he already out-witted the rookie detective twice, and so quickly.

A few minutes later, Robert returned to the holding tank with a gourmet dinner of a diet cola and chocolate chip cookies. Robert soon realized he had screwed up. One of the few simple orders -YOU NEVER LEAVE LUKE HENRY ALONE.

"Hey, if no one sees the violation, it didn't occur, Robert thought to himself, which is similar to the theory, *"if no one finds the body, then a crime has not been committed."*

He felt assured that Luke was not privy to the rules, but Robert underestimated his opponent.

After handing the food through the food port in the door, Robert began to walk away, but Luke Henry was apparently in the mood to socialize. Luke asked the detective questions, but got little to no response. Luke knew the angle to pursue next.

"Robert, if I would have asked for a steak dinner, would you have driven to the restaurant and picked it up for me?" Henry smirked.

Detective James did not reply.

"Let's see," Luke continued, *"that would require leaving me alone for about an hour, instead of three minutes. Robert, Robert, Robert, Captain Hill would be very disappointed in you! Robert, would you like a bite of one of my cookies?"*

Luke's smirk turned into an all-encompassing smile, knowing that he had probably just pissed off his young detective.

Without hesitation, Detective James again left the room, returning a short time later with more cookies and a cola. He then walked over to the cell and handed the two items through the food port in the cell door.

"I just saw Captain Hill at the vending machine and he sends his regards. You can thank him for the extra items on Monday."

Mr. Henry seemed bewildered and amused over what he witnessed from the detective, which was a brazen violation of the rules, again! Detective James was, indeed, a boy scout in the public's eye but a bad boy at heart. Luke was beginning to enjoy the game in which they were now engaged.

As Robert began to walk away, Luke asked him to stop. He began to explain how he knew Robert's first name, as well as his lust for chocolate chip cookies. In law enforcement, rookies learn at the academy that the world is black and white, night and day, with no gray areas. They are not taught that somewhere in between, a foggy area may exist, which is one area where good and bad or white and black meet and blend without either party having to cross completely over the line. A professional mutual respect, one might have it-both men had just met in that gray, foggy area.

"Want to chat, detective?"

Without a reply, Detective James pulled up a chair and a long and interesting evening was about to begin.

CHAPTER 2

Before the night was over, the vending machine was out of cookies and the stack of diet colas was piling up. Luke found Robert incredibly easy to talk with. He did not possess the arrogance of the federal agents or homicide detectives, who tried to implement training or psychology techniques to extract a statement.

To Luke, Detective James was intelligent, but uncomplicated; experienced, but still learning; harsh, but compassionate. Robert seemed to be a man who enjoyed his job but did not put work first in his life. The trait Luke liked most - a cop who enforced the law but had a little touch of "bad-boy" inside. Now, Luke Henry had someone with whom he could really communicate with. He liked the young detective, which became apparent from the information Luke shared freely this evening.

Detective James was all ears. He spoke few words, except to acknowledge the facts of Mr. Henry's confessions. These renditions were much too bizarre to be fabricated. One confession Luke told involved the murder of a college student who was working at a local hardware store. This young man was only two weeks away from college graduation when Mr. Henry chose to end his life.

According to Luke, just before sunset three years ago, he was traveling from Jonesboro, Arkansas to Kansas City, Missouri when he ran out of money. He only had a few dollars in his pocket, which was not nearly enough to buy gas to travel the last two hundred miles.

Initially, Luke intended to rob a convenience store, knowing though that it would only yield a limited amount of money. Next door to the convenience store was Courtland's Hardware. A sign on the door indicated that it closed at seven P.M., only ten minutes away. Knowing the store would have a day's supply of money available; Mr. Henry made it his target. It was time for payday. Luke never mixed business with pleasure, but this day was going to be an exception.

Upon entering the store, Luke noticed a slim, young man behind the counter, who appeared to be working alone. Immediately, Luke was attracted to him. Not in a homosexual way – but as a ripe victim, ready to be plucked from the vine. His motive soon changed. It would be murder first, robbery second.

The store clerk's primary focus was preparing the store for closing. When Luke refused the offer of assistance from the unsuspecting young man, the clerk continued his calculations at the register. Meanwhile, Luke Henry browsed the store, searching for an ideal weapon. In front of him was a smorgasbord of weapons, a display of hammers of different type for any occasion imaginable.

Luke looked for a claw hammer, with nice padding on the handle and with a head made of polished chrome. Luke figured the young clerk was deserving of the best, so he picked out the most expensive one. Right before he left the display, Luke noticed a small, wooden handled tack hammer, just like the one he used on this first victim, his sister Sarah. For memorabilia purposes, Luke removed the smaller hammer from the shelf, too, and slid it into the front pocket of his jeans.

It had been a good day at the store; the clerk had over three-thousand dollars in cash lying on the counter, and this amount did not include credit card receipts. The owner would be proud.

While the clerk sorted the bills into proper denominations, Luke managed to sneak up behind the young cashier. At this point, he drove the claw portion of the hammer into the young man's skull. Blood began to spurt in all directions, including onto Luke's face and body. The fluid was warm to him, to the point of even being sexually exciting. Luke maintained a firm grip on the handle until all life was drained from the young man. He was now dead, number 46 for Mr. Henry.

Much to Luke's despair, in his one and only move of attempted survival, the clerk reached toward Henry, at which time he grabbed the small tack hammer that Luke had stashed in his pocket. The victim was unable to do anything with it, but now he had an inanimate object to comfort him through his journey of death. Luke tried to pry the hammer from the grips of the young man but found the task to be difficult, due to the fingers locking when he died.

Desperate not to leave without a souvenir, Luke briefly left the victim to search for a tool he could use, preferably a pair of pliers. He knew where they were, right next to the hammers. As Luke passed the hammer aisle, he debated grabbing another tack hammer but no, the one in the dead man's hand was a real souvenir; it was saturated with the victim's blood.

Luke Henry found a pair of pliers he felt was fitting for the task. Returning to the victim, the murderer used the tool to pry loose the tack hammer. Upon doing so, all five fingers had to be broken.

Up until now, this event was a true dilemma for the original investigating detective but not anymore. By chance, Robert was the backup officer for this call several years ago when it occurred. He remembered it like the murder had taken place yesterday. This was yet one of the calls that made him second-guess his choice of profession, but today, it all made sense.

This was one of many stories Detective James listened to that evening, as Luke Henry revealed his evil soul. Every word of each confession was captured on tape, as Luke had requested.

Monday morning would come soon, and the homicide detectives and FBI Agents would have little work to do. Robert could hardly wait! Now was the time to call Captain Hill and deliver the news to him.

Before parting, Luke asked Robert for a small piece of paper and pen. An unusual request — but considering what he had just been told, Luke got his wish.

A note was then passed off to the detective, containing two words — a man's name, 'Gene King'. Robert looked at Luke with a bewildered face.

"This is the path to your next promotion, Robert."

"What...uh...why?" asked the bewildered detective.

"He's an evil killer, unlike me, who is just a misguided artist," proclaimed Luke Henry as he turned his back and became silent.

It was obvious that Luke's conversation with Detective James was over.

Gene King?

CHAPTER 3

At 7 A.M. on Sunday morning Robert felt the need to attend a church service. Any denomination, any location, he just needed to cleanse Luke Henry's demonic confessions from his mind. This time, wine and women were not capable of doing the job.

It was time to talk to God since he had spent the past evening with the Devil.

To church Robert went, with a Walther PPKS pistol tucked under his shirt, being unsure that even God could protect him from the evils just revealed by Luke Henry. The next sixty minutes flew by, despite Robert's inability to pay attention to the pastor's sermon. Just being in a place of God, a palace of good, was ample enough this day. At one point the pastor mentioned the devil.

"I just spent the evening with him! If only that pastor knew that I personally know the demon he was preaching about. No, only special FBI guys would understand, maybe."

After the service, the remainder of Sunday seemed to crawl by, due to the anticipation of what the next morning would bring.

After a short night's sleep, Monday morning finally arrived. It was 6:30 a.m., and Robert's phone rang.

"Get your ass down here now, rookie," the voice on the line all but screamed.

"FBI, maybe? Homicide Detective, probably, Robert thought."

It was Monday morning and Robert did not have to report until 3 P.M. He drifted back to sleep, intentionally being defiant to the caller.

Forty-five minutes later, the phone again rang. This time it was Captain Hill.

"Robert, we do need you down here, so get up. See you shortly."

The detective crawled from bed, jumped into the shower, dressed and drove to the station. Captain Hill was a no-nonsense type of guy-a good man to have on your side and Robert would make sure it remained that way.

Word made it to the FBI and the Homicide Unit on Sunday that Luke Henry had given Robert a lengthy confession that cleared six cold-case files. Strictly against his marching orders but still six in the bag, the defiance of their orders selfishly outweighed the accomplishment that the young detective achieved. They were pissed and wanted to take a chunk out of Robert's ass.

Captain Hill was proud of his young detective and gave orders that NO ONE was to contact Robert on Sunday. They would not have found him anyway. Robert was at church, a location that none would have thought to look.

It was Monday morning and today in the media's eyes, Detective James would be law enforcement's superman.

Word leaked to the press about what had occurred. On Friday in a quick briefing, the media was told that little progress had been made and that Mr. Henry was not being cooperative. Monday morning, 6:30 a.m., six cases solved over the weekend. What happened?

As Robert pulled into the parking lot, he observed a feeding frenzy of media. Fortunately, no one yet knew who had cracked this murdering monster.

Detective James walked into the captain's office. Inside were several FBI agents, along with their own reputable homicide detective. Each looked like a starved lion, and walking in was their prey. Overseeing this pack of hungry animals was Captain Hill, sitting behind his desk wearing a sheepish grin. Robert then knew that everything would be OK.

As expected, the ass chewing commenced. Robert did not care. He knew what had occurred over the weekend. No special tactics had been deployed and no deception skills used, just the right man at the right place. Success was his and no pissed-off, ego driven cop could take that away. It was Monday and today was his day.

A few minutes passed. Despite mentally zoning and blocking out the abusing rhetoric, enough was enough. Robert's self-fulfillment from this accomplishment would not be spoiled by reprimands about his reckless conduct. He was not going to take this from a detective of the same rank and two FBI agents whom he had never met.

Robert made contact with Captain Hill's eyes. An almost undetectable nodding of the captain's head gave signal to Robert that he was good to go. It was obvious that Captain Hill was proud of his young detective.

"Excuse me gentlemen," Robert said as he slowly walked past the men and headed to the door.

The agents and the homicide detective were aggravated, but they knew there was nothing they could do to stop, Robert.

"Watch your ass, you glory hound, hot dog!"

After hearing the comment, Robert knew the reason for this meeting. These seasoned veterans were jealous of his accomplishment, so they wanted to burst his balls.

The young detective could not help looking back to reveal a "kiss my ass" smile to his comrades as he walked out the door.

It's definitely time for one of Sgt. Park's cigars.

CHAPTER 4

Two Years Prior

"701, be in route to a 10-50, J-2 at the intersection of County Road 114 and Interstate-44."

Dispatch had just sent Patrolman Robert James to an accident scene located just south of the Springdale City limits. In a 10-50, J2, major injuries should be expected. As usual, James was not looking forward to responding to this type of call.

Patrolman Robert James was a recent college graduate. In college, Robert redirected his career intentions from computer technology to law enforcement. During the late '70s, the computer field was still in its infancy but rapidly developing. Despite the growing industry, the thought of sitting behind a desk, watching reels spin and cards shift, bored the hell out of him.

If foresight and maturity had been present at the time, this career path may have been pursued. But who gives a damn about computers and money at the age of twenty-one? A more exciting career path prevailed. Robert's best friend attempted to get him to enter into a federal law enforcement position, such as his own in the intelligence community. Not right now, not at this time; Robert's immediate desire was to be a street cop.

The best part of the call was here. As a rookie cop, there was no bigger thrill than being behind the wheel of a Buick LaSabre Police Interceptor patrol car, with a screaming four-hundred and fifty-five cubic inch motor under the hood. Patrolman James acknowledged the directions of his dispatcher and placed the microphone back on its hook. A glance down at the control panel helped guide his hand to the switch, transforming the sedan into a well-lit rocket on wheels. With red lights illuminating the night and headlights engaged in an alternating flashing sequence, the wail of a two-hundred-watt siren just added to Robert's desire to drive faster.

The screaming patrol car, mixed with a steady flow of adrenaline, was expediting the young officer to a scene he would soon regret. With his heart racing and respirations per minute almost doubled, James was rapidly closing in on the scene of the 10-50. Or maybe he was about to create one of his own while traveling at speeds in excess of one-hundred and twenty-five miles per hour. The rush from adrenaline and anticipation of the unknown made Patrolman James oblivious to the lethal weapon into which he had turned his vehicle. Hopefully, a safe arrival at the scene would follow.

As Robert pulled up to the accident scene, he caught sight of flashing lights from two Missouri State Highway Patrol cars. The presence of blood and mangled bodies was still a difficult sight for the rookie cop. Usually, a late-arriving officer was assigned to direct traffic while the first cop on scene was responsible for tending to the injured and completing all reports. This was not the case at this accident scene.

Upon arrival, Patrolman James was not thrilled with the assignment from Sergeant Bret Parks, who asked him to disregard the traffic post and meet him on the scene. Being out of the norm, Officer James proceeded with reluctance to the accident site so he could meet with the trooper. As Robert approached, he noticed a yellow Ford Pinto virtually wrapped around a tree. It had come to rest approximately two-hundred yards from the roadway, down a small embankment and into the woods. Smoke was still steaming from the engine and the smell of engine fluids filled the air. Without a doubt, it was not possible anyone survived this accident.

Robert came to a sudden stop. He could hardly breathe. Hopefully, no one was watching as he contemplated edging back to his patrol car and leaving. Officer James suddenly realized that the Ford Pinto belonged to Debra Watts. He knew the beautiful young woman well and had recently ended a dating relationship with her, in a less than friendly manner. Despite this, James could not fathom seeing the mangled body of his ex-lover lying beside the roadway.

It was too late. By this time, Sergeant Parks has already noticed that Officer James had arrived on scene. Parks was a large man, riveted with muscle and about as emotional as a rock. A country boy by birth, his rigorous chores of farming alleviated the necessity for a fitness program. Representative of his character, an ever-present cigar

26

dangled from his mouth. In a building or most other locations, the tightly rolled smoking log would remain unlit. While in the field, smoke would bellow from its end.

Most who knew Bret, believed this choice of smoke was not a crutch to divert him from the adversities of his job but instead, to represent his boldness and undaunted emotions. If God ever allowed a demon and angel to mate, Sergeant Parks was truly their offspring. A seasoned veteran, he had seen and experienced anything known to law enforcement during his twenty-two-year tenure. Before becoming a state trooper, Bret served two tours of duty as a Marine in Vietnam, which surely helped mold him into the unemotional icon he was today.

Just last week Sergeant Parks had again bared his soul during an automobile accident where the driver had been decapitated. After a short search in a nearby field, witnesses observed Parks walking out of the woods carrying the deceased's head with a lit cigar stuffed in the man's mouth. Paramedics, firemen and police officers all stood in shock. Not a word was spoken, only the chuckles of Sergeant Parks broke the silence.

"I figured this poor boy would have wanted one last smoke," remarked Parks as he handed the victim's head off to a rookie state trooper.

The rookie trooper immediately turned pale, just before his knees buckled under him as he hit the ground. Sergeant Parks used the uniform of the unconscious trooper to wipe the blood from his hands, right before directing the accompanying training officer to take care of the rookie.

Everyone remained silent as Parks pulled out a new cigar from his pocket. Following it was a metal clip, which encompassed the tip of the smoking log. With a quick snip, the cigar's tip flew off and all watched as it glided to the ground, almost in slow motion. A snicker could be heard from the sergeant as he walked to his patrol vehicle, knowing the symbolism of his actions.

"Is this man a person of total control or total insanity?"

This was a question for everyone who witnessed Sgt. Park's sick display.

27

When Sergeant Parks heard Springdale P.D. dispatch Unit 701 to the scene, he recognized that the responding officer was Robert James. Recently, Debra was almost arrested for trying to ram Robert's patrol car with her own vehicle. The incident and Robert were the focus of many jokes among the local law enforcement brotherhood. Robert had definitely pissed off the wrong female, who cared more about revenge than she did for human safety and the patrol car Robert was driving. All local cops knew the name of Debra Watts and the vehicle she drove.

It was again time to screw with a rookie. As Sergeant Parks observed Robert pulling his cruiser up to the scene, he radioed for the officer to meet him at the wrecked car. Giving his orders over the radio ensured compliance from the rookie. As Robert began his journey down the embankment toward the sergeant, the anticipation of what he would soon witness was very noticeable. The walk seemed to take forever for both men, but for difference reasons. The rookie dreaded the horrors he was soon to see; the Sgt. could not wait for the opportunity to screw with another young cop.

As Robert neared the entangled body of the Ford sedan, Sgt. Parks gave a slight grin as he pointed toward a nearby tree. The force of the collision had propelled the driver from the car into a tree in the ravine below, coming to rest on a branch about twenty feet from the ground. Despite being mangled, the lifeless body was still identifiable and was not that of Debra Watts. Instead, a visiting relative had borrowed her car. Although a relief, the grotesque body took its toll on Officer James. A smiling Sergeant Parks seemed pleased as he watched the rookie vomit beside the roadway.

A few minutes later, Officer James looked up and saw the sergeant approaching him. The young officer was attempting to regain his composure before this cigar-yielding immortal reached him. As the men met, few words were exchanged as Bret handed Robert a newly lit cigar.

"Here, son, you can smoke this while you're cleaning up this mess. I need to leave now. My favorite diner will be closing soon, and I'm way too hungry to let that happen."

Clearly, Bret Parks took great pleasure in his actions and words.

"Asshole!"

Robert was silently bellowing as the sergeant walked from the scene. These words were unthinkable to say aloud, out of self-preservation, but they were warranted.

Someday, just someday, I will have my revenge, Sergeant Asshole!

"Blood, gore, death and ASSHOLES! Did I really sign on for this," the young officer asked himself as he tried to steady a nervous hand enough to write his report.

CHAPTER 5

Robert James was the youngest child of four and a third-generation native of Springdale. Robert's father was a successful commercial pilot. He was a man of large stature, naturally strong, but supporting the sometimes deceptive appearance of a quiet, gentle man.

The James' household consisted of three younger siblings, one other boy and two girls. Robert was the oldest of the four; therefore, Mr. James expected him to be the man of the house in his absence. Responsibility came fast for Mr. James' oldest son, especially after the premature death of Mrs. James.

Mr. James' family always came first, and he was a diligent supplier of their needs, but business took him from home a lot. In his absence, Mrs. James was very capable of being the solo parental figure in her husband's absence. Despite having four children, Mrs. James was able to tend to all their needs, which required mastering the art of multi-tasking. School, extra-curricular activities, sports, meals and individual attention were all done in a skillful way. When it came to discipline, this was the one task that Mr. James was the primary household figure for. Even though his airline job required many days of absence throughout the month, each child knew the consequences of dealing with their father regarding such matters. Each child, especially the boys, did not want to be the recipient of a spanking from their muscular father.

Respect was never an issue in the James' house. Despite Robert's athletic build and notable strength while maturing, the thought of challenging his father's authority always eluded the teenager.

Being a religious and moral man, Mr. James required compliance of numerous rules of ethical issues from his children, with his wife being the enforcer. Hard work, honesty and integrity were three simple words emphasized in the James' household.

When Robert was in sixth grade, Mrs. James died of cancer. The James' children had fond memories of their mother. Mrs. James was the June Cleaver type, a woman who cared for and nurtured her family. Chocolate cakes and backrubs seemed to be two of Robert's favorite memories of her. Despite being young, Robert could remember how devastated his father was from her death. For the first time, Robert saw his father weaken, confirming that indeed he was a mortal as well.

Robert resented the fact that he was not able to bid a proper farewell to his mother. At the funeral, Mrs. James' casket remained closed and her body was not available for viewing. According to Robert's father, his mom's cancer had consumed her body to the point of leaving it grossly disfigured. Before her death, Mrs. James was confined to a renowned hospital located in Chicago, which prevented visits from her children. Mr. James told the kids that it was best that they all remember a healthy mother, not a sickly one. According to him, that is the way their mother wanted it, good memories instead of horrible and sad ones.

After the passing of Mrs. James, a nanny assisted in the role of enforcing house rules and raising the James children. If she were unable to gain their compliance, the matter would be passed on to Mr. James. A few times the siblings tested the system, but Robert never tried. Whether this was the result of witnessing the repercussions experienced by the others or maybe common sense prevailed, obviously Robert had made the right decision. His father was not a man to be challenged.

Robert never forgot the time two drunken men made the mistake of slamming into his father's car while engaged in a street fight. In a cool and collected manner, Mr. James exited the car and rapidly pulverized the men who violated his property. His response was almost effortless, making his father's six-foot one-inch; two-hundred and forty-pound stature seem larger than life. For a young boy, these actions added a point in the respect column for his father.

After his wife's death, Mr. James never remarried. His children weren't sure if this was due to his devout love for his deceased wife or the avoidance of another potentially heart breaking relationship. This question always intrigued Robert the most about his father.

At an early age, Robert noticed how women reacted to his father. One such incident occurred in eighth grade when Robert was visiting a schoolmate, Billy Stone, during summer break. Billy's mother was almost invisible while the boys played that day. Around the time

Mr. James was due to retrieve his son, the boys detected a sweet aroma. Shortly afterward, Ms. Stone entered the room and it was evident that the sweet musky scent was coming from her, but she was even more noticeable. This was the moment Robert became aware of her beauty and appeal. The young man's eyes were affixed to this stunning woman, dressed only in cut-off blue jean shorts and a tight shirt, pulled up and tied, exposing more skin than young Robert had ever witnessed.

For the next ten minutes, Robert was adrift in his own world of fantasy with this older woman. The doorbell rang, and Robert watched in bewilderment as Billy's mother stood inches from the doorknob, but she would not reach down and turn it. In the next few moments, she inhaled a large breath of air, letting it out slowly as she reached for the doorknob. With her face aglow, she opened the door to greet Mr. James.

Ms. Stone's interest in Robert's father was apparent. As his father walked through the door, the scantily dressed admirer greeted Mr. James with a hug, which seemed to last an eternity. Once the bodies separated, Mr. James engaged in a conversation like one never witnessed by Robert. His father was suave and sophisticated, yet seemed to be intentionally elusive in his conversation with Ms. Stone. This appeared to make the woman want him even more.

After a brief conversation with Ms. Stone, Mr. James looked at Robert and nodded toward the door. As Robert began walking out, the conversation between the two adults reached a low tone, almost to that of a whisper. Despite this, Robert overheard Ms. Stone's dinner invitation to his father. Robert never knew how his father responded.

A lesson in relations between man and woman had just been taught to the young spectator. Robert believed that his father intentionally did just that. Similar examples followed but soon Robert became aware that even temptations of beautiful women would not affect his father's desire to remain a bachelor. In a way, this was somewhat confusing for him. Robert could not figure out the reason for his father's elusiveness. Was his dad still in the mourning stage or was there another factor? At the age where hormones and testosterone were raging, Robert did not ponder on the question long. Instead, his mind shifted to this pleasure of life he would someday enjoy.

CHAPTER 6

The house was over eight-thousand square feet in size. The mansion contained modern electronics, hot tubs, a swimming pool and game room among its amenities. About a dozen guests occupied the home, mostly young women and exotic dancers. The music was almost deafening, but the home had been built on secluded acreage outside the city limits of Ft. Worth, thus the volume did not matter. The party was comprised of two men and five women—odds that were only a dream for most men. This dream was reality for Gene King.

The evening party favors were booze, pot, cocaine, ecstasy and speed-indeed, a smorgasbord of iniquity.

As the evening progressed, clothing disappeared, and sex became the sport of the hour. Each man had his pick - one, two or three women at a time. Man and woman, man and women, women with women; it did not matter. The party was a scene straight out of Sodom and Gomorrah, and continued into the early morning hours at the home of 'King Gene'.

Back in Springdale on the same evening, Officer Robert James was working patrol in the central portion of the city next to the university. Clements Bar was a locally owned establishment known for selling cheap drinks to attract the college women. This was also the formula for adding another number to Robert's black book. Almost every night of the week, the club was packed with young women, and men in search of young women. This was a product-rich environment for those seeking companionship. Robert's shift ended at 2300 hours, which was only thirty-five minutes away. It was time for a bar check.

"Unit 701 to 715," Robert announced over his police radio.

When 715 responded, Robert directed him to meet at Clements Bar for a business check. Robert knew that the uniform attracted women. Combined with Robert's charisma, this little tour of the bar would certainly yield him companionship for the evening.

"The badge can get you women, but the women can get your badge."

This was an important adage taught in the police academy that Robert never forgot. Robert soon found the first part to be true. A quick walk through the bar resulted in two possibilities. With confirmations from both females they would remain at Clements until he returned, Robert and his partner concluded their business check.

Patrolman James then drove to the station, turned in his paperwork and was about to walk out the door. The midnight shift sergeant approached Robert, begging him to work overtime due to a shortage on his shift. Robert quickly evaluated his options. Work or date, money or companionship? Help a fellow officer or a hot, young female?

"No thanks, Sarge." He quickly passed on the overtime offer and walked out the door.

Still in uniform, Robert pulled into the parking lot of Clements Bar, took off his uniform shirt and shed his gun belt and weapon. Robert reached for a shirt he always kept in his vehicle for situations such as this. He swiftly evolved from a police officer into a civilian, and entered the bar. A quick stroll through the club and a tap on the shoulder allowed Robert to escape almost unnoticed. He soon left with his prize for the night.

The woman was a tall slender blonde, a sophomore in college. Once the couple entered Robert's apartment, the drinking began. It did not matter that she was only twenty-years-old, and the young officer was supplying alcohol to a minor. After a few glasses of wine, the college student became another statistic for Robert, and was well worth the risk.

Five hundred miles separated Gene and Robert but both were sampling some of the same fruits. Both had a passion for women, a drive worth almost any risk. Both had similar personalities, appealing looks and a lust for the pleasures of life. The men traveled down opposite paths but obtained similar rewards. The finer pleasures of life were usually worth a risk for both.

The next morning Robert woke to an empty bed. A note left behind thanked him for an eventful evening and produced a telephone number. He had scored again, but at the price of neglecting his department and fellow officers. This was an event the midnight shift sergeant would not forget, but Robert had been willing to risk the consequences. It was not just the companionship and sex. At times, this was necessary to make the unpleasant memories of his job disappear for an evening.

CHAPTER 7

Patrolman James began to acclimate to his new career. As with any law enforcement officer or soldier engaged in combat, mental adjustments are made to accommodate the adversities of the job. The recurring, horrific dreams of witnessing a massive fatal accident and human carnage were becoming less frequent. The sleepless nights were beginning to go away. Despite these adjustments, life as a cop could still suck at times.

Robert had the personality, intelligence and physique to take him about anywhere he desired. Most individuals at work seemed to like him. The rookie cop noticed he was winning the trust and admiration of a majority of his peers and supervisors. Minor accomplishments were being acknowledged and praised including letters of accommodation and award ribbons for the uniform. Soon to follow was a promotion to Corporal and then Detective.

Life was good. Robert now had a gold shield in his wallet. There were no more blood and gore calls. Working accidents in the rain and snow, along with refereeing domestic disputes, were things of the past. He would work eight to five most of the time, with very few call-outs. His assignments would mostly involve property crimes and fraud cases. Life was definitely good for Robert-no more Sergeant Parks!

Despite his professional accomplishments, Robert's personal life remained status quo. Many of his friends and buddies at work were meeting that someone special, marrying and having babies. Not Robert. Women were creatures of art: smooth, soft and sensual. Nights filled with body massages, wine and intimate encounters were the only things on the menu for him. Changing diapers and picking up kids at daycare were not on the agenda. A meaningful, spiritual relationship with a woman was out of the question. Robert was proud of the multiple names in his black-book and looked forward to adding more names to the list.

Another successful night at the bars, and Robert was on his way home with the newest entry in his little book sitting next to him. No car wrecks today, no blood or gore. It was just a simple day at the office and a night comprised of wine and women.

On the same evening in Ft. Worth, Gene King finally received the recipe. Gene was a multi-millionaire, who was about to get richer.

CHAPTER 8

In a secluded lab in the Dallas-Ft. Worth area, a new drug had been formulated. Gene King named it Formula-X. This substance was a close, but more potent form of the drug Ecstasy. The best part of Formula-X was that Gene's friend and lieutenant, Bradley Dean, had invented the drug. The rest was simple. Gene owned Bradley and financed the project, making him the sole possessor of the formula for one of the most desired drugs in America.

Working with the Cartel smuggling cocaine into America was becoming a risky business for Gene and others in the drug trade. The Federal Government's newest law enforcement agency, the Drug Enforcement Agency (DEA), was starting to bear down on drug smuggling into the U.S. It seemed as if the government had given them an unlimited budget. The DEA had all the nice toys. Jets, helicopters and modern surveillance equipment were just a few of the items in their arsenal. In addition to these efforts, the government had allocated millions to set up drug task forces across America, which the DEA would oversee.

Just recently, one of the Cartel's 'family members' landed on the cover of Time Magazine for being the largest cocaine dealer ever apprehended in America. Gene felt somewhat fortunate since this individual was one of his colleagues and close friends. He knew it was just a matter of time before the heat would be on him as well if he remained in business with the Cartel. Formula-X was his ticket out. Gene would develop the drug and supply it to the Cartel for distribution throughout Central and South America. This would add to their profits without requiring a total break from their organization, which could have deadly repercussions. In addition, the flow of Formula-X into the south would be a lot safer than attempting to smuggle and distribute the Cartel's cocaine in the United States.

Formula-X was a euphoric, mind-altering drug. It was like combining cocaine, speed and LSD all into one pill. This potent little pill had not been reviewed or regulated by the federal government. Undoubtedly, Formula-X would add millions to Gene's bank account. The precursor chemicals required to manufacture the drug were readily available in any quantities to a licensed professional in the chemical or scientific field of employment. After speaking with his own chemist, Gene estimated they could produce seven to ten thousand pills a day. (Simple math-ten dollars per pill street value, multiplied by ten-thousand. Damn!)

With the only existing copy of Formula-X in hand, Gene walked over to his safe and secured it inside. The smoking room would be his next stop. There would be no diet colas tonight, just a good cigar while nursing a glass of an imported red wine. Life was good for Gene King.

Simultaneously, approximately fifty miles east of the Florida coast, a private vessel floated unnoticed. Larger than a yacht, this small ship was strategically located in international waters. In the distance, a helicopter was approaching. The chopper circled the ship several times before making its approach to land. Clearly, permission was required before this aircraft could set down. As it descended, a melody of colored lights above the deck revealed not one, but two helicopter landing pads.

The evening was dark as the sky had evolved into a new lunar phase, robbing the earth of the moon's florescent light. This gave an advantage to those watching to the incoming air traffic. Looking to the west, another set of flashing lights was visible against the dark sky curtain-evidently a second helicopter.

As the first helicopter landed, several men appeared from the ship's shadows and approached it. The doors of the aircraft opened to reveal three men; all appeared to be financially affluent. Despite being dressed in expensive suits, it soon became apparent these men were not here on business. With cocktails in hand and loud voices reflecting a moderate level of intoxication, the three would soon be enjoying an evening of recreation. Perhaps 'pleasure' would be a more fitting description for the evening.

As the men exited the helicopter, the men who had just emerged from the ship's shadows greeted them. They each shook hands and exchanged friendly words as they walked from the landing pad and made their way to a door leading into the ship.

As the three entered the ship, darkness that just enveloped them was left behind for a room similar to one on the strip in Las Vegas. The area was well lit, with bars and gaming tables providing the main décor, and large enough to host an inaugural ball. The room was occupied by approximately twenty men, each accompanied by at least one female. It did not take an FBI profiler to analyze the situation. The men were all financially fruitful; the women were ready to harvest the fruits.

After the three visitors from the helicopter entered the room, they were escorted to a smaller area in a corner of this vast, floating casino. The host instructed the guests to take a seat on one of the many couches in a somewhat secluded section off the larger room.

The roar of voices and machines made it impossible to know what the visitors were told, but whatever the host was conveying appeared to be protocol. During the briefing, each man was served cocktails of their choice. When visiting this ship individual needs were known in advance, allowing each guest to be catered to as if he were the captain of the vessel.

The short briefing ended, and the host walked away from the three guests, leaving them on the plush couches to nurse their cocktails. Despite being amid such a carnival atmosphere, the men remained seated, enjoying their drinks. Only a few moments passed when a side door opened, and several women entered the area. Each was a beauty in her own way; none were the same size, shape or the same ethnic background. The commonality was that each female wore expensive, revealing clothing-short shirts, clinging fabric and breast-baring tops.

The women engaged in conversation with the guests, and after a few minutes, the group began to disburse. Each man left the small reception area with two women of his choice and faded into the crowd to enjoy. A night of gambling, drinking and sex- all one could expect for a mere twenty-thousand-dollar investment.

While the three visitors were being indoctrinated into the ways of this floating "Sodom and Gomorrah," a second helicopter landed. As it approached, there was no circling of the ship, waiting for clearance to land. The direct approach and rapid descent made it clear this chopper had a VIP on board.

As the skids hit the pad, two men exited the chopper and continued in a direction different from the previous three visitors. There were no hosts to greet them. It was evident that the King had landed. The occupants aboard this helicopter were Gene King and his Lieutenant, Bradley Dean.

Gene proceeded to his private quarters where he was met by several other men. As usual, it was business before pleasure.

"Take me to them," Gene ordered.

Gene was soon led to a room in the ship's belly occupied by only four women; they were not like the women in the grand room. These females were obviously of Central American descent and poverty-stricken. None could speak even a word of English. The women were opposites of the escorts that normally inhabited the ship. Their faces were ordinary, their bodies unflattering, and intelligence was a word none could spell or probably even understand. Each had her own reasons for being on the ship, but the one thing in common was that each had a financial motive.

Despite their lack of beauty, the young women were surprisingly healthy considering the environment from which they traveled. Gene began visually inspecting each female; they, in turn were examining him. Each understood that the man supplying this opportunity for them had just materialized. Due to their cultural backgrounds and inherent feelings of inferiority, none would look directly into the eyes of this American.

Silence prevailed during the visual inspection, but soon a smile appeared on Gene's face. In a tongue native to these women, Gene began to speak. This was just one of the twenty-plus languages Gene could speak, and all were self-taught.

Each woman knew not to engage in a conversation with Gene, but each was delighted to hear the words that reinforced their desire to travel. The women were accepted and welcomed into the kingdom. As Gene spoke the words 'five-thousand dollars', the women's eyes twinkled so brightly they could have lit up the dark skies surrounding the ship. This amount of money would support each woman's family for a year in their native country; they were pleased.

"Send in the doctor," were Gene's last words as he exited the company of the four women.

After Gene's departure, the women remained silent despite the excited nervousness within each of these contestants. They were not

41

certain what lay ahead, except that an opportunity to make some substantial money was near. However, each of the women would make an individual sacrifice to obtain the financial reward.

One week prior, these women were in their native country of Belize, a small country located just south of the Mexican Riviera and close to the Panama Canal. This area was fertile ground for Gene's search. The population of Belize consisted mostly of individuals equal to or below poverty level. They are hard-working individuals whose family members are their most cherished and valued possessions.

The country of Belize is geographically located along the route that some have labeled the 'Trail of Cocaine'. In the late nineteen-eighties, the U.S. Government began a project labeled 'Snow Bird', involving the DEA and U.S. Special Forces on a mission to alleviate the drug labs and Cartel in the region. Following the commission of this task force, agents and troops silently invaded numerous areas of Central America and Columbia. Their mission was simple: to eradicate the cocaine problem. For eight months, the special warriors located and destroyed cocaine labs, along with several hundred criminals associated with the manufacturing and distribution of this product.

The United States heard very little about this project, with the first information being a small blurb in a San Antonio newspaper almost one year later. Back in the target zone, this mission did not need the media to broadcast the results. America's war on drugs was being felt.

As Belize was centrally located around the Trail of Cocaine, the impoverished citizens had the opportunity to see the wealth available to those associated with the Cartel and their drug operations. If one could just have a small taste of this forbidden fruit, their families would be set for life.

For Gene King, Belize served multiple functions. With the country's close proximity to the Mexican Riviera, Gene could slip into Belize without being noticed or tracked by U.S. officials. Planes flying into Cancun, Mexico were mostly filled with Americans who did not need a passport to enter. Once there, Gene would have one of his associates meet him at the airport and they would travel the remaining one-hundred and sixty miles south to Belize in a private auto or helicopter.

Traveling in this manner was protocol for Gene King. His primary objective was to elude the American agents and any tracking programs they implemented. After heading south from the Mexican border, once again he became King Gene.

Following seven years of conducting joint business ventures with the Cartel, Gene knew he had carte blanche in Central and South America. He could attribute about half of his financial success to the drug lords of the south. The Cartel supplied the cocaine and, for the past seven years, Gene offered the means of distributing their product in the states.

King Gene knew this was fertile ground for recruiting help needed to supplement his operations. He was looking beyond the cocaine. Formula-X was now the focus of his attention. Neither cocaine nor prostitution were the purpose of this visit.

His objective during this voyage to Belize was to find a few female recruits. In the previous two visits, Dr. Robert Perez accompanied Gene to assist with the selection process; he was no longer needed. Gene was a quick study and soon adapted to a procedure for selecting these women. Consistent travel with a business associated was too risky, especially with such a valued associate as Dr. Perez. Adding to this concern, Dr. Perez was a family man with a private medical practice in Florida that also demanded his attention. Normally, Gene would not tolerate any outside interferences for his employees, but Dr. Perez was too critical to his operation to argue this point.

Gene wanted healthy women who could not speak or understand English. Young women with families and children were the prime targets and most were pre-selected by associates of the Cartel. These women were trustworthy and loyal, and all had a hunger for money. They were also completely unaware of their expendability if their mission were ever compromised.

The four women on board were selected in Belize by Gene and transported via boat to his ship.

The door to the small room where the women were waiting opened, and in walked Dr. Robert Perez.

"Come over here, young lady," the words muttered from Doctor Perez's lips in Spanish, as he pointed to one of the waiting women. The final process of this selection had begun.

It was almost midnight and Gene's workday had yet to be completed. He proceeded quickly to his private quarters to shower and

43

change clothes before joining his new guests in the gaming room. Gene began shedding clothes as soon as he opened the door to his quarters and walked toward the shower. In the background, a silhouette reflecting the curves of a naked woman could be seen. Apparently, the King had company and the gaming room was void of one its finest escorts.

Despite a companion being present, Gene knew he needed to make an appearance soon. The gaming room was full of life and awaiting his arrival. He wanted to make sure his guests were being pampered in the manner required for making such a large investment in pleasure. The naked female in Gene's room would have to wait. She was there to please the King, but women and sex were something he never lacked. They were always available at his disposal, so it was business first tonight.

A short time later, Gene made his entrance into the gaming room. It pleased him to see his guests were being well treated. The twenty-thousand-dollar fee paid by each man was only for the services of the women and party favors. Gene knew that only those with deep pockets could afford a visit to his floating palace of pleasure. It was customary that once a visitor arrived, free alcohol and recreational drugs, primarily cocaine, were readily available. As their intoxication levels would rise, so would each man's need to boost his ego by outspending the others in attendance. Before the night's end, the poker and blackjack tables would devour an amount of money that made the twenty-thousand-dollar initial fee appear minimal.

Conversation with each guest was limited. Gene knew these men were here for the women and gambling, not fraternization with other men. After making the rounds, Gene secured a light beer for an evening cocktail. The King was a health-conscious, fitness freak who closely monitored the poisons he allowed into his body. Even though surrounded by drugs, Gene knew better than to mix business with pleasure. Too often, he saw the white party powder become the downfall of the men disbursing it. Gene would much rather reap the financial benefits of these vices, than succumb to the simple, short-term pleasures they provided.

As Gene settled into a chair in the corner of the room, he sipped his beer and visually inspected the gaming room. After running a quick calculation, he estimated the proceeds from the evening would come close to the one-quarter of a million-dollar mark.

Not a bad day's earning, not a bad day at all," Gene thought as his workday had finally come to an end.

CHAPTER 9

Southern Missouri was rapidly evolving into one of the nation's hotspots for methamphetamine labs. This unprecedented rise was for several reasons; one of the primary reasons is the result of poorly staffed law enforcement agencies, their untrained officers, and the lack of federal funding for task forces. Because the numbers in drug lab seizures are lower than other states, funds are not as readily available for the smaller agencies to combat methamphetamine producers.

The use of amphetamine throughout the Midwest is comparable to a runaway freight train. At this point, the drug had become so popular that it affects every nationality, race, social and economic class. Methamphetamine is now the first drug of choice for those accustomed to using illegal substances. The supply and demand of illegal drugs were now having a major economic impact throughout the nation. Even the simpletons of the drug world realized there is a vast fortune to be made by manufacturing and selling meth.

In addition to funding issues, geographic factors also make the Ozark Hills a haven for meth cooks. The Ozarks are blanketed with rolling hills draped by large oak trees, which naturally obstruct visual invasion from public roadways. This environment is an improvement from the flat, shrub covered land of Texas, where one would see for miles on a clear day. In the Lone Star State, privacy is a sacred commodity. In addition to the flatlands and sparse vegetation, the prevailing southern winds carry the P2P stench to the neighbors who finally were acquainted with the odor, therefore, alerting law enforcement.

The vast expanses of rocky hills were worthless to most farmers and property owners, so they welcomed the opportunity for land rental to the southern invaders. The sparse population of the Missouri hills also make detection from a "nosey neighbor" highly improbable.

Once the "cooks" nestled in the Ozark Hills, access to their properties became very limited. The small roadways that led to these secluded acres and farms were easy to monitor and block access. Most of the locals in this part of the state are old school, private people. They didn't want anyone knowing their business, and likewise, do not want to know about anyone else's business. A meth operation is conducted here with little threat of detection.

These were the hills where Robert James had spent many hours in as a youth. As teenagers; hunting, fishing and camping were weekly events for Robert and his friends. The Ozarks supplied an abundance of secluded places to escape from the thoughts of school, or to repair the bruises from last night's football game. Mother Nature always seemed to hold the ingredients for healing mind, soul and body. Now, there was a completely new type of ingredient enclosed in the Ozarks Hills; one that destroyed instead of healing.

Law enforcement, or what typically symbolized a police department or sheriff's office, is practically non-existent in this area. The small law agencies run on bare-bone budgets, and responding to calls for service is the primary objective. Being a proactive department was not possible for most of these agencies. Not only is being proactive expensive, but it is also dangerous in this part of the state.

Many law enforcement officials in the remote areas are minimum wage employees. This makes 'greasing the palm' a common practice to get the cops to ignore the illegal drug operations. Most of these men and women were hard-working, moral police officers, but for some the newfound money for ignoring a situation was welcomed.

The southern hills of Missouri are also encompassed by lakes and rivers, providing a high degree of humidity during the summer months. This warm, humid climate has been recognized for decades as a suitable environment for the growing of marijuana. Thousands of acres of hemp plants line the Ozark Hills each summer. Unless observed by helicopter or turned in by a pissed-off competitor, the marijuana gardens are cultivated each year without fear of detection. They are a valued commodity for the financially deprived citizens in this part of America.

As fellow entrepreneurs, the marijuana farmers welcomed meth cooks from the south. Each had a product the other could use, so the welcome mats were extended without hesitation. This type of hospitality was an unusual event in the drug world, whereby the invasion from a competitor usually results in turf wars.

47

The vast array of lakes and rivers also supplies additional routes of transportation to and from the meth labs. One could produce the meth on some remote acreage and afterwards load the product onto a boat. The vessel would carry the methamphetamine to a vehicle located miles away. This in turn protects the location of the illicit laboratory if a seizure of the product occurred.

The Ozark Hills rapidly became the new safe-haven for methamphetamine labs and the accompanying criminals.

CHAPTER 10

Texas was putting the squeeze on some meth lab operations, forcing the cooks and investors to seek virgin territories for their improprieties. Missouri rapidly became a safe-haven for the Texas meth crowd, and had recently caught the attention of Gene King.

It was not his intentions to ignore other drugs while he capitalized from the sales of Formula-X. Gene King was a knowledgeable businessman. He knew it was just a matter of time before legislation finally caught onto his game and made Formula-X illegal, along with regulating its precursor chemicals. This was an expected casualty, so contingency plans were made. Methamphetamine was one of his sacred sources of income. To Gene it was his security blanket: safe, fast and easy to manufacture, and a product in constant demand.

Southern Missouri was his next target. After recently making a joint purchase with a local judge of over two-thousand, five-hundred acres in the Ozarks, Gene was ready to set up shop. The magistrate was a trusting, and unsuspecting man who believed the joint business venture would yield him a small fortune in mineral products. Gene set his safety net, so the possibility of being detected deep in the Ozark Mountains was extremely remote, especially on a judge's property. Besides, his employees were both dedicated and fearful of their boss, knowing that breaking their vow of secrecy or loyalty would most likely be a fatal mistake.

Gene King was a street savvy individual, whose intelligence level appeared to be equal to that of a Harvard graduate. He could understand and fluently speak over a dozen different languages, all self-taught. Gene was a suave and good-looking man—a class act, for a product of evil.

Five days a week, first thing in the morning, Gene was in his personal gym, working out until he could barely move. His evenings were devoted to business dealings and parties. After Gene's workout, he visited his pantry, which contained more vitamins than the nutrition section of most stores. His daily ritual was usually necessary to revitalize his body after a previous evening ingesting his poisons.

Over the years, Gene had witnessed his competitors fall to the addictions of these substances. The result would be their financial ruin, along with a free trip to the Federal Country Club.

Gene King enjoyed money and the pleasures money brought him. Wine, women and rock-and-roll were his preferences. Being someone's bitch in prison was not on his agenda. In his mind, Gene believed that he was intelligent enough to elude the unpleasant consequences. He assumed he was untouchable.

However, the past several months, Gene King began to change, taking a small step at a time toward using the chemicals he once would not touch. A line of cocaine here and there was becoming a daily routine. The burden of running such a huge operation was beginning to take its toll. Despite having numerous business associates, Gene trusted few. The only exception was his Lieutenant, Bradley Dean. Day and night, 'King Gene' was at the helm.

Taking supplements accompanied by working out, supported his illusion of health. Gene believed that his morning routine would chase away the demons from the night before. This ritual seemed to be working, at least for the time being.

"The King" was a believer and practitioner of mind manipulation, particularly with women, who both lusted and loathed him. Over the years, many women had become his victims. Most of his relationships began normally. Gene had the combination of looks and money, which attracted gold diggers, some romanticists, and a few who were dope whores. It did not matter which one to him, since all types were needed for his operations and personal pleasures. Gene was like an evangelist seeking a flock. He knew that women, if worked right, could be great business assets, to run his drugs, attend social events or become party favors for clients. Their ethnic backgrounds or intelligence level did not matter. He had a place for all and needed many.

Once Gene trusted a woman enough, school began. Most of the women he attracted and needed for his endeavors could be profiled as young, slender-built and self-absorbed. The women who think the world revolves around them are perfect. He knows this type of woman was the easiest to mold because this type is so predictable. With his experience, money and drugs, Gene knew that many such women are within his grasp.

The manipulation training game begin with expensive dinners, week-end trips and limousine rides. Money is no object for Gene King. He is initially a charming man—courteous, polite and seemingly subordinate to their needs and desires. This behavior continues until his victims grow to expect pampering and endless bankrolling. Regarding the dope—coke, weed, speed and pills—it was all there. Each woman's weakness is soon to be discovered and played upon. Gene knows that any addiction may be fed, and he comes up with the woman's formula.

Most women take only three-to-four weeks to reach the point of conditioning where Gene wants them. Once there, his disposition changes. The suave and debonair man evolves into a narcissistic, manipulating demon. What the women need, want and crave is no longer at their immediate disposal. Whether it is drugs or money, it is now time for them to earn it.

The dope whores are the easiest. With a few lines of cocaine or a small bag of meth, these women do just about "whatever", "whenever." Some become the female mules for his drug operations and others, prostitutes. The best part to Gene is the women are easily expendable.

Gene knows that most drug agents must profile a male drug pusher ten miles away, but they are usually blind to an attractive, young woman. Sex appeal is a powerful weapon and he knows it. Gene recognizes that when putting a cop face-to-face with one of his women, wearing the usual short skirt and revealing blouses, the officer's attention is soon diverted, as thoughts of sex immediately become primary-a primal instinct, indeed. These dope whores have no limitations.

Others take a little more work but are just as, or even more, important to his operation. King knew if he captures a woman who has some moral ethics and respect for the law, he has a person who could be trusted and depended upon. A major thrill for Gene is to convert a "saint into a sinner." He slowly involves the women to a point of no return. Once they eventually realize what they have become a part of, it is too late. They are already a member of his organization and by now have probably committed numerous felony offenses. Some eventually realize these improprieties. Upon doing so, Gene made sure that each knew every illegality they were a part of, along with the legal repercussions if ever detected by law enforcement.

Another faction of these women were the dope whores, who have no concern for the law or improprieties. The others, who have some semblance for morality, were frequently told of the legal ramifications of their crimes. Gene owns both types, and makes sure that each knows their place.

A primitive lesson, which is most enduring, is the last factor. While in the presence of his student, Gene finds someone to use as an example. They may be either male or female, but always a member of his organization. The victim is always a person who questioned his authority or someone in whom Gene had lost confidence. Maybe this person recently disobeyed him or become so stoned on drugs they became an embarrassment and a liability. Whatever the reason, it did not matter; an ass kicking would commence! Blood, bruises and even broken bones were observed after each incident. Gene was an equal opportunity employer in this area-male and female both suffer the same consequences.

Gene's father, who spent weeks at a time working offshore on oilrigs, raised him, which left the young man to tend to himself on many occasions. Working for money to buy most of his clothes and food was necessary for Gene to survive. Growing up on the gang-riddled, poverty-invested streets of East Dallas introduced Gene to the survival sport of "street fighting." Gene had no desire to become a gang member, and this caused more undue abuse from the younger gang members. Gene taught himself survival skills, which included killing a seventeen-year-old boy in self-defense when he was only fifteen years old.

Gene's crime was never discovered, and neither was the body. Gene knew that without the body of a victim, a crime does not technically exist. Many locals suspected Gene of being responsible for the missing teenager, which helped Gene earn his right of passage and to be left alone. The streets of Dallas proclaimed Gene a man, despite his youthful age.

Gene King and Bradley Dean first met and became friends on the dangerous streets of Dallas. Both had only one parent, both living in poverty and both teenagers had similar likes and needs. These common traits led to an immediate friendship.

Being a street fighter was not enough for Gene, however, he soon earned a black belt in martial arts. Now the physical confrontations could reach a level of violence necessary to send a message. An audience was always present to witness Gene annihilating his opponent. There was always a lesson for someone to learn. On occasion, the person who became the brunt of his aggressions was never seen again. Again, without a body, there was no crime.

No man or woman was an exception to Gene King's displays of violence. Out of either fear or respect, no person dared to report the assaults to the authorities or challenge King's madness. Gene King owned them all.

CHAPTER 11

"Adam-321, be in route to 725 Jefferson Street, Lot 26, in reference to a welfare check," the radio squelched.

The police dispatcher continued by advising the beat officer that a female real estate agent had left her office late afternoon to show a potential client a listing and never returned.

"10-4. Show me in route," Adam-321 responded.

No back up was needed for a routine call such as this.

District 321 is in the middle of a booming, bedroom community located just outside of Ft. Worth, Texas. The area was thriving with lakes, parks and homes inaccessible to citizens other than the financially successful. Crime in this area was moderate, which was unusual in the mid-1980s in Tarrant County, which carried the label as the meth-amphetamine capital of the nation. Here, meth and crime were as analogous as cream is to coffee- one usually did not exist without the other.

Located in one secluded block in the middle of District 321 is a small, mobile home park. When the surrounding properties were being bought out for development, the third-generation, financially secure property owner refused to sell. The mobile home park is where the owner lived as a youth; therefore, the area would remain sacred. The eyesore would remain.

Adam-321 knew this area way too well. Almost daily, officers responded to calls in the mobile home park. Domestic disturbances, thefts, alcohol and drug-related matters all occurred here.

Lot 26 was just ahead. Occupying the property was a doublewide trailer that was only a few years old. A for-sale sign was planted in the front yard.

"Adam-321, show me out on call."

"10-4," the dispatcher replied.

Adam-321 was a seasoned officer who knew there was no such thing as a routine call.

Upon arriving, no vehicle was observed in the driveway but after conducting a visual check of the property, the officer noticed the front door ajar. This was unusual as the customary procedure for real estate agents was to lock the door and return the key to the lock box before leaving the property.

"Adam-321, I have an open door, so I will be going in," the officer notified dispatch.

"Adam-322, be in route to 321's location for a backup."

"10-4. Show me in route."

It was obvious by the complacent tone of 322's voice that he too expected this to be a routine call.

Adam-322 then made a U-turn in his police cruiser and proceeded toward Jefferson Street.

"No emergency lights or siren needed for this call," so thought the officer.

As Adam-321 approached the front door, his instincts began sending out an alert. Something just did not feel right. The officer's gut feeling told him to back out and wait for Adam-322's arrival. These actions define the character of a true police veteran. No one can actually explain what sparks this intuition. Gut feelings and instincts are not used in police reports or referred to in courtroom testimony. This intangible object is discussed many times in rookie school though. For this officer and other veterans, many years of street survival teaches one to trust instincts. Statistics do not exist that account for the many times instinct alone has saved a police officer's life; without a doubt, many more times than ballistic-vests can contribute to. Again, his gut-instincts would prevail. Adam-321 waited.

Within a few minutes the second patrol cruiser pulled into the drive of Lot 26.

The officers were taught to stay together when performing a building search. While one officer was conducting the search, the other would cover his blind side. For safety's sake, this would continue throughout the search, despite the slow pace it required. These officers were veterans who knew that keeping safety first is a necessity.

Despite being late afternoon, the residence was dark from all the shut blinds, which blocked out the intense mid-summer sunlight. This was not a good sign. Just two months earlier, Adam-321 had placed his own house on the market. His listing agent recommended to keep his home as radiant as possible by leaving the blinds open. For some reason, this was not the case here. Accompanying the dark and quiet was an unpleasant odor. This odor was a distinctive one that both veteran policemen had detected many times throughout their careers.

The officers conducted their search one room at a time. The mobile home was immaculately clean but as they approached the back bedroom, the scene began to change. A small painting from the wall was lying in the hallway. Dozens of scuffmarks tainted the shine and cleanliness of the tile floor. Not far away, a woman's shoe was strewn. And there was that odor again, but stronger than before. The officers imagined what discovery awaited them just beyond the door. It was just a matter of the type and appearance of evil that would be revealed this time. Upon entering the room, their suspicions were confirmed.

"Adam-321, we need a Crime Scene Unit, a supervisor and notify the Homicide Unit."

Adam-321's voice depicted what was found. It was not necessary to air that Trailer 26 contained the body of a homicide victim.

The female, approximately twenty-eight years old, was lying on the floor just beyond the bed. For what they were witnessing, the room did not appear to be in much disarray. Yet it was obvious the victim had been involved in a violent struggle. She was nude with the clothes torn from her body. The victim's eyes were wide open and still outlined with dark makeup. A small stream of tears mixed with mascara ran from her eyes downward toward her navel. The young woman's mouth was open, with both corners forced downward by her locked jaw muscles. Dozens of stab marks accompanied by a massive amount of blood covered her entire torso, arms and legs.

Acting like a small dam, a scar on the victim's lower stomach disbursed the blood stream toward both of her pelvis bones. It appeared there could be additional victims of this crime scene. From the signs of her apparent C-section scar, it was believed this victim would leave at least one child behind without a mother.

Next to the victim was her blouse with an identification badge still attached. Printed on the badge were the words 'Clear Water Realty' accompanied by her name, "Jessica." It was obvious Jessica had suffered an excruciating death that was far from an immediate one. Her thirty-eight stab wounds appeared to come from a large butcher or hunting knife. It was later discovered why Jessica died in the fetal position. Her agonizing death was evident from the embedded expression on Jessica's face.

This was obviously not a typical murder, and probably not a rape or robbery. Jessica had just been taught a lesson, an unimaginable one given by one of the devil's own.

It did not take long for Trailer 26 to transform into a gather point for countless law enforcement vehicles and the media. Police and detective cars lined the driveway, along with a feeding frenzy of media eager to violate the boundaries of the crime scene tape. Most reporters were focused on the white van parked near the front door, which displayed the name of its owner "Medical Examiner's Office".

At this point, the only information the media had been given was that Trailer 26 contained a single body, which was the area's most recent homicide victim. To imagine that such a horrific event would soon entertain those watching the evening news seemed almost sacrilegious.

After several hours of waiting, the news crews were about to be rewarded. Being wheeled through the front door was one single stretcher containing a lifeless body that was encompassed by a large white sheet. The persistence of the remaining reporters had paid off. For those who waited, the cameras were now allowed to capture the first glimpse of the dead body. This poor victim would give these reporters a few coveted minutes of television news fame.

Soon after the medical examiner's van left the driveway, a police spokesperson exited the trailer to give the media a very brief summary of what had occurred inside.

"A dead female, whose identity is being withheld, was found murdered inside earlier this date. There are no suspects in custody at this time and additional information will be disseminated in the near future."

The scripted report is very predictable for this type of crime scene. Many reporters questioned the fact that they remained at the scene to hear these redundant words. Each was probably hoping for a brief conversation with a rookie cop leaving the scene, who has not yet learned about media mistrust and the no-tell rule. This is often a valuable source of information that was always worth an effort for reporters at a major crime scene. On this day, there was no such luck.

The cameras began to fade away and the clusters of vehicles were thinning out. Those few who remained in Trailer 26 were the crime scene officers and detectives looking for any trace of evidence left behind. For these men and women, hours of non-eventful work lay ahead.

The exterior of Trailer 26 soon lost its circus type look and took on the appearance of its lifeless victim.

The body was transported to the Medical Examiner's (ME) Office, where an autopsy was performed. The medical examiner conducting the procedure soon made a grim discovery. The murderer's final thrust had embedded the knife deep inside his victim, probably while she was still alive. This ME's office had a national reputation for being one of the best. The scar on Jessica's lower stomach was then classified as the result of a caesarean birth. In this case, this noted medical examiner made an error, and a major one at that.

As detectives interviewed her co-workers, it was learned that Jessica was new to the Clear Water Realty Agency. From the first day, they knew Jessica would be one of those aggressive new agents. She was always hungry for that next sale and the large commissions check. However, Jessica was one of those drug-related success stories. Apparently, in Jessica's prior life she was involved with elements from the dark world of drugs, but no one in her office knew. This was part of Jessica's secret past and it was apparent she wanted to keep it that way.

In the real estate industry, each agent is usually on his or her own, which was no exception for the employees of Clear Water Realty. Shortly after lunch, an unidentified male caller contacted the agency and specifically asked for Jessica. After a brief conversation, the young agent was out the door and in route to Jefferson Street. When she failed to return to the office a few hours later, the police were called, but it was too late; by then Jessica had already met her demise.

Frustration set in after three months of working on the case. Homicide detectives were no closer to solving Jessica's murder than they were on day one. It was difficult to call it quits on such a horrific crime, but the detectives had no choice. The file went to the cold case cabinet, with hopes that someday a lead would come.

"Another cold case file for law enforcement - another memory for Gene King."

CHAPTER 12

A case such as Luke Henry's comes around only once in a lifetime. Evil walks the face of our earth daily, but few like Luke, remain predators on the loose for years. Cases came and went, with Detective James enjoying a clearance rate of almost forty-five percent. These statistics were practically unreachable for even the hardest working detective, a distinction not used to describe the young rookie.

Robert enjoyed his job and the excitement, along with notoriety that came with solving criminal cases. The press seems to feed off the misfortunes of others, along with the apprehension of their violators. Robert appeared to have found his niche. Still not able to comprehend completely the reasons for his success, Robert knew he was in a good place for now. Law enforcement work was becoming gratifying, despite some of the experiences and scenes that it unveiled.

Shortly after the Luke Henry case, Springdale P.D. formed a long overdue Organized Crime Unit. The unit was to be comprised of four detectives and one supervisor. Robert was Captain Hill's first choice for the squad, even before he made his decision for the unit's supervisor. On numerous occasions, Captain Hill tried to talk his young detective into taking the promotion exam, but Robert refused.

One fear of a newly promoted police supervisor is that he would most likely be assigned to the graveyard shift, supervising a group of cops consisting mostly of rookies. Captain Hill assured Robert that this would not be the case. If Robert would just take and pass the promotional exam, Captain Hill had the assurance of the police chief that Robert would remain in the Criminal Investigations Department.

Despite the promises and the fact that Robert knew he could pass the exam, he was not interested. Not now, but maybe someday. Life was just too easy at this point. Detective James could work his

Monday through Friday job, and coast right through it. There would be a few exceptions — but none that would interfere with his weekends of chasing women and checking out the local bars.

CHAPTER 13

On Saturday morning, at approximately 6:45 A.M., when Detective James' phone rang. He had to struggle to find the portable phone, because of another late weekend night; Robert retired shortly before 3 A.M.

> *"Detective James, this is Wanda in Dispatch. Captain Hill instructed us to give you a call. We have a Signal 18 in Memorial Park. Can you be in route?"*

Robert's weekend began as soon as he left work on Friday evening. Several of his buddies in the unit called a 'choir practice' at a local tavern. This event is universal to the law enforcement community, where cops pick a place to drink and converge on the bar as soon as possible. Once all have arrived, the drinking commences until the participants are intoxicated to the point of singing with the jukebox tunes.

Once at the bar, Robert participated in the camaraderie, but after a few beers, his attention became diverted.

"Who will be my victim tonight," Robert thought as he scanned the room for the most attractive female.

Hanging out with the guys on occasion was fun, but this activity was not going to get him laid. Robert decided to set out on his own, soon to find a target. The remainder of the evening was fruitful, with Robert getting several phone numbers and before midnight, leaving with a luscious twenty-two-year- old vixen.

Robert usually wanted to party at the female's house, keeping his own home sacred for the few women he dated on a regular basis. Robert did not like surprise visitors, so his home remained off-limits to most. This was easily accomplished, after explaining to his companion the nature of his job and the necessity to keep his life as confidential as possible. Leaving his fellow comrades behind, Robert and his new woman left for her house.

After playing for a few hours with his new friend, it was time for Robert to leave. Remaining at a woman's house all night would signify to some women that the meeting meant more than just a physical encounter. Snuggle time with his latest black-book addition was out of the question. Robert wanted to awaken in his own bed, no matter the hour he was required to drive home.

After a short good-bye kiss accompanied by a few words of appreciation, Robert left her house and walked briskly to his pickup.

"An escape without a future commitment; always a good thing."

A few hours later, the early-morning phone call was unexpected and unwelcomed.

"Show me in route," mumbled the detective as he struggled to find the base for the portable telephone.

A signal 18 was a priority call.

"A dead body had been discovered. But why call me? Wasn't there a homicide detective available?" Robert wondered.

This was not for Robert to question. His job was to get dressed and go.

A five-minute shower, absent of a shave, was all time would allow. This was a necessity though, to bring him out of his slumber, along with washing the scent of the female from his body.

Detective James was now on duty. Slipping into the unmarked detective car and with the movement of a few switches, lights and sirens were blaring. The usual twenty-minute drive across town to Memorial Park would be cut in half, with his emergency equipment activated.

"Move over, dumbass! Can't you see the pretty lights and hear the nice loud siren, you moron?"

The detective was amazed how ignorant drivers could be when confronted with emergency vehicles.

"Just pull the hell over. If I must be out here hauling ass this morning, you should at least be able to pull your car to the right lane and let me pass; jack ass!" Robert's tone reflected his early morning mood.

Despite his amazement at the inability of drivers to yield to an emergency vehicle, responding Code-3 to a crime scene was part of the job the young detective enjoyed.

Obviously, the detective was feeling the pain left in his body and mind resulting from a sleep-deprived night of pleasure and alcohol. Taking on the task of being a detective put you in a position of occasional call-outs, any hour of the day or evening. However, this hour and day would not have been Robert's choice.

As Detective James approached Memorial Park, it was not necessary to radio to the on-scene patrol officers to obtain the location of the victim. Fire trucks, ambulances and police cars lined the path to the scene, with one large pumper truck blocking the entrance to the park.

Detective James drove his vehicle as far as he could before the road ended and the crime-scene tape began. Captain Hill was already on scene, along with several of the detectives from the Homicide Unit. As he exited his vehicle, Robert was approached by Captain Hill.

"Robert, we have two victims here; both are females of Spanish decent. Be prepared, this is not the prettiest crime scene you have ever seen."

Both men then proceeded down a bike trail to the bottom of a small hill. As they approached a nearby creek, an unpleasant odor soon overwhelmed the scents of Mother Nature. It was the smell of burned flesh, which was very familiar to Robert.

The eyes soon revealed what the nose had already detected. Silently greeting him were two partially burned, nude female bodies. One could conclude by the initial viewing that this had been the earlier scene of a torturous criminal act. The women were both tied to chairs, with hands bound behind them. They had bullet holes in their legs, accompanied by a few knife-slashes to the face, which were easily detectable on each victim.

64

What appeared to be the lethal wound for both victims was a large cut to the stomach; stretching from the left pelvic bone to the right one. The wounds were like that of a C-Section birth but obviously not administered by a surgeon. Once the stomach was opened, the demon poured gasoline into the stomach cavity and struck a match. The significance of the creek appeared to be a ready supply of water, which was used to douse the fires shortly after they were set.

Both women were then left to die in excruciating pain. It was obvious that the suspect(s) wanted the victims to be identified, for whatever reason.

A message to someone had definitely been delivered.

"This is a crime scene that would shock even Luke Henry," the pale detective thought to himself.

"Why was I called out?" Detective James asked his captain.

"You need to find the answer to that question. All that I know is the FBI received a tip yesterday that a woman had contacted their office and was going to turn over some information to them. The only information the agents were initially given was that a drug-lord was using women for his operation and serious injuries and even deaths were the results of this man," Captain Hill advised.

"This morning, the woman never made her appointment with the FBI, and these bodies showed up. There is more to the story than what the Feds are telling, but it is their belief that one of these two women is the one who called them yesterday."

Robert just nodded in response to his captain's narrative.

The Crime Scene Unit was processing the scene. Their members were true professionals at this part of police work, much more so than Robert. The Medical Examiner was also present, preparing to take the bodies to the morgue so autopsies could be performed at a later time. Nothing more could be done today. Monday would begin a busy week for Detective James.

"I told the Feds that I would assign my best to the case, so here you are, Robert. Go home, Son, and get some rest. See you Monday."

Captain Hill's parting orders were confirmed by his young detective.

The weekend was shot. There would be no more bars, liquor or women. Robert could not get the thoughts of these two new victims out of his head. Monday morning would be a welcome distraction. At least his work would help overshadow the scene that was now embedded in his mind.

It was only 10:30 P.M. on Sunday, normally an early bedtime for Robert. However, tonight he felt the earlier bedtime was necessary because tomorrow would be a busy day. The detective knew that a case such as this required many working man-hours. Early days and late nights were in his foreseeable future for the next couple of weeks.

As Robert's eyes closed, pleasant visions of beautiful women that usually serenaded him to sleep were replaced by visions of his two new victims. Robert felt that their hollow eyes and pain-filled faces that had previously begged for mercy, were now asking for his help and vengeance.

The voices continued their silent requests until Robert finally drifted to sleep in the early morning hours.

CHAPTER 14

The sun was just rising in the east as Robert finished his shower and began to eat breakfast. It was a light breakfast at that, due to his loss of appetite since Saturday morning. He wanted cereal and fruit to eat, nothing that had to be cooked, especially toast. He did not want to run the risk of over-cooking or burning anything in an oven or toaster.

7:15 A.M. and Detective James was at his desk. Robert wanted to review the Crime Scene Investigator's report and photos before contacting the FBI. It would take several days for the Medical Examiner to complete the autopsy on the two victims, but these deaths being ruled a murder was definite.

Captain Hill arrived thirty-minutes later and observed his young detective reviewing reports at his desk. A small smile could be seen on the captain's face as he walked away, not wanting to break the mind-set of Detective James. He knew that the right man had been assigned the case.

"It's 9 A.M. Those Fed boys should be finished with their frou-frou coffee and in the office by now," thought the young detective.

Instead of calling to make an appointment, Robert rapidly left for the FBI office without making his warning call. No lights, no siren; but Robert made the five-mile trip in what seemed to be a matter of seconds.

The Feds occupied one of the finest office spaces in town. Larger budgets meant better equipment, training and facilities for these guys. This was a good thing though for the local law enforcement community who at times solicited their assistance. Many police officers have aspirations of someday becoming a Fed, but not Robert. He was exactly where he wanted to be.

Area law enforcement officials respected most of the local FBI Agents, but not the two with whom Robert would be meeting, due to the work ethics these two practiced. The locals would do all the hard work, and the two Feds would assume the case and file it in federal court, thus more likely assuring prosecution. Once the criminal was found guilty, the two agents would take credit for the catch and add it to their stats. In addition, all monies seized would have to be divided with the federal boys. The Feds portion added to their nice offices and large expenditure budgets. The local's money had to be put into the city or county coffers. This situation was the making for a love-hate relationship with these two local FBI guys.

Detective James was well known among the federal agencies. Springdale was not a large city and crossing paths during major investigations was common.

"I'm here regarding the homicides in Memorial Park this weekend," Detective James informed the receptionist in the FBI Office.

"Have a seat, Detective; an agent will be with you momentarily," she replied.

A few minutes later, two FBI agents appeared in the lobby and escorted Detective James to an interview room.

"Captain Hill has assigned me to lead the double-homicide investigation, and I have been told that you may have some information for me," Robert advised them.

The two FBI agents began a briefing with Detective James that lasted only fifteen minutes, a short time for such a horrific murder. The agents advised that when the informant was to meet with them on Saturday morning, she would come forward with information about a major player in the crime industry. Apparently, the individual the informant was going to get information on was heavily involved in the drug and prostitution business, along with white slavery.

The woman also advised us this player was leaving behind a trial of dead bodies, mostly women, and that she and a friend feared for their personal safety. The only information that she would tell us over the phone was the name of Gene King, also known to them as

'King Gene'. It was obvious that the female informant was of Spanish decent.

Detective James sat silently, but his mind was racing a million miles an hour.

"Gene King, Gene King. Luke Henry briefly mentioned this man at the end of his interview with me. Detective James' mind was now in overdrive.

"Does that name ring a bell, Detective?" one of the agents asked.

"No," Robert replied, *"not at all."*

"Gentlemen, thanks for your time. Please keep me posted if you get any additional information," the detective said while exiting his seat.

As the detective departed, both FBI agents knew that they had hit upon something when mentioning Gene King's name to Detective James.

"We'll have to stay on top of this one. That rookie detective knows something."

CHAPTER 15

"Has word gotten back to Belize yet?"

"Yes, sir. They all know about the birds being roasted. I personally made sure of that."

A look of contentment reflected on Gene's face as Bradley Dean reported to his boss.

Apparently, a couple 'birds of the flock' wanted to sing to law enforcement officials about one of the most secretive aspects of his operation. The King was first notified of this by a Cartel member from Belize. One female recruit had a sister die while working for the King, and her family was not reimbursed for the completion of her mission. The King informed them that the agreement was made between him and the deceased, not the family. She swore to avenge her sister's death.

The sister was too emotionally involved to back out, so she and an associate would be completing their mission in the United States. Once there, the women would contact the FBI and tell them all they knew about Gene's operation. Having some knowledge about how U.S. officials work, both knew that reward money for snitching on drug dealers could be very lucrative, enough to live the remainder of their lives without working for the drug world. The women believed once they were in the presence of the FBI, their worries would be over. Protection would be provided, and her sister's death vindicated.

Once Gene was made privy of their intentions, a carefully, laid plan was activated. The King instructed his trusted lieutenant to allow the women to proceed to the states and make their delivery. After their package was delivered, Gene wanted the women to be taken to a location where their painfully executed bodies were sure to be found.

"I want those bitches to suffer," Gene demanded. "But we need to leave the bodies intact, so they can be easily identified. I want this one to hit the press, so an example can be made."

"One last thing, Bradley. I will be there to help you. I want my face to be the last thing those whores see," Gene exclaimed with an enthusiastic but demonic tone.

A response was not required from Bradley. Without a doubt, Gene knew that his orders would be carried out.

CHAPTER 16

A few months had passed since Gene King traveled to Missouri. Several months prior, his trip included a journey to the Lake of the Ozarks area, which is nestled in the central part of the state. He was looking for another safe-haven for one of his meth operations. This area was a perfect place: situated deep in the Ozark Hills where the chance of an operation being discovered was minimal.

The King was attracted to this area for more reasons than just business. Recently, he discovered what a vast area of recreation this lake is for adults. It is a haven for boating, resorts, women and nightclubs, this was definitely a place to relax and play.

Gene's last trip to Missouri was for business but this trip would be different. It had been a while since Gene had taken any time off to relax, so relaxation was overdue. He would fly into Springdale and then drive to the lake, which was just a little over an hour drive away; then playtime would begin.

It was Saturday afternoon at the Lakeside Bar. Gene drove directly to the bar after checking into his resort room, located a few miles away from the bar. Upon arriving at Lakeside Bar, he sat at a large table in the far corner of the bar. This allowed him a view of everyone entering or exiting the establishment; Gene, always wanted to alleviate any element of surprise.

Soon, everyone at Lakeside knew Gene was a man of money, drugs, or both. At his table, numerous women were back and forth, laughing and pawing at him. On occasion, Gene allowed a few of the "princesses" to accompany him to the car, at which point a session of 'powdering the noses' would commence. A year ago, Gene would have watched this activity, but now he was a participant.

"Hell, I am not conducting business, this is just pleasure."

Gene justified in his mind, while sucking each line of powder into his nostrils. *"Nothing but pleasure!"*

Detective James spent five grueling days at work; some progress was made, but very little. The first step of any investigation is to identify and conduct a background check on your target suspect. Gene King had been identified. King, a Texas native and resident, had only a minor arrest record. Evading Arrest and Failure to Identify to a Police Officer was it, and both occurred over fifteen years ago. One item of interest was that Gene used the name "Bradley Dean," when arrested for one prior offense.

The Medical Examiner had already completed both autopsies and submitted his report, revealing the obvious. After being bound, both women were shot in their legs with a small twenty-two-caliber pistol, disabling them immediately. A knife was then used on both women, probably during a torturous interrogation session, attempting to get the women to talk.

The last assault on the women was a large cut, from one pelvis bone to the other. A slight bit of gasoline was poured into each wound, and set on fire. The ME estimated the fires only lasted five to ten seconds, but long enough to send excruciating pain throughout the bodies of both women.

The reasoning for the stomachs being cut in such a manner remained a mystery to both Robert and the Medical Examiner.

"Why were they set on fire? Robert thought. *"Had they not been tortured enough? Or was there something else that we did not find that the murder was trying to cover-up?"*

The fire destroyed some tissue but was extinguished before it consumed much of either woman.

"What were the murderers trying to do?"

Robert was trying to make some sense of this brutal execution.

It was now one week later, and he had only the names of two victims, one possible suspect and little evidence to go on. Detective James was at wits- end after a sixty-hour work week.

"Doesn't your dad have a cabin at Lake of the Ozarks, Robert?" asked Captain Hill.

"Yes sir, he does," replied, Robert.

"Then get your ass down there for a couple of days, have a few cocktails and relax. If I see you in this office over the next two days, I am going to put my boot up your ass, young man." Captain Hill smiled as he walked away.

Without further delay, Detective James decided he would take Captain Hill's advice and head to the lake.

"It's a Saturday at the Lakeside Bar. Not a bad place to be, considering the week I just had," Robert thought to himself. *"Nice weather, cold drinks and women everywhere. If it weren't for the obnoxious loudmouth in the corner, this place would be perfect."*

"What's up with this dude," Robert mumbled as he watched the man at the corner table.

The man who caught Robert's attention was surrounded by hot women, all groping for his attention. Robert's cop instinct kicked in and this woman-rich individual became a focal target for Robert.

Robert sat about thirty-feet from him and could hear most of the conversations between the entertainer and his flock. Everyone who was close by was witnessing the touching of bodies, along with their provocative verbal intercourse. To some men, this display would cause jealousy but not for Robert. This loud exhibition was beginning to invade his privacy.

On numerous occasions, their eyes met. Robert's facial expressions were simple for anyone to decipher, especially for his opponent with his master of people skills. This loud boisterous man knew that he was being watched, and was enjoying the fact that he could piss off someone without even saying a word. He also figured that soon his observant opponent would engage in some type of contact with him.

Thirty minutes at the Lakeside Bar was about all that Robert could handle. The loudmouth playboy in the corner was taking his toll

74

on him. After finishing his beer, he began to watch for his waitress. When she finally came into view, Robert motioned to her in a manner with his hand that signaled he wanted his check. This was a disappointment to his opponent in the corner, who was now paying more attention to Robert than the women around him. For some reason, he could not let this opportunity pass. He felt compelled to have some type of contact with his rival before he left the club.

"You like?" a loud voice was heard.

In an even louder tone, the voice again said, *"You like?"*

Robert looked up to see "Joe Playboy" holding up a margarita glass in his direction.

"You have been watching me ever since you came in. Are you possibly a little envious, my friend," the boisterous man thundered.

The cynical smile of this guy blocked out the view of the scantily clad women sitting beside him, which normally would be the focus of Robert's attention.

After his week at work, Robert was in no mood to be messed with. A twenty-dollar bill hit the table to pay for his drinks, and Robert began his exit.

"Screw you," Robert responded while walking toward the door.

The man smiled with contentment as he turned to his female companions.

"That asshole does not want any part of the King, does he?"

It was obvious to Gene that he had prevailed in his little game, inflating his ego to an even higher state.

75

CHAPTER 17

The little episode at the Lakeside Bar ended the day for Robert. A small altercation like this usually would not bother him, but for some reason this one had got under his skin. What confused Robert was that he could not figure out why this upset him so much. Had the long hours of the past week mentally beat him down? Was it just that he couldn't get the thought of the two murdered victims out of his head? Maybe there was something about the guy that rubbed him wrong. Whatever the case, his mood was broken, and Robert decided to call it quits for the evening.

Back at his dad's lake house, Robert could not stop thinking about his case. This was the first time in a week that the young detective had any down time, allowing his idle mind to be fueled by thoughts of this horrific crime.

Silently, yet incessantly, the women seemed to be crying to Robert for help. The burden of solving this case was on his shoulders. The victims needed him, and he could not let them down.

Thinking about how the women had been set on fire sparked an unpleasant memory from several years earlier. Just two months out of the police academy, Robert received his first 'baptism by fire'.

As a rookie patrol officer, Robert was driving down the service road to Interstate-44 when something caught his eye. A crowd was gathered around a trailer in a small mobile home park. It didn't take long for Robert to see what was happening. A small stream of smoke was emerging from each window on the east side of the trailer.

Robert immediately called for the fire department and EMS to be in route. As he pulled onto the street where the mobile home was located, Robert noticed a tall man running toward the side door of the trailer. The slender, muscular man began fervently tugging on the door, but it would not open. Being persistent, the individual continued his efforts until he was finally able to break the seal that was keeping the door locked. When the door began to open, it allowed the building pressure in the trailer to release its fury through this small air hole. The escaping pressure blew the man about twenty feet through the air before he came crashing to the ground on his back. Robert thought for sure that the motionless individual was seriously injured.

As Patrolman James swiftly parked his vehicle, he saw the man regain his senses, stand up and again charge the burning trailer. This hero was on a mission, and one that he valued over his own life. It then became obvious that someone was trapped in the burning home.

"102 to dispatch, we have individuals trapped inside. Notify the fire department and have them expedite," Patrolman James shouted through his microphone.

Recognizing the anticipation and fear in his voice, the responding support teams could tell that the rookie cop was about to face something he would never forget.

"Sir, stay back!"

Officer James was shouting to the man who kept putting himself in harm's way.

"I can't. I can't. My nephew is inside!" The crazed man yelled while charging the building again.

Immediately, Robert could hear a voice. A small child was screaming for help.

"Please, help me! Help me! I'm on fire," the child screamed repeatedly.

With complete disregard for his safety, Officer James joined the uncle in a futile battle to enter the mobile home. Later, they discovered the trailer was built in the 1950's, with not one piece of material that was flame retardant. The fire chief concluded that the temperature inside the burning trailer was almost nine-hundred degrees when the rescue was being attempted. It was a burning inferno that was almost twice the temperature of the hottest setting on an oven.

When charging the building, Officer James and the victim's uncle were confronted with an impenetrable wall of heat. Numerous times they attempted to enter the trailer, but the wall of heat would not allow them to even get close. There was nothing they could do.

"102 to dispatch; where the hell is the fire department," Robert screamed into his microphone. *"We have a child trapped inside!"*

"They are in route, 102."

"Contact the fire department again and tell them to expedite, and I mean EXPEDITE!"

Dispatch was unable to reply, probably due to choking back the tears from the horrible situation at hand.

Officer James knew that it would be too late once the firemen finally arrived.

Both men, along with the gathering crowd, were forced to stand and listen with horror as the child's pleas for help diminished.

There was nothing any human could have done to save the four-year-old child trapped inside. The young victim was laid to rest a few days later and the trailer was bulldozed to the ground. The child had been buried and the trailer no longer existed. However, the pleas coming from inside would never be forgotten.

" Please, help me! Help me!"

These words would not fade from Officer James thoughts. This event was still vivid in his mind. The sights, smells and screams were as if they repeated, but this feeling is not usual. How does one erase such a memory?

Although, now in a completely different scenario, Detective James again encountered a fire victim. Robert heard the same pleas, but in a different tone this time. Several years ago, there was nothing he could do to help the young child, but with his two recent homicide victims, he could vindicate their deaths. The demon responsible for this had to be brought to justice.

A bottle of tequila sat on the table where it was easily available to pour into a glass and mix with some lime juice. There would be no margaritas tonight for Robert. Straight tequila, until he slipped off into a slumber. The cries for help finally subsided.

CHAPTER 18

"It's almost noon! Man, how did that happen?"

Robert cursed himself as he focused on the alarm clock sitting next to his bed.

With the taste of tequila still lingering in his mouth, the answer to his question was obvious. Robert did a quick scan around his bedroom to reassure himself that he was not alone.

"A night of drinking and I slept alone? What a waste of good tequila!"

A solid night's sleep was an elusive luxury for Robert since he took over this homicide case. The rest was welcomed, despite the method necessary to achieve it.

In his mind, thoughts of the day shuffled around before he decided on his agenda. Robert decided today would be void of any work on this case-Sunday would truly be a day of rest.

The morning shower caused the alert on his pager seem dim to almost non-existent.

"Surely not. It's Sunday." Robert ignored the interruption and continued his shower.

Curiosity took over once the shower ended, and the towel removed the moisture from his body. Robert looked to see whose number the device revealed.

"998-223-1019-1976."

"What the hell? Chad Cooper?"

The first ten digits reflected the phone number. The last four were the year that Chad and Robert graduated from high school together. This was a code that each used when paging the other. A personal ID for both, which assured a return phone call.

The call had to be returned ASAP. Chad was an inpatient man, and his idea of having fun was not hanging out next to a pay phone for thirty minutes, waiting for someone to call.

Out came the calling card and the phone call was placed. The voice on the other end of the phone confirmed the identity of the recipient.

"Eagle one to Eagle two," the voice responded with a chuckle.

"You in the states," Robert asked.

"Of course, would I be calling if I weren't," Chad asked sarcastically. *"I'm at Lambert Field in St. Louis. When can you be here?"*

"Let me clear all the women from my room and I will meet you at the main door of Terminal-One at 2:00 P.M. sharp," Robert responded.

"Then your fantasy should only take five seconds. Just open your eyes and those imaginary women will disappear. See you at two, my friend."

Chad was a lifelong friend since the early days of elementary school and continuing through adulthood. Both men chose similar professions for their life's work. Both desired to enter the law enforcement field. Robert's inherent fear of flying prevented him from going to the federal level, but this was not the case with Chad.

In 1979, Chad entered an internship with the CIA after completing his three years of college, which was important for his resume, since his dream of becoming an FBI agent began in middle school. Somewhere along the way Chad became caught up in the cloak-and-dagger games, and decided to join the agency once he earned his diploma.

After his training, Chad's assignments took him to places far away, to countries with names one could barely pronounce, let alone spell. In addition, working for the CIA was a single man's sport, which was not a problem for Chad, since his and Robert's commitment to women ran a parallel path. Both had a taste for the fast life, which was

81

conducive to Chad's lifestyle. The excessive travel and requirement for secrecy negated a permanent relationship for an intelligent agent. However, this was not the case for Robert. Maybe a spouse was exactly what he needed. A companion to confide in and discuss the ill effects of the job could have a positive effect on this young detective's life, but this thought was not a welcomed one for Robert James.

Once or twice a year, the agency would turn Chad loose for a month, which was the only time Robert heard from or saw him. During the yearly event, Chad journeyed back to his home state of Missouri and contacted Robert.

For several weeks, bullshitting, drinking booze and chasing women were the main objectives of the day. Though both men had similar careers, when it came to conveying professional war stories, Robert usually had to do most of the talking.

Chad conveyed little to Robert about his working life due to the confidential nature of his job. Nothing that Robert learned about Chad's assignments in Eastern Europe was ever repeated to anyone. This trust was protected out of self-preservation as well as respect for Chad. Even though he was never part of the federal system, Robert knew of the possible repercussions if anything Chad said was leaked. Without a doubt in his mind, the little information that Chad relayed to Robert remained confidential.

At 1:45 P.M., Robert exited Interstate-70 in north St. Louis, and turned onto Lambert Field Road. Five minutes later, he parked and walked into Terminal 1. Much to Robert's amazement, Chad had already arrived at the meeting point, which was unusual for the man who would undoubtedly be late for his own funeral.

"Amazing, simply amazing! This is the first time in your life you have ever been on time for anything."

Robert was smiling while extending a hand to greet his friend.

"Well, there was this little hottie who just left the plane, and I had to stalk her for a while. This is just where we ended up," Chad said with a snicker.

"Hey, Buddy, I hate to do this, but this trip is going to have to be focused around family business. My father is critical."

"His kidneys?" Robert asked.

"Yes, and if the doctors are correct, Dad has only a few weeks left. Robert, can you be my taxi to the Veteran's Hospital? Lunch is on me along the way. We can stop, have a few beers and catch up on each other's lives during the trip."

It was apparent this visit would be different from trips in the past. Instead of the festive, uninhibited, immature demeanor both exhibited during those visits, the mood was now more solemn. Chad's father was on his deathbed and Robert was working a horrific homicide case. The imminent situation for both was not a good mix for the normal two weeks of partying.

Once Chad's luggage was loaded, Robert steered his car back toward I-70 and accelerated toward Kansas City. An abnormal silence was noted between each topic the men discussed. Obviously, Robert was consumed in thought.

"Okay, Robert. What's eating at you? I thought I would be the boring one on this visit."

The four-hour ride gave the men a chance to discuss many aspects of Robert's case. Chad's professional venue was different from Robert's, but when it came to resources, Chad prevailed. The CIA had access to records and databases like no other agency in the world.

"What about suspects? Do you have any names yet," Chad asked Robert.

"Gene King. About all I know is, he lives in Ft. Worth, Texas. His criminal records are limited, but I just feel there's something more to this guy."

Robert continued giving Chad information he currently had on Gene King. Robert was a firm believer that the more information a cop accumulates on the suspect; the better he will understand and predict his target.

"Give me a few days with my dad, and then I'll contact Langley and see what we can come up with on Mr. King."

"That old gut feeling is working overtime here, Chad. I know there is more to this guy than what I have heard. In addition, there are two FBI guys who are somewhat involved in the case. I know without a doubt they have more information than what's being told to me."

"You have to go easy on them, Robert. They are just disgruntled CIA wannabes," Chad replied with a chuckle.

The four-hour drive to Kansas City seemed to pass in minutes. Robert and Chad were so involved in discussing the case that both forgot about stopping to eat. As they approached the Veteran's Hospital, Chad extended his offer to Robert for lunch.

"No thanks, Chad. Just get in there and take care of your dad. There will be many more days for us to find sinful things to do. Your father needs you, Buddy. Give him my best regards."

"Will do, Robert, and I appreciate the taxi service. I will call you in a couple days after I run this clown. We'll find something on ole' Mr. King for you."

As Chad walked away, Robert was confident that his life-long friend would come through for him.

CHAPTER 19

It was 6:40 P.M. Things were beginning to wind down at Gene's room at the lake. When the King left the Lakeside Bar the night before, he was not alone. His hotel suite looked like a scene out of the movie "Scarface." Cocaine, wine and women littered the room.

"Get these whores out of here," Gene barked orders to Bradley Dean. *"We have work to do."*

"Will do, Boss Man."

The night before, the five women who left the bar with Gene were treated like queens. The night was filled with all the drugs, alcohol and money the girls wanted, and they had one price to pay for the party favors-sex. Today was different; Gene's temperament had changed. The lack of sleep, accompanied by a hangover from excessive amounts of cocaine and alcohol caused the King's true colors to show. Gene got what he wanted from the women and like so many before, he had no further use for them. Bradley shoved the trespassers out the door like beggars on a street corner. The women got what they wanted, and so had Gene and Bradley; it was time to move on.

Once the women were gone, Gene and Bradley hurriedly packed their bags and were soon in route to the Springdale Airport. The 100-mile journey passed rapidly, as one might expect from a person being chauffeured in one of Europe's finest built sport coupes. A short encounter with a Missouri State Trooper did little to interrupt the trip. In an odd way, Gene enjoyed these little encounters with law enforcement officials. The thought that these cops had no idea they were dealing with one of the nation's drug lords was somewhat amusing to him.

Bradley slowly pulled the sports coupe into a private hangar at Springdale International Airfield. Sitting with its crew waiting was a private jet. Being an impatient man, Gene was pleased to see the aircraft was ready to depart. With his moody demeanor and short temper, causing the King to wait would have been unpleasant for the pilot. The full night of party and pleasure reflected in Gene's unpleasant disposition.

"Take my ass back to Texas," Gene barked his orders to the pilot.

The jet engines began to hum as the pilot propelled the aircraft down the runway. The noise was comforting for Gene, who had not slept for over forty-eight hours. The plane made a safe flight, but Gene would be crashing.

In addition to the euphoric effect that cocaine provides, it also diminishes the need for sleep while continually medicated. When the body is no longer being fed this poison, the user becomes tired and somewhat depressed. For the past two days, enough powder had gone up Gene's nose that it formed a thin-white crust around each nostril, but Gene could care less. The effects of the drug had finally worn off and he was sound asleep. Gene dozed off before the plane made it to the end of the runway.

Bradley Dean was sitting across the aisle from his boss during the trip back to Texas. Like so many before, it had been another wild weekend with Gene. Many thoughts were swirling through Bradley's head about his childhood friend and employer. These were not memories of the wild times the weekend had brought. Something else was going through Mr. Dean's mind.

Bradley was Gene's lieutenant. In the streets, this non-military title is tied to the individual in a drug operation who is the boss's right-hand man. In work and play, both men saw each other on a daily basis.

In play, Bradley was the cameraman during the small orgies that two would have with multiple women. Gene cherished these 'crime scene photos'. The pictures were always Polaroid shots of women engaged in acts of sex with Gene, and then photos of the girls together. The King was an impatient man, so these instant snap-shots were very pleasing to him. If he did not like the results of his instant photos, the women would again engage in whatever sex act Gene demanded, as the photo session continued.

In business, Bradley was always there for Gene to bounce off ideas and schemes. Although a confident man, the King needed to have others reaffirm his work. In addition, if something went awry, Gene had a scapegoat close by.

Gene King was also extremely private and untrusting. Bradley was the only person in Gene's life who was aware of all aspects of his organization. This trust provided great financial rewards but also great danger; and certainly, the job was not one you could quit if you weren't happy. If Bradley ever expressed his desire to leave, or if Gene became suspicious of his loyalty, Bradley would be physically retired by his boss. The King made sure that Bradley knew that everyone is expendable-even him. The two men were friends for life, but Gene had control over what this meant for Bradley. Yes, Gene owned his lieutenant.

Looking at his boss that afternoon, Bradley witnessed a once-rare sight that was evolving into a common event. Until the past six months, Bradley had only seen Gene use cocaine and crash a few times-maybe three times in the past twenty years-until recently. The last time before Gene's recent spree, was when he and his wife divorced.

"The divorce party -- an event worthy of a celebration after being married to a bitch like Gene's ex," Bradley remembered. *"That situation was justifiable, but things were now beginning to change."*

CHAPTER 20

The thought of The King becoming a cocaine addict was terrifying to Bradley. He knew if this cycle began, it would compromise and possibly lead to the demise of Gene's empire. Bradley had become accustomed to his extravagant lifestyle. Despite his livelihood being funded through criminal endeavors, Bradley knew Gene's operations were shielded; however, if Gene continued the cocaine binges, Bradley feared the binges would cause holes in the shield and the operation may be in jeopardy. He had worked too long and hard to be locked up in a federal penitentiary or to work a nine-to-five job.

Their lifestyles were funded by The King's operation, which was fed by the sale of cocaine, meth, marijuana and Formula-X – in addition to prostitution, white slavery and gambling. People did not call him The King for nothing. He was one of the most successful independent criminals in the nation. No mafia, organized crime or other similar group had aided in his success. Gene worked his way up from the streets to become a king on his own. He owed no one and nobody owned Gene King.

Just like his boss, Bradley Dean was an intelligent man, a trait recognized early by his mentor. Gene barely made it through high school, despite having an IQ that would embarrass most college graduates. He could discuss politics, business ventures, financial investments and foreign issues. Yet despite his knowledge on these topics, Bradley was shadowed by his master.

Gene began his criminal career by stealing thirty-five pounds of marijuana from rivals who lived nearby. He didn't even plan to take the stash. The change began after Gene was attacked and beaten by a local street gang. After he recovered from these injuries, Gene went on a mission of revenge. Upon learning where one member lived, Gene placed the location under surveillance. His plan culminated one evening when all five individuals who attacked him were together in the house.

Revenge was simple and quick. With a Glock 45 in hand, Gene burst into the room and killed all five of the men. Before leaving the scene, he noticed his victims had gathered to divide a large bale of marijuana. Gene made his decision. He quickly slid the pistol into his belt and carried the marijuana from the bloody, body-littered room.

Gene estimated that his newly acquired stash had a street value of over three-hundred thousand dollars. His journey had just begun. With this money, Gene was able to establish and evolve a simple drug operation into an empire. Revenge was indeed sweet for Gene King.

Another gift Gene possessed was his ability to recognize talent in its early stages. Gene knew that his friend and now business associate, Bradley Dean, was an intelligent man. In school, Bradley excelled in science, which was just what Gene needed after branching off into methamphetamine and cocaine. An obvious investment for Gene was to fund Bradley's college education for four years in order to obtain a chemistry degree. Like investing in an ROTC program, but with a much longer reimbursement, Bradley had to commit his talents to Gene's endeavors.

After several years of working together, Gene began the manufacturing operation of Formula-X, the brainchild of his protégée, Bradley Dean. In the early 1980s, the drug Ecstasy was running rampant in nightclubs and bars in both the Dallas and Houston areas. The drug was comprised of many readily-available components, most which could easily be replaced by similar chemicals when lawmakers attempted to outlaw the substance. What made Formula-X unique was that it contained a chemical that Bradley discovered and that was virtually impossible to trace or identify.

Although Bradley invented Formula-X, both the drug and its creator were owned by King Gene. In an agreement close to that of a blood contract, Bradley swore that the drug would be manufactured only under the direction of Gene, and never without his consent or knowledge.

When controlling the amount of such a highly-desired product, there was no ceiling on the price of this drug. Formula-X was an exclusive product of Gene King. To safeguard his prized possession, the chemical composition of Formula-X was transcribed on only one piece of paper, which was stored away safely in Gene's safe. Even though Bradley had the formula memorized, Gene required it to be put in writing, in the event something happened to his lieutenant. In a subliminal way, by doing this Gene was sending a message to his chemist.

The flight back to Ft. Worth's Municipal Airport was only an hour from Springdale International. Bradley looked at his boss with thoughts of both disgust and concern during the trip. There was the King, crashed out in a seat across the aisle. A crusted nose, very slow respirations and saliva running from his open mouth-certainly Gene was not the icon he was six months ago.

Bradley knew it was time to start making contingency plans. This once-steadfast pillar was beginning to weaken.

CHAPTER 21

The National AFIS (Automated Fingerprint Identification System) came through again. Both homicide victims from the park were identified. Several years ago, the two deceased females had been detained by U.S. Customs and Immigration, so their prints and photographs were on file. One woman was twenty-nine years old, the second only twenty-one and both were from the country of Belize.

Detective James had two simple questions to answer; first, was to learn why the women were in Springdale. The second task was to identify the killers. When saying *killers,* the Crime Scene detectives did conclude that there was more than one person who contributed to the deaths of these women.

With more than one victim, logic dictates the assumption that it took more than one person to handle and control them. In addition, both women had their hands and feet tied to small, portable chairs. These chairs had to be carried to the scene, along with the women. The location where the victims were killed also required a four-hundred-yard hike from the nearest road or parking lot. Lastly, the ropes that bound both women were tied with different types of knots.

The final piece of information listed on the Crime Scene Report reflected that each woman had bruises on both arms. The investigator concluded that one suspect probably held the women while a second person interrogated and then tortured them with a knife. This conclusion was based on a series of small cuts on the women's faces and torsos.

Reading the report was enough to nauseate Detective James and rekindled the voices in his head that were asking for help.

The phone rang at Detective James' desk.

"Detective James, how can I help you?"

"Hey dude, it's me. Sharpen your crayon; I have some scoop for you."

The voice on the line was that of Chad Cooper.

The conversation lasted about ten minutes. Chad was able to access FBI files detailing a decade long, failed investigation that their agency had initiated on Gene King. One of the FBI's narcotic agents had opened a case file on Gene back in 1974. At that time, he was suspected of ripping off and killing five gangsters in East Dallas along with stealing a large amount of marijuana. Since these were what a law enforcement agency would classify as 'misdemeanor killings', detectives did not put much time and effort into the investigations. Five scumbags were dead, so complacent attitudes prevailed. Their investigative file was open for three weeks and then sent to the storage room.

Apparently, one of the murdered gangsters was an informant for the FBI. The Feds then began an informal-covert investigation, due mostly to them not having any jurisdiction over a homicide case. Their quest took them to the streets of Dallas, where they were advised of an altercation these five victims had with a local teenager a few days prior. This was when the name of Gene King first graced the files of any law enforcement agency.

Chad continued by explaining to Robert how the FBI monitored Gene for several years, watching his drug operation get large enough to meet the guidelines that would allow them federal jurisdiction. Once this occurred, a female informant was sent to infiltrate Gene's operation. Initially she was funneling information back to the FBI, but after a while, their informant dropped off the radar. Rumor has it that one evening Gene got the informant stoned, at which time she confessed to Gene that she was a FBI informant. This was the last anyone ever saw or heard from the informant.

"Over the past years, Gene King has built an empire. Any vice, all over the world, Gene's got it covered."

"Gene also uses the alias of Bradley Dean at times. Bradley is believed to be Gene's lieutenant and lifelong friend, who will do anything for the man. Ring any bells," Chad asked.

Chad was snickering as he passed along this bit of information, comparing Gene and Bradley's relationship to be like his relationship with Robert.

"And, one last thing, Robert. Be careful. This guy is an international criminal whom even the feds have been unable to topple. Gene is wealthy, has an extensive organization, and he has built an empire. Robert, this also means that he probably has a few politicians and judges in his hip pocket. Gene has a lot to lose, which makes him very dangerous and capable of anything. Did I also forget to mention that he is suspected of being involved in several homicides along the way?"

"If I can be of help, Robert, page me on my beeper. Things don't look good regarding my dad, so I probably only have a few days left here."

"Goodbye my friend and thanks, Chad."

Pleased and pissed were the two emotions going through Detective James' mind after hearing Chad's report.

Captain Hill looked up just in time to see his young detective storming out of the office.

"Where are you off to, Robert?"

"I feel the need to have a prayer meeting with two FBI Guys, Captain. I will be back shortly."

The receptionist at the Springdale FBI office knew Detective James by sight. She was young and single, and this rising young star was a target of interest for her. As Detective James burst through the door, a person did not have to be a seasoned investigator to figure out that this was not a social visit. This detective was definitely a man on a mission.

"Do you have an appointment, Detective," the receptionist asked.

"Gee, I forgot to call. Just tell Asshole #1 and Asshole #2 that I am here to see them!"

"Will do, Robert, I mean Detective. Just have a seat and they will be right with you."

Only a few moments passed before the receptionist instructed Robert to go on back; that they would be waiting in the conference room.

As Detective James entered the room, both agents knew what was coming. Somehow, he had become privy of their long-botched investigation involving Gene King.

"I appreciate all of the information guys," Detective James remarked in a condescending way.

"Now, how about the truth, or is it too embarrassing to tell another cop that the FBI has been unsuccessfully chasing a ghost for the past eight years."

There was no second-guessing that Detective James was pissed-off about not being told about their investigation.

"That information was on a need-to-know basis, Robert. It was part of a federal investigation."

"Bullshit! The fact that two women were tortured and killed, along with your boy Gene King's names surfacing in the case, and you don't think I need to know? I'm trying to bring the demon to justice and you're withholding information. Can you tell that I am pissed-off?"

Robert was yelling as he continued to pace the floor.

"Either you be straight with me and let me see your files, or this will be the last time I walk through your door. And gentlemen, I will solve this case and once I do, I will be glad to sit down with the local news reporters and give them all the facts of this case."

"Just calm down detective and give us a few minutes, alone. We will be right back." The two agents then exited the room.

A few minutes later only one man returned.

"Follow me, detective."

The agent then led Detective James down the hallway, into a vacant office that had four file boxes stacked in one corner.

"Everything you need to know about Mr. King is in those boxes. You're welcome to take notes, but NOTHING, I mean NOTHING, leaves this office. Understood?" the agent ordered.

"Nothing will, and thanks."

"Captain, this is Robert. I will be at the FBI office for the next few days, reviewing files on my homicide case. If you need me, please call."

"Should I call for Pizza?"

Captain Hill chuckled as he hung up the phone.

Reading the files of Gene King was like attending the crime-buster movie of the year, except there had been no crime-busting going on. On the other hand, there had been a lot of crime. Apparently, the FBI had been chasing this guy for years. Coming close at times, Gene King was always able to elude the grips of the feds. The case being either luck or intelligent, or a combination of both.

Without a doubt, Gene built himself a financial empire. Records show he owned numerous homes, office buildings, condominium complexes, along with legitimate businesses. Play toys were also included on the list. A few that captivates the male gender is his lust of old muscle cars, along with the cigarette boats and a ship. Chad's suspicions were confirmed. Gene made joint investments with several politicians throughout the U.S.

"And I thought only Elliott Ness was untouchable," Robert reflected while reviewing the files.

Two days of staring at Gene's files was about all Robert could take. Despite the vast amount of material, the notes that the detective took were somewhat limited. Having an almost photographic memory, Robert was depending on memory to store information on this guy.

95

Taking a vast amount of notes only meant a delay in getting back to the investigation. The notes would have to be minimal.

Robert knew that his abilities, or lack thereof, would soon be put to test. For the first time in his professional career, Detective Robert James had a mission: to give those voices crying for help priority in his life.

CHAPTER 22

Six months passed since the gruesome murders of the two women from Belize. Never had Detective James been so frustrated in his work. Still enjoying a higher case clearance rate than any other detective on the job, a black cloud lingered above him. Robert felt he had let his Captain and department down; and most importantly, those cries for justice from the murdered women still went unanswered.

Six months passed and not a single lead, other than the name of Gene King. This is practically unheard of in law enforcement work. After a crime, the criminal always talks to a girlfriend, cellmate, or some trusted friend. Not in this case — not a single word had leaked.

The only lead that Detective James had was the name of Gene King. With Gene living in Texas, there was little chance of interaction between the two or any of his associates. Robert tried to schedule an interview with Gene, but his request was answered by a telephone call from a Dallas attorney. In summary, the attorney refused the interview for his client. He advised Detective James that Gene could be interviewed only if an arrest warrant was issued for his client. Robert knew he lacked the probable cause of getting any judge to issue a warrant for Gene.

Robert was beginning to realize that his murder investigation had just reached a stalling point.

CHAPTER 23

"Hey Bradley, get a load of this. Some hillbilly cop from Missouri wants to question me about a murder investigation."

Gene King appeared to be somewhat perplexed by this request.

"What did you tell him, Boss Man?"

"I had my attorney tell him to go pound sand," Gene said in between laughs.

Even though Gene's face reflected a sarcastic smile, it bothered him that somehow, his name was in some police homicide file. Someone had defied him.

Bradley too seemed to find this scene humorous, but concern formed in his stomach. Not just knowing that the cops had a viable tip, but how did they find the information. Was the Boss Man starting to become a liability to him?

CHAPTER 24

Out of curiosity, Detective James watched as two unescorted men entered Captain Hill's office. Dressed sharply and with an air of confidence, both seemed at ease in being present in a cop-shop. However, other than their apparent comfort level, both looked out of place. The men had long hair, facial hair, and wore cowboy boots. Despite their appearance not being the typical cop look, neither fit the profile of a suspected criminal, attorney or witness.

"Unescorted and just a little arrogant. Who are these guys?"

The young detective monitored Captain Hill's office with a heightened state of curiosity. Once they left, Robert would find a reason to speak with the captain, and, with any luck, the identity of these men would be revealed to him

Forty-five minutes later, Captain Hill's door opened. The captain escorted his visitors to the side-employees exit door. Robert could overhear one man informing the captain of their lodging accommodations, and he said they would be in town for a few days before returning to Texas.

When the door shut, and Captain Hill began walking back to his office; Robert quickly turned his head to a file on his desk and acted as if he were reviewing it.

"Robert, in my office," the captain ordered.

Obviously, the identities of the two visitors would be revealed to Robert without him having to ask.

"Yes Captain."

"Have a seat Robert, we need to talk," Captain Hill replied.

"Still interested in Gene King son?"

"Hell, Yes. I mean, yes sir, I am," Robert replied.

"Then I have a story to tell you, and some of it I am probably going to regret."

The private conversation between Captain Hill and Detective James lasted over an hour. The captain began by explaining that the two men who just left his office were from a federal drug task force out of Texas. This task force was dedicated to the investigation and apprehension of major drug dealers and their operations in a multi-state region. Their unit was comprised of local, state and federal agents, along with several assigned federal prosecutors. Since this was a federally funded program, jurisdictional issues were not a problem. No matter what agency the investigator came from, all were commissioned as Deputy U.S. Federal Agents and would fall under the umbrella of the Drug Enforcement Agency.

"These guys are after the big fish, Robert, and they have an opening in Dallas for someone with an organized crime background. Your name came up son, so here they are."

"But how and why, Captain? I'm somewhat baffled."

"Robert, you underestimate yourself at times. They are looking for the best in the field, and the glass slipper fits you."

A proud smile was reflected on Captain Hill's face as he addressed his detective.

"Texas is a long distance from Missouri," Captain.

"But Gene King isn't, Robert. Apparently, he knows how to get here. And yes, those task force boys know you have been investigating Mr. King."

"But how," asked, Robert. "The details of my investigation have gone unpublished."

"One of the agents that was just in here transferred to the DEA from the CIA a few years back. It appears he wanted more of a family life (ha). He said you two have a common friend."

"Chad; that son of a bitch! Five-thousand miles away and still helping," Robert said to his captain.

"Robert, I know this is a last-minute deal, but you only have twenty-four hours to decide. When those two get back on the plane Thursday morning, they want you with them. This is a once in a lifetime opportunity, Robert. The task force is a four-year assignment. You're still one of us when you're done, or there is the possibility you could sign on with them permanently. Of course, the choice is yours. I wish I would have had such an opportunity when I was younger."

"And, Robert, go home. The rest of the day is yours. Those guys will be back tomorrow and want an answer."

"Thanks, Captain," and out the door Robert went.

The drive home was somewhat foggy for Robert. His mind was not on driving or anything else around him. Tunnel vision was the best description of his state of mind.

"No wife, no kids, hell, not even a dog. I rent an apartment, I own nothing and the only responsibility in my life right now is to find the killers of those poor women from Belize."

"And I can be a federal agent and I don't even have to fly. Maybe not a bad gig!"

The icing on the cake was that Robert had Captain Hill's blessing and encouragement. His decision was made.

Robert only dozed through the night, due to his excitement of what tomorrow would bring. Despite his lack of rest, he was up at dawn and preparing for work.

101

This day was filled with mixed emotions. Robert would accept a position in an elite law-enforcement unit-one most cops would almost kill for. He also would say goodbyes, at least for the next four years, to Captain Hill and his co-workers, and friends at Springdale P.D. This would be a day to remember.

As Robert entered the Detective Division doors at 6:55 A.M., he was surprised to see Captain Hill was already at the office.

As he entered the Captain's office, he was stunned to see that his boss had traded in a suit and tie for blue jeans and a button-down work-shirt. As his eyes scanned the room, numerous cardboard boxes were stacked in one corner.

"I bet you never knew that Self-Move opened so early in the morning. By the way, their moving boxes are quite a bargain."

"How did you know what my decision would be, Captain," Robert asked.

"I see a lot of me at that age in you, Robert. I know what my decision would have been, and I was betting you would make the same one."

"I am going to miss this place, Sir."

"As it will you, my son, but not quite as much as I will miss you."

The clock had not yet struck 9 A.M., when the two Texans came walking through the door. Captain Hill was in Robert's cubical, helping him box up his personal belongings, as the men came through the door.

"Come on, Robert. Let's go meet your new boss."

"Special Agent Michaels, this is Detective Robert James. Robert, meet your new boss," Captain Hill conceded.

With a smile, Agent Michaels responded, *"Welcome aboard Robert, welcome aboard."*

"Robert, this is Ronnie Bays, who is the senior investigator on our squad. He will be your training officer for the next month. By the way, everyone on the squad has a street name-for some reason, Ronnie's

street name is the "Crazy Cajun." Ronnie and I have no idea where that name came from," Agent Michaels said with a snicker.

Detective James extended his hand to shake the hand of his new colleague and training officer. Without a word being spoken, by looking Ronnie in the eyes, Robert immediately knew why this man was referred to as the Crazy Cajun.

"Welcome to the club, uh, Robert. God, that name sounds like an Ivy League male cheerleader. Got to think of a street name fast, Robert," Ronnie said with a slight laugh.

Determined not to let Ronnie get the best of him, Robert's mind raced.

"Well, ole Crazy one, let's go back to my college days. While there, I earned, I mean was given, the nickname of "Mad Dog." Will that work?"

"Well, I was thinking of something that either began or ended with 'Hillbilly,' but what the hell. 'Mad Dog,' it is."

Both men could tell that the ensuing years would be interesting.

"Robert, I will take a promissory contract over to your city manager's office today, and the federal government will pay to have your personal contents stored. While on assignment, we will take care of your accommodations. Due to the volatility of your position, you will be moving about every six months."

"Boss Man, I thought we agreed not to tell the rookie about the hazards of the job, yet," replied Ronnie.

"That's just so you won't know where to find him, Ronnie."

"Men, that's what happens when you let the animal out of the cage. I just can't take him anywhere. Let's go, Ronnie, and let the new hire say his goodbyes. Robert, I will be by to pick you up for your flight to Dallas at 9 A.M. tomorrow," Agent Michaels instructed.

"If you don't mind, sir; I will drive; Robert and flying are not synonymous."

"You can take the Hillbilly to the city, but he's still going to be a Hillbilly." Ronnie muttered to his boss, but intentionally loud enough for Robert to hear.

"Like I said Robert, I can't take Ronnie anywhere. Here is my business card with our office address on it. See you bright and early on Monday. For us, that is anytime before noon."

"See you, Rook."

Ronnie Bays pulled his hat over about a foot of long, wiry hair and accompanied his boss out the door.

"Well Captain, I guess this is it," Robert said with a noticeable amount of remorse.

"Son, this will be an experience of a lifetime for you. Plus, Robert, you will still be working for me, just in a district way south. When you come back, I expect to hear all of your war stories, especially the one about bagging Gene King."

"That I will do, sir, and thank you for this opportunity."

"Godspeed, Robert, Godspeed."

CHAPTER 25

Leaving the Springdale area was difficult for Robert James. After living in the area his entire his life, Robert was soon to be introduced to a lifestyle that was one-hundred and eighty degrees different.

There would be little opportunity for Robert to say his goodbyes to fellow detectives and family members. There was no time for the department to organize a going-away party for Detective James, so another choir practice was scheduled for that evening immediately after work. The group consisted mostly of detectives, but the Homicide Unit failed to send a representative. This was no surprise, especially after the Luke Henry case. Being the new star on the block certainly came with a price.

Many who attended Robert's event came with a date or spouse, but he was one of the few solo acts. At this point in Robert's life, a significant other was beyond the realm of possibility. This was indeed a good thing, for Robert was about to embark on a journey toward a new chapter in his life. A woman at this point may have excluded him from this opportunity. In addition, his new position came with inherent dangers-not something one wants to expose a loved one to.

While in the bar, Robert noticed a few possibilities for a black-book entry, but not tonight. After choir practice, the family visit was next on the list. Farewells to his father and siblings were necessary before going south; only the lack of time prevented the possibility of female companionship for the evening.

Choir practice concluded, and the half-sober future Fed made his way to his father's house. Robert had the complete support of his dad; he understood his son's desire to advance his career. This new opportunity would certainly put him on the fast track of doing so.

The meeting at the James' residence went by quickly. Each knew Robert needed to return home to prepare for his move. Twenty minutes after arriving, Robert was walking out the door consumed with his family's blessings. This was, indeed, a sad but exciting day for the James family.

CHAPTER 26

Robert veered his pickup truck south onto Oklahoma Highway 75 and headed toward the Texas line.

"Damn, the Red River sure looks nasty. Nothing like the White or Jack Fork rivers in southern Missouri, which are spring fed and clear," Robert thought to himself as he crossed over the river into Texas.

"Dallas, 85 miles," the road sign reflected.

With each mile, Robert's heart rhythm seemed to increase. The cities of Sherman, McKinney, and Plano lined the roadway into Dallas.

"This place is wall-to-wall concrete," Robert thought as he continued his trek into the city.

Springdale was a city of approximately one-hundred and fifty-thousand people. The Dallas-Ft. Worth area had a combined population of over six-million, with over two dozen cities that were just as large as or more so than Springdale.

"Welcome to the jungle," Robert said aloud.

The intersection of Highways 75 and 635 in Dallas appeared to be a huge spider-web of concrete. To the west and south, Robert could see nothing but large buildings and bumper-to-bumper traffic.

"Did I make the right decision?" Robert began to question himself. *"I feel like a fish out of water."*

As he reached downtown Dallas, Robert veered off the highway and onto a city street. He was amazed at the cluster of tall buildings that lined the city skies. His mind began to race.

"Six-million people, which equates to over three-million women. I like those odds. I might like this gig after all. DFW, here I come!"

Robert took out a road map and began looking for the street address of his new apartment. This task alone was an early test of how this visitor from the north would adapt to the big city. One of the first thoughts in Robert's mind was how the Dallas cops get anywhere in ample time to help the citizens. This city is a maze of streets that were almost unimaginable to him.

10255 Southwest Parkway. Robert inched his way to the address. He reached his destination by stopping every few miles to view the map to be assured he was following the proper route. At last, he had arrived at the new apartment.

After a quick visual tour of the property, it was obvious to Robert that the Feds had an abundance of financial resources. The new apartment complex was nothing like he saw in Springdale. Here were new buildings, tennis courts, three swimming pools, along with other amenities. The accommodations helped convince the new arrival he made the right decision.

Robert had few things to unpack. His personal items consisted mostly of clothing. A benefit of being a JDLST member was a fully furnished apartment. It soon became obvious there would be few wants or needs for the young detective while assigned to this elite unit.

CHAPTER 27

6:30 A.M., Monday morning came early; Robert prepared himself for work. Suddenly, he began to panic.

"Okay. Agent Michaels said to be at work sometime before noon. What the hell does that mean?"

By the time the clock struck 10:00 AM, Robert was crawling out of his skin. Being consumed with both anticipation and curiosity, he pulled out Agent Michael's business card and looked for the address on the map.

"14250 Highway 121, Suite 500, Las Colinas, Texas." Into his Ford F-150 Robert left, in route to his new office.

At 10:30 AM, Robert walked up to the office door. On the door were the words "Southern Construction Engineering." Confused, Robert took a second glance at the card. There was no error; he was at the correct address.

"Maybe a misprint? I don't want to be late; I better make a phone call."

Robert entered the offices of the Southern Construction Company and approached the receptionist's desk.

"May I help you, sir," she asked.

"This is sort of embarrassing, but this is my first day of work and I can't find my office. Is this by chance 14250 Highway 121, Suite 500," Robert asked.

"Yes, it is. May I ask your name, sir?"

"Certainly, I am Robert James."

"Ah, welcome to the JDLST Headquarters, Robert. I am Cynthia Green, the unit's Administrative Assistant. It looks like the sign on the door works," she said with a smile.

"The sign is necessary to protect my boys, and keep the riff-raft out. Come on Robert, I will escort you to your new office."

Cynthia buzzed the door, so Robert could enter the office area. She was a woman in her mid-fifties, who had worked for the federal system her entire adult life. After a few minutes of conversation, there was no doubt in Robert's mind that this woman ruled the roost around the office. Intelligent and on top of her game, Robert quickly formed a favorable opinion of Cynthia.

"None of the guys are here yet, Robert. Looks like you're the early bird of the group, but believe me; that will soon change. Just relax and get familiar with your new office. Over the next week or so, I will spend time acclimating you to our computer and paper-flow system."

Robert spent the next hour admiring his new office. His fifth-floor window overlooked a man-built stream that snaked its way through a maze of tall office buildings and restaurants. A new desk, computer, recording equipment and television set; were part of his new office.

"If only those FBI guys in Springdale could see me now," Robert chuckled to himself as he sat comfortably in his padded-leather chair.

It was 11:30 AM before Agent Michaels entered the office. After welcoming Robert to Texas, the first item of business was to take the new investigator to the Federal Courthouse in Dallas. At this location, Robert would be sworn in as a Federal Agent and would receive his credentials.

"Do you swear to......."

Those were about the only words Robert could remember the judge saying. This process and environment was all encompassing, leaving his mind in a fog-like state. At least Robert was coherent enough to hear the final words and reply.

"Yes sir, I do."

"Robert James, I now commission you as a Federal Agent for the United States of America."

"Thank you, sir."

"I wish you the best of luck and may God walk by your side," the Judge concluded.

Robert's new boss led his rookie investigator down the hall to a separate office, at which location Robert received his badge and ID card.

"Now for the fun stuff, let's get out of here," Agent Michaels said as he led Robert out of the building.

The next stop was the armory. Both men showed two forms of ID to enter the building. Once in, Robert understood why.

"You will be issued a Sig-Sauer 45 auto pistol, an H&K MP5 submachine gun and a Remington 12-gauge sawed-off shotgun. Then we will head out to the range before they close, so we can get you qualified. Can you handle this machinery, Robert," asked Agent Michaels.

"Yes sir!" boasted the new investigator. *"One thing we Hillbillies can do is handle a gun."*

On this day, Robert was riding on cloud nine.

CHAPTER 28

The first week passed quickly for, Robert. He spent time organizing his office and learning the federal system. Familiarizing himself with Dallas and his new home also consumed time; there were no idle moments in Robert James' life.

The guys in the unit would be great to work with—talent abundant and all very knowledgeable in their jobs. The first week was all office work, but the second week he would work the streets. Robert was initially assigned to Investigator Ronnie Bays for training, and later his permanent working partner.

Friday afternoon arrived, and all team members had made it into the office for briefing. As Robert entered the briefing room, Special Agent Michaels was there to greet him at the door.

The room was comprised of law enforcement talent from around the nation. First, there was Ronnie Bays, a Dallas P.D. detective, who was the most senior on the squad. Ronnie had been on the task force since its inception seven years earlier. A Chuck Norris look-a-like, Ronnie was just about as bad. After years of martial arts, it was questionable if he actually needed to carry a firearm. Ronnie had a reputation on the streets as being "one crazy Cajun." After a person had the opportunity to work around Ronnie, they realized the appropriateness of his title.

Next was Mike Bales, a New York transplant who came to the unit from the ATF's Denver Organized Crime Task Force. Mike was on a temporary assignment with the unit, due to his immense involvement with the biker gang murders related to the amphetamine world. Mike was a specialist in both areas of crime.

The third man was someone out of the norm for an undercover drug agent. Adam Ainsworth, a street cop from Ft. Worth, thought of himself as someone worthy of being featured in "GQ" magazine. Adam refused to take the appearance or demeanor of a doper, like most others in the unit chose to do. It was apparent Adam had his own agenda, which consisted primarily of visiting the gym and chasing women. Working drugs was an entry on his resume requiring little of his own effort. His charm and ability to bullshit anyone, including his supervisors, provided his route to this prestigious assignment.

The fourth man, Blake Waterman, was the newest member to the unit. He was a transfer from the Drug Enforcement Agency (DEA). Federal agents and state law enforcement officers usually mixed like ammonia and bleach but once on this team, each was willing to give the task an ivy-league effort. The mixing of agencies seemed to have little effect on Blake, as he conducted his daily investigations, with or without assistance.

To dispel questions about rank and file, once assigned to the JDLST, each person was given the title of Investigator. No more agents, detectives or sergeants—just investigators.

Commanding the unit was "Agent Michaels" or "Boss Man." His first name, Adrian, did not seem to fit a man in his position. Special Agent Michaels was on temporary assignment from the Los Angeles DEA Office. His reputation for combating the methamphetamine crime world in California earned him national recognition. After accepting the assignment, Michaels joked about buying all the California meth cooks a plane ticket to Texas, so he could hang out with his old buddies.

Robert felt he was an unusual addition to the unit. Texas had many detectives who had a better handle on the drug world. However, the fact that the team supervisor personally recruited him intrigued Robert and the other investigators.

"Your work week is over, Robert. Go home, enjoy the weekend and we will see you back here at 1:00 P.M. on Monday. Robert, you need to lose the razor for a few days and don't shower before coming to work Monday. One last thing, find a Goodwill store over the weekend and do a little shopping. We want you looking your worst when you come in on Monday. See ya, pal."

Robert received his orders from his new boss. Feeling somewhat ostracized but filled with curiosity, Robert left his new office behind and headed to the parking lot.

"Three-million plus women." Robert knew what his mission would be over the weekend.

"Where's the black-book baby? It's time to add to the numbers."

The weekend passed quickly. Robert spent most of it organizing his new apartment, along with doing a little shopping, as instructed by his boss. Exploring the city and taking care of necessary chores consumed most his time.

On Saturday night though, Robert did make time to check out a nightclub that was located close to his apartment. When he initially arrived, Robert sat in the parking lot watching men and women entering the club. It did not take him long to realize that his blue jeans would not work here. A trip back to the apartment for a quick wardrobe change was necessary.

A short time later, Robert returned to the club with proper attire and made his entrance. Once inside, it did not take long for him to realize that he was no longer in Springdale, Missouri. The club was packed. Men and women were practically shoulder to shoulder- certainly not the typical bar or club Robert was familiar to. The women did not resemble women he labeled as his prey back home. They were somewhat older, not the typical college crowd Robert was accustomed to. Most appeared to be intelligent, professional women, many of whom probably had higher paying jobs than him.

Using his routine line of being a detective was no longer available. Robert was now a federal task force investigator, which required a certain level of confidentiality. He would now have to work for a date, just like the normal-Joe.

Robert always remembered dating advice his father once gave him. *"Women like looks, power and money. The man, who possesses all three, is certainly a lucky one. The person who has none is, indeed, unfortunate."*

Robert had good looks, but the other two attractions were not within his scope this evening. He knew having a badge, especially a federal one, represented power. Robert convinced himself that this avenue would not be pursued. The third attractor being money, Robert knew he lacked. After spending a short time in the club, he soon became aware that the money factor was important to the women in Dallas. Robert's work would certainly be cut out for him tonight.

The next two hours, Robert mingled among the crowd and engaged himself in conversation with several women, but there would be no additional tallies in his black book this night. Robert felt fortunate to leave the club with two telephone numbers he collected during the visit. Tonight, Robert experienced something that was a rarity to him; he would go home alone.

CHAPTER 29

At 1:00 P.M. Monday afternoon. Robert was eager and waiting at the office when Ronnie Bays entered.

"You ready, Rookie? Got bullets in that gun, or have they not issued them to you?" Ronnie's own words seemed to amuse him.

Investigator Bays led Robert into the parking lot, and pointed to a white, Z-28 Camaro with T-Tops. This was his car of choice for this week. During one of the information sessions last week, Robert was given a credit card, and with the name of a car dealership. The card would pay for any purchases he needed, including the weekly rental of the car of his choice-within reason that is.

Robert would work with Ronnie Bays for the next few weeks, learning the drug world on the street. Once Robert learned the streets, he would work on cases involving criminal organizations. Investigator Bays was an undercover street operative, an assignment he personally chose. Recently, Ronnie infiltrated a biker gang notorious for manufacturing and distributing meth-amphetamine. During the training period, Robert was to work with and assist Investigator Bays in these endeavors.

"Mad Dog, you've heard the words 'baptism by fire' haven't you?" Ronnie asked. *"Well, tonight, it's time to go to church, but not in the traditional way."*

Evidently Ronnie was just as excited about this training mission as was his rookie, but just in a different aspect. Ronnie knew that this new cop was a virgin when it came to working undercover, so it was his duty to change this as soon as possible.

"Mad Dog, I've got a question for you. What does a doper look like?"

"Like you, of course," replied, Robert.

"Wrong answer, Rookie. They come in every shape, form and fashion. From street scum to attorneys, from teenagers to grandmothers. There is no such thing as a typical profile for a doper."

"For you to survive out here, you need to take visual and mental notes on everything I do. If I fart, you fart. If I drink, you drink. If I smoke, you smoke. Get the picture, Mad Dog? One last thing, learn to lie your ass off and remember your lies. Your life depends on it!"

The rumble of the Camaro's modified four-hundred cubic inch engine could be heard for blocks as Ronnie Bays put the car into motion.

"Buckle up, Rookie; you're in for one hell of a night!"

During the first few weeks Robert spent in the Dallas-Ft. Worth area, he did not visit Ft. Worth. This city of approximately one-half million people lies about thirty miles west of Dallas. From what Robert was told, the city had the appearance and attitude of a West Texas town. Many compare Ft. Worth to the Texas towns of Lubbock and Odessa. Having a cosmopolitan city like Dallas located just a few miles from Cow Town was an oddity.

"So, I understand you have never been to Ft. Worth, Mad Dog. Is that correct?"

"Nope, this will be the first."

"It's still early, so here is what we will do. I need to talk to you about many items before we actually go to work. Being the nice guy that I am, I will give you a quick tour of the city before we start crawling with the cockroaches."

"Sounds like a plan, Ronnie."

"Mad Dog, once we leave the nice office in Las Colinas, I am the Crazy Cajun and only the Crazy Cajun, understand?"

"You bet, sorry dude."

"By your looks, you were an athlete in school, right? It all goes back to what your coach preached to you. You play like you practice, so practice like you're playing. All that it takes is one little slip-up and you're toast. Got it, Mad Dog?"

"Got it, ole' Crazy One."

The thirty-minute drive from Dallas to Ft. Worth was a crash course for Robert. Investigator Bays loaded him with information and instructions, all of which was critical, such as how to simulate the use of marijuana or how to shoot dope. In addition, there were instructions on what to do if someone is carrying a gun, how do we protect our identities and when is an arrest conducted when working undercover? These are vital questions that needed to be answered.

Robert was not too thrilled with his training officer's first response. Investigator Bays prefaced his reply by telling the rookie undercover cop that almost everyone in the drug world carried a gun. When going into a drug deal, an undercover cop should never try to hide the fact that he is carrying a weapon, if asked. If a gun was detected and one did not confess, the crooks would immediately become suspicious of you being a cop.

Another factor that could rapidly blow a cop's cover is one's reluctance to use dope, when offered. Simulating marijuana was simple. When offered a joint, it was easy to take on the pretense of smoking, just by blowing out, instead of inhaling. This would cause the cigarette's tip to fire up and send a stream of smoke into the air, just as it does when one inhales.

"Okay, Mr. Crazy., then what about injecting dope?"

"Mad Dog, first, people on the streets do not use the words 'injecting dope'. You must be careful to use street lingo when working around these scumbags. It's referred to as "shooting," "running" or "hitting," but NEVER "injecting!"

118

Investigator Bays pulled the car into an empty parking lot.

"Let me show you something, Rookie," as Ronnie reached under his car seat.

Investigator Bays then revealed a velvet Crown Royal bag, with surprising contents. In the bag were syringes and several small containers of liquid Vitamin-B that Ronnie had obtained from his doctor.

"Doing the job right determines if you get to go home at the end of the shift, Rookie."

Robert watch intensely as Investigator Bays loaded two syringes with the liquid Vitamin-B.

"I always carry two of these in my sock. That's one of the reasons I wear boots out here. Shooting dope can be a very private ordeal. It is almost ceremonial to some of the scumbags, especially the big, and bad ones. Methamphetamine is bigger and stronger than the meanest man here, Robert. That is why some of these men make shooting dope a private ordeal, because meth's empowerment makes them look inferior."

"When someone asks you to run some meth, they usually load the syringe for you. Once you have the syringe in hand, it is not uncommon to excuse yourself and find a remote corner of the room to run the stuff. No one looks over your shoulder at this point. This is when I slide the syringe with loaded dope into my sock and pull out the clean one that is loaded with Vitamin-B. Now, watch this, Rookie."

Investigator Bay pulled up his jeans to expose the lower portion of his leg. A piece of cloth was wrapped around his upper-calf area, causing his veins to bulge. After a few seconds, the syringe slid into one of Ronnie's veins. Robert cringed but continued to watch.

Once the syringe was in the vein, Ronnie pulled a little blood into it, ensuring a vein was hit and the vial was stained with blood. Then, slowly and methodically, Ronnie pushed the vitamin-B potion into his vein. After the syringe emptied, he took out another small container and poured a little substance onto a cotton ball, as one would do with rubbing alcohol.

"Now, what the hell is that, Ronnie?"

"Just some type of acid I picked up at a DEA narcotics seminar. The substance is harmless, but after rubbing it on the same area for a few minutes, it actually causes bruising."

"Now look, "Mad Dog."

Robert looked closer at Investigator Bay's leg. Obviously, the needles' point of entry was a blood dotted pimple, along with a nickel-sized bruise.

"Perfect," remarked Investigator Bays. "Mad Dog, we have to be the masters of illusion out here. To the dopers, we appear to be one of them, but are as opposite as night is to day. For me, having needle marks and bruises on my arms and legs gives one the illusion that I am a meth-junkie. After your training is complete, this exercise will probably not be necessary for you organized crime boys."

"Plus, Vitamin-B helps one get through the late-night hours."

The reason Investigator Bays was nicknamed the "Crazy Cajun" was becoming obvious.

The shock factor to the rookie investigator was worth the time given for roadside class of shooting dope. Investigator Bays drove with a slight smile as he guided the Camaro toward downtown Ft. Worth.

The sun finally set, and allowed lights from the tall buildings in downtown Ft. Worth to give a bright greeting to the city. Being several times smaller in size than Dallas, Ft. Worth still dwarfs the City of Springdale.

Investigator Bays quickly gave his young rookie the fifty-cent tour of downtown. The night crowd was beginning to line the streets of the city, in route to their favorite bars and clubs. Women, tons of them, scantily dressed, were scurrying in all directions.

"Are you sure we have to work tonight?" Robert asked his training officer while watching short skirts sway across the street.

"Yep, Rook," that we do. But believe me, Buddy, there will be plenty of time for that activity later."

"Mad Dog, have you ever heard the term 'speed-whore'," Ronnie asked.

"Nope," he replied.

"That will change soon, my friend."

After leaving the cosmopolitan area of downtown Ft. Worth. Investigator Bays drove north to "Cow-Town." This is the location of the famed "Billy Bob's Honky-Tonk," located on a brick-lined street that still carried the same aroma of cow manure as it did in the late 1800s. Cowboy boots and hats seemed to be the common attire for the people here. Now, Robert began to understand why some think there is a huge diversity between the cities of Dallas and Ft. Worth.

Indeed, Robert was in Texas.

"Okay, Rookie, your fifty-cent tour is over. It's time to go to work."

Investigator Bays turned the car to the south and cranked up the stereo. The Phil Collins song, *Into the Night*, was playing from a cassette Ronnie slid into the stereo.

"Gets me into the mood," Bays muttered.

"We are headed to a bar just west of downtown called, "Scooters." It should not be hard to figure out what kind of bar we are going to Mad Dog. Once inside, follow my lead and listen to EVERYTHING I say," instructed Investigator Bays.

"Will do, ole' Crazy One."

A few minutes later, the Camaro turned into the motorcycle-lined parking lot and found a place in back to park.

"Stick your pistol down your drawers, Mad Dog, and let's go in."

"Aren't you going to lock up the ride, Ronnie?"

"Nope, everyone knows if you get caught stealing in the parking lot, you may have just signed your death warrant, literally! That is one of the cardinal rules for dopes; you don't steal from your brothers."

As the doors to Scooters opened, Robert entered a world unlike any other place he had been in the past. The bar was packed, and smoke filled. Bikers were everywhere; most were wearing leather vests with markings of the motorcycle gang to which they belonged-a member of, the Bandera's.

Oh, shit!

Robert had attended many seminars where the Banderas were discussed, he knew running dope was their primary forte', and anything or anyone who threatened interference would be exterminated.

Last week, Robert read a story in the Dallas newspaper about a North Texas police officer who was shot and killed by a Bandera biker gang member. Apparently, the officer had just stopped the biker for a traffic violation and put him in his patrol car to write a ticket. Unknown to the cop, the biker had a felony warrant out for his arrest. The felon pulled a pistol from his waistband and shot the officer in the head, killing him instantly.

A manhunt ensued, which involved hundreds of cops from North Texas. Assisting in the search were members of the notorious law enforcement agency, the Texas Rangers. Several days later, the suspect was found by one of the Rangers, outside of a small town near a creek, with a bullet hole in his head. According to the Ranger, a suicide note was left next to the body, in which the biker apologized for the crime and said he would not live with this burden any longer.

In some biker gangs, such as this one, a member achieves status when injuring or killing a law enforcement officer. Many people questioned the suicide to be abnormal behavior for a biker, but no one cared, the officer's murder was vindicated.

As Ronnie and Robert entered Scooter's Bar, all eyes were upon them. Crazy Cajun was obviously no stranger, and he brought a new face into their den.

"Hey Crazy Ass, what the hell's happening, Brother," one biker shouted.

"Time to wash the dust from the throat," Cajun replied.

"Who's the girlfriend with you, Crazy One," the same biker asked.

At this point, the bar was almost silent; all ears were listening.

"This is "Mad Dog," he's my cousin from Missouri that was just booted, I mean discharged, from the Army. "Mad Dog" feels Texas was a good place for a new start, so here he is."

There was no response, as Robert and Ronnie bellied-up to the bar. Chatter filled the room, but not to the level it was when the two men entered. Obviously, some were suspicious of Mad Dog, who did not resemble them in any way. Mad Dog was sporting short, groomed hair. The grubby clothes he was wearing were purchased from Goodwill. Despite the common attire, Robert could not completely hide his professional demeanor, or the hands which reflected clean fingernails.

"What can I do for you, Crazy Ass," asked the bartender.

"Give me a Jack and Coke."

Robert leaned over and in a low voice asked Ronnie if it was wise to be drinking on duty.

"You've got to be kidding, Rookie, drink up. We are no longer driving a patrol car. Welcome to the real world, Boy."

"Sounds good to me!"

Robert stood at the bar over ten-minutes, watching the bartender mix drinks and then handing cold beer to customers. Despite being bellied-up to the bar, and signaling the bartender several times, Robert could not get service.

"What the hell is up with this guy, Ronnie," Robert asked.

Investigator Bays looked at his rookie and shook his head.

"He does not know you, so he's going to make you work for your drink. I will help you with the first one, but you take over after that."

"Hey Earl, Mad Dog has some dust in his throat, can you help him out here," Ronnie said to the bartender.

There was no reply as Earl approached, Robert.

"What's you need there, Mad Puppy?"

"I will take a wine cooler."

Earl stood in shock as he pulled out a broken pool stick from under the counter and started banging it on the bar. This got the attention of everyone and once again, all eyes were upon, Robert.

"This sissy ordered a wine cooler, A WINE COOLER!"

The room was silent.

"Now why does the little Mad Puppy want a wine cooler? Is that the only drink his mommy will let him have?"

At this point Investigator Bays froze in his tracks and began silently praying for some type of miracle, so they both could escape alive.

Thinking quickly, Robert took both hands and ripped open his shirt, exposing his hairless chest.

"Because it puts hair on my chest," Robert said loudly.

A long period of silence prevailed and finally...

"You little shit. Hey, Crazy Ass, your cousin is quite the comedian," Earl said in response, actually believing that Mad Dog ordered the wine cooler as a joke.

"Hey, whatever it takes to get a beer around here, I'm game," responded, Robert.

"A beer on tap and it doesn't matter what type."

For whatever reason, Robert managed to escape his predicament. Apparently, Earl was a biker who was respected by his fellow patrons.

After Earl served Mad Dog a beer, the bar began to return to normal. Ronnie edged toward his rookie and put his arm around his shoulders.

"If you ever do that again, I will shoot you myself, got it!"

For some reason, Robert believed his training officer would do just that.

Several hours passed as the two investigators remained in the bar, going table to table meeting various members of the Bandera biker gang. Many bikers let down their shields and allowed Robert to participate in the conversations while drinking. The ice was broken, but there would be no meth buys tonight.

It was easy to distinguish the 'who's who' in the bar tonight, as they were the men surrounded by the "biker bitches." Most women were slender, wore either jeans or cut-offs. Tank tops, exposing their breasts, seemed to be the female attire for the evening. These women were at the complete disposal of these men; they brought drinks or food, and did everything but taking a piss for these men. There was no doubt who had the power here.

After several hours, Ronnie decided to leave; his mission was accomplished. Robert had been tested and apart from the opening line, he performed well. The bikers accepted his rookie, especially after telling the story about being kicked out of the Army, due to his flunking urine tests on numerous occasions and assaulting one of his drill sergeants.

As the men returned to their car and set sail for Dallas, Ronnie asked his rookie what he had learned that evening.

"Two things, Ronnie. The first; NEVER order a wine cooler at a biker bar. Second, I now know what a "speed whore" looks like"

Both men laughed and fell silent as Ronnie again cranked up the stereo to the sounds of *"Into the Night."*

Robert survived his first night as an undercover cop and he had a good story to pass along to his grandchildren.

CHAPTER 30

Several months passed since Robert James' assignment to the JDLST and the move to Dallas. Except for hunting, the remainder of the outdoor activities Robert enjoyed in the Ozarks, such as fishing and boating, were abundant and easily available in Texas, also. Robert was becoming use to the conveniences of a large metropolitan area, and the broad expanding social life the city made possible.

Investigator James was beginning to make his mark and establish a reputation with his new boss and fellow employees. He was solving cases and securing large cash and property seizures, which were coveted almost as much as putting criminals into jail.

Robert never realized how large Texas actually was until he went to work for the JDLST. Due to his federal jurisdiction, accompanied by the fact that criminals have no boundaries, Robert drove many miles during the past months, due to his traveling to Houston, El Paso, Austin and San Antonio; it seemed as if he were working cases in adjoining states. At almost one-thousand miles from El Paso to East Texas, the distance was almost unfathomable to be in only one state.

Robert James was beginning to make his mark in the JDLST.

After completing training with Investigator Ronnie Bays, as with most of the team, Robert started working solo. When a team approach was needed, each investigator had an assigned partner, which was typically a team member with similar experience who wanted to work the same hours.

Investigator Blake Waterman was assigned as Robert's team partner. Blake was one year older than Robert and he was also a transplant from another state. Blake was born in New York, but moved as a young child to Nevada, where he remained until completing college and joining the DEA. Houston was his assigned duty station, until accepting a position on the JDLST.

Blake and Robert worked primarily organized crime cases. Most involved putting together cases on drug-lords, who were making a fortune in Texas from methamphetamine labs, along with the trafficking cocaine that was coming in from Mexico.

This assignment took planning and patience, traits that some on the team did not possess, such as Crazy Cajun. On the other hand, the crazy one supplied valuable information from the streets not obtainable to most law enforcement officers. For a cop to penetrate the Bandera biker gang was almost unheard of, a feat that none wanted to attempt, especially after the recent murder of the Arlington Police Officer. The street criminals not only respected the Crazy Cajun, but many also feared him. For example, during Robert's undercover training after first coming to the unit, Investigator Ronnie Bays received a page from one of his confidential informants (CI). After a brief conversation, the stage was set. The informant set up a drug deal with a major distributor. This meeting was to take place in a sleazy motel on Harry Hines Boulevard in Dallas.

The investigators met the informant in his room, which was a room typical of what a speed freak may rent. $19.95 a night, complete with cockroaches and possibly clean sheets. Once in the room, Robert found it littered with used syringes, dirty clothes and half-eaten food. Also, discovered was a sixteen-year-old, strung-out female teenager who lay half-naked on the fifty-one-year-old informant's bed. The sight of this young girl being in such a position angered Robert.

"What should we do with the kid? We can't leave her here-or do we?"

The drug deal went quickly; Investigator Bays handed the dealer two-thousand dollars cash for an ounce of his brownish-white meth. As soon as the deal transpired, the dope pusher was out the door. Once he left, Bays handed the informant a few hundred dollars cash, and turned his back while the man sampled the fruits of the purchase.

"Good shit, ole Crazy Cajun, good shit," the informant exclaimed in an almost drooling manner.

Obviously, the drugs were more meaningful than his financial reward.

"Hey, guys, what's mine is yours, so have at it!" The CI then pointed toward the young girl on his bed.

"Not tonight, we have got to head out but appreciate the offer," Crazy Cajun replied.

Just as soon as Robert and Ronnie left the informant's motel room, a car pulled up and stopped in front of it.

"Oh God, here's trouble," Ronnie said in a muffled voice.

Four men, two of whom Ronnie knew as meth and gun dealing street thugs, were in the car. Ronnie sensed trouble, so he stopped, pulled out a cigarette and lit up. Two of the men who exited the car carried wooden-sticks at their sides; it was obvious that Ronnie's suspicions were correct.

"You have business inside," Ronnie asked as the men approached.

"What business is it of yours," replied one of the men.

"There are two friends of mine inside."

"You mean there is only one of your friends inside, because the other will be a dead mo-fo here in a few minutes. By the way, who in the hell are you? Either get out of my way or maybe I will request that you join the party inside."

"People call me the Crazy Cajun."

With these words, all the men stopped in their tracks.

"As in Bandera Biker Crazy Cajun?"

"That I am."

At this point, the tone of the conversation rapidly changed. The thugs then asked the Crazy Cajun for permission to go inside and kill the informant. Apparently, he had violated the unbreakable rule of

129

'thou shall not steal from your fellow criminal'. The informant had stolen about a dozen guns from these men, and revenge was heavy on them tonight.

"*Are you guys packing heat?*"

"*Hell, yes, don't we all?*"

With an arrogant chuckle, Ronnie turned to his rookie.

"*Mad Dog; let me see your piece.*"

Investigator James was caught off guard by the request but recovered quickly to ward off any suspicion. Robert reached under his shirt and wrapped his hand around his Sig. 45. With reluctance, Robert placed the weapon into Ronnie Bay's outstretched hand.

"*Does this answer your question,*" Ronnie asked while sending an overconfident smile toward the opposing group.

"*Mad Dog and his little buddy here takes care of my light work. Believe me; you don't want to see my shit!*"

A message had been sent to his opposition. It was obvious that Ronnie's authority would go unchallenged.

"*My last request, just don't kill him, and throw the girl out first,*" Ronnie ordered while calmly sucking on his cigarette.

"*Will do Crazy Cajun; you have our word.*"

Both investigators watched as the four men entered the CI's motel room. In just a matter of seconds, the young girl was literally shoved out of the room, with only a few items of clothing in hand. Instantaneously, loud noises and moans of pain were heard coming from the CI's room.

The ass kicking had commenced.

"As the two investigators got into the car and began to drive off," Robert had to ask:

"What do we do now, Ronnie?"

"Nothing, Rookie, just let nature take its course. In their world, this is comparable to you sending a murderer to prison or the death chamber. You just let it happen. Those guys know if they cross the line, their asses will be mine. So, the informant will live, but will be wishing he were dead."

"What about the young girl Ronnie, we can't just leave her there, can we?"

"Robert, she is a sixteen-year-old female. In a perfect world, the girl is still a kid. In the dope world, she is a young woman who is here by choice. The newest little speed whore on the block, is her new title now. There is little that either of us can do to change that. If we did take her in, it would be just a matter of days before she is right back out here. Once again Robert, at times we just have to let nature take its course."

The young investigator did not necessarily agree with his training officer, but knew that Investigator Bay's reasoning was correct. The young addict should remain in her little world.

This little experience was an eye opener for Investigator James. He was beginning to understand Ronnie Bays, and how this man must adapt to survive his assignments. It was rapidly becoming obvious to Robert that no undercover cop could work the streets as well as Ronnie Bays.

CHAPTER 31

3:05 A.M.

For a July night in Texas, Mother Nature was being kind to its inhabitants. The extreme temperatures from the previous day, accompanied by the rapid fall of temperature after dusk, led to a cool evening that caused the grass to glisten from the dew. Eleven law enforcement officers were converging on a house in a quiet, southwest Ft. Worth neighborhood, camouflaged by the early morning darkness. Strangely, the crickets, which are known as the alarm system of the outdoors, continued their chirping as if they were there to assist this law enforcement endeavor. Any loud or miscalculated footstep would be covered up by the singing of these creatures. Besides this, the Earth lay silent, like a night blanketed by a winter's snow.

Six of the waiting men were SWAT officers draped in black Ninja-type uniforms, each armed with H&K MP-Five sub-machine guns. These guns are capable of total devastation to any living being who challenge the officer's authority. On one side of this weapon was a lever with three settings. When the gun is engaged in the first mode, it is only capable of firing a single shot. The second position allows a three-round burst to be sent. The third setting gives the triggerman the ability to spray dozens of nine-millimeter bullets in the direction of the target in a matter of only a few seconds. These SWAT officers had the third mode engaged.

Accompanying SWAT was a team of five detectives from the Joint Drug Lab Suppression Team (JDLST). Their reputation placed them in the ranks of the elite when dealing with the nation's methamphetamine problem. Not a statistic to be proud of, Tarrant County, Texas was ranked as the county infested with the largest methamphetamine problem in the entire country. JDLST was a federally funded program with a two-fold directive. One was to assist in the detection and eradication of this problem. The second was to focus on the criminal organizations or drug lords who were funding these illegal operations.

The JDLST team was comprised of some of the finest and most reputable narcotic detectives in Texas and beyond. Amid this group stood Detective Robert James.

The air was moist and filled with the odors of wet grass combined with the rotting contents from trash containers residents had placed at curbside. Another odor also filled the air. Coming from a two-story, middle-income residence, was a pungent smell. The odor was distinctive to all present. It was unquestionably Phenyl-2-Propanone, also known as P2P. This substance was the desired result from mixing several precursor chemicals needed to produce liquid amphetamine. Once the heating or cooking of these chemicals begins, a foul odor is released. This odor, once smelled, is never forgotten or misinterpreted as anything other than P2P. These chemicals are volatile, but not as much as the individuals who plague society when they began making their evil potion of methamphetamine.

The combination of sleep deprivation and the sampling of their own product would make these violators a dangerous force with which to reckon. It was well known in the law enforcement community that methamphetamine (a.k.a. speed) users are the most dangerous of all criminals. Each day, law enforcement officers in Texas are burdened with dealing with the devastation left behind by these drug offenders.

The time was now perfect. The JDLST was about to put their plan into action. The confrontation between good and evil was about to awaken this silent, suburban neighborhood.

3:15 A.M.

Despite the cooler temperatures, the armed officers were sweating profusely from the amount of armament each was wearing. The increased metabolism of each officer added to the amount of perspiration escaping from the men. These modern-day warriors were highly trained and in peak physical condition. But with the anticipation of the unknown, their bodies were now met with biological conditions not experienced during training. With each passing minute, the SWAT officers were losing nutrients from their body, but when the time was

133

right, Mother Nature would make up for this loss with a huge rush of adrenaline being pumped through each man's veins.

Just one week prior, a hostage situation at a local convenience store reflected the capabilities of this elite unit. Two masked and armed suspects stormed the store one evening with the intentions of robbing it. Their plan was immediately botched by a night shift police officer who stopped in for a cup of coffee. Bullets soon began to fly, leaving one uniformed officer wounded, two customers dead and the masked gunmen in possession of two young female hostages. When negotiations failed, SWAT elected to make entry by blowing out a portion of the rear wall of the store. After lining a section of concrete blocks along the back wall with C-4 explosives, the detonation occurred.

The SWAT officers later described the situation as if they were running through a burning hell after the charges exploded. With pieces of cinder and burning ceiling tile still filling the air, SWAT Officer Joseph Burns recalls displaying super-human strength as the one hundred and sixty-five-pound cop took hold of both hostages. With a sub-machine gun strapped over his shoulder, he easily lifted the young women off the ground, with one hand on each. Officer Burns then carried the two young women to safety through a section of the missing back wall. As Officer Burns and his hostages were running from the store, an eruption of gunfire ensued. The MP-Five sub-machine guns once again began to sing their song of death.

In the succeeding silence, it became obvious that the officers who yielded the machine guns prevailed. Two masked gunmen lay dead and two hostages were virtually unharmed. This was certainly a story that would be told repeatedly by these high school students when they returned to school.

These same men lay in wait, like soldiers awaiting the orders to charge. In the background were the five JDLST investigators, one of whom was the Agent-in-Charge. For some reason, most SWAT officers seemed to be cut from the same mold; however, the JDLST investigators are anything but.

In the distance, the faint sound of a car door shutting was detected. Appearing from the shadows was DEA Special Agent (SA) Michaels. The time finally arrived. In hand was a signed search-warrant.

"Game on!"

134

Protected by night's darkness and crickets singing, four of the black-clothed SWAT officers crept toward the house, splitting off in pairs and disappearing to the opposite sides of the building. The remaining two officers stood in wait, one yielding a fifty- pound battering ram and the other providing his cover, with the H&K MP-Five in hand. Their orders were soon to come.

"*SWAT One, green light,*" whispered Agent Michaels' voice over the police radios.

Two of the SWAT officers then burst into a sprint toward the front door. The silence of the night was interrupted with crashes and explosions. First, windows were broken and 'flash-and-crash' percussion grenades were thrown into the house. This move was sometimes risky when running warrants on drug labs, but since the P2P process was not volatile to percussion grenades, this procedure was used as a means to stun the occupants of the house. If the methamphetamine were in the process of being powdered, this procedure would have resulted in an explosion killing all those in or near the house.

Numerous percussion grenades could be heard exploding as the two charging SWAT members ran to the front door and broke through it with their battering ram. One swing from the huge device was all it took to splinter the door into pieces, as it swung open. The battering ram was thrown to the ground as both officers stormed into the house. The other four soon followed.

Time always seemed to move the slowest during the period it takes the SWAT team to secure the premises. JDLST investigators were impatiently waiting as they surrounded the exterior of the building with weapons ready.

Investigator James sat behind the wheel of an older-model Camaro with a pistol in one hand, and an evidence kit in the other. This was his search warrant, his case, his responsibility. If the information and probable cause were correct, the weeks of work to get to this point were worth the effort. If not, indeed, everyone's time was wasted.

A shot rang out, then another.

"*Oh, shit,*" exclaimed Special Agent Michaels.

"Dispatch, we have two shots fired. Have EMS in route and staging," the boss yelled into his police radio.

Thoughts were already running through Robert's head.

"Why didn't I wait until tomorrow, or the next day? Here I am again with another officer shot in the course of one of my search warrants. Why the hell did I sign up for this job?"

Not once but twice over the past six-months, law enforcement officers had been shot during the service of one of Investigator James' search warrants. The first occurred out of state, in Oklahoma. For some reason, a local judge decided to issue a 'knock warrant' requiring officers to knock and announce their presence before making entry into a building.

This issue made absolutely no sense, especially on a suspected drug lab operation run by a meth cook. In addition, the suspect had an outstanding Texas arrest warrant for charges of attempted murder and kidnapping. On this occasion, the occupant's response was a twelve-gauge shotgun, which disemboweled Oklahoma State Trooper Chris Moore. His death was not instant. Watching the life fade from a fellow officer was a haunting chapter in Investigator James' life. A shootout then ensued, with the suspect eventually taking his own life.

"This guy took the cowardly way out."

A law enforcement funeral then followed; one Robert too frequently remembered.

The second incident was not as critical but still haunts Investigator James. During a search warrant at a local hotel, a patrol officer shot a SWAT team member in the leg. This officer should not have been there, but SWAT was short a team member that evening. Therefore, an additional uniformed officer was necessary for the warrant. Investigator James picked the assisting officer, which nearly proved to be a fatal error.

Despite being a non-lethal wound, the SWAT officer was medically retired at the youthful age of thirty-one. He never again would use his leg. This is yet another unpleasant chapter in this young investigator's career.

"A fellow officer shot and because of me?" Robert pondered this thought until total confusion caused him to dismiss it.

CHAPTER 32

Even though each investigator wanted to enter the house to learn the reasoning behind these gunshots, standard operating procedure required them to remain outside the house until the building was secure. The radio silence was excruciating, but the call came, finally!

"Building secure, we need you guys in here ASAP!"

The radio was silent for only a moment.

"I have one on the ground, running south from the building. The suspect is a white male, approximately thirty-five years old and he is armed with a pistol."

Investigator Ronnie Bays was in pursuit on foot. As the SWAT officers entered the house, one of the crooks inside decided to abandon his sentry post and exited through an open window. While SWAT makes its initial entry, the duty of the JDLST investigators is to secure the perimeter.

"SHOTS FIRED, SHOTS FIRED," Investigator Bays yelled.

The radio was broadcasting what each of the officers at the scene heard.

The suspect chose to fire a few warning shots at the pursuing officer, hoping the officer would assume a defensive position and stop the foot chase. The situation was dangerous, but more for the suspect than the investigator. This is another example why Investigator Ronnie Bays had the reputation of being a crazy Cajun.

Ronnie was born and raised in the bayous of southern Louisiana, where alligator hunting was as common for him as quail hunting to others. Ronnie had no fear, or maybe he lacked common sense, or possibly a combination of both. Whatever the case, he was relentless. Investigator Bays also held a fourth-degree black belt in martial arts and according to rumor, Ronnie never experienced defeat in a match.

Having a pistol-packing, crazy Cajun who wants to do nothing but kick your ass is an ingredient of an unpleasant ending for this suspect.

The radio was silent. The SWAT officers and the investigators were in swift pursuit of Investigator Bays and the suspect, but without further directions from the pursuing investigator, a direct interception was not possible.

"I have one in custody. Have EMS in route to the scene for the suspect," Investigator Bay's ordered through his radio.

Without a word being spoken, the law enforcement officers on scene knew what just occurred-the fleeing suspect experienced the wrath of Investigator Bays. Two broken ribs, an eye swollen shut and a jaw incapable of moving enough to speak one word were the results of this suspect's sin.

Police brutality? Not to a scumbag who just shot at a cop.

CHAPTER 33

Investigator Robert James and his team were facing the rewards and possible horrors that awaited them. SWAT gave the all clear signal and requested investigators to enter as soon as possible. By now, the quiet neighborhood had come to life. With calls coming in to the 911 Center, patrol units were dispatched to the scene to calm the fears and concerns of the neighbors. No one could blame them though, just minutes prior, the entire block was awakened by sounds of percussion grenades and blasts from several machine guns.

Sympathy? Not from the JDLST group. It was unimaginable how the local residents could fail to notice or report such obnoxious odors coming from this residence, along with all of the late-night activity. A blind man could see what was going on here. The activity brought many people out of their homes and into the street, asking questions about what occurred.

Soon, Investigator James heard a patrol officer calling him over the police radio. "Investigator James, the neighbors are wondering what's going on here. Can I release a little information to them?"

"Without a pause," Robert's reply was a simple. *"Just tell them it's the same thing that has been going on for the past three months, but 'John Wayne" is here tonight to exterminate the rodents."*

This response was not quite perfect public relations expected by the neighborhood residents, but Robert didn't care. No matter how naïve a person might be, anyone could decipher the activity that had been taking place at this residence for the past few months. One might not be able to understand what was happening, but this was not rocket science. Illegal activity was the only feasible answer which all chose to ignore. Therefore, on this evening Investigator James felt comfortable to ignore the neighbor's request.

A simple '10-4' was received, indicating the officer knew the inquiring neighbors would not be satisfied with Investigator James' response.

It was time for the investigators to make entry and conduct a search of the residence. The JDLST members were curious about the gunfire but at this point concluded that neither a suspect nor officer was shot; since there was no request from the SWAT officers for paramedics. All of their questions were answered upon stepping through the front door. Lying motionless in the middle of the living room floor was a full grown, one-hundred and thirty-five-pound pit bull. The canine was surrounded by a pool of blood, indicating the SWAT team member had to terminate the animal in order to defend them, a tragedy to most involved, knowing that similar dogs often fall victim to this demise. These animals were doing the job for which they had been trained-protecting the drug lab and their owners.

This pit bull was probably raised being abused. Gunpowder and amphetamines were common additives to their food. This unique diet, accompanied by daily beatings and the constant weight of a forty-pound chain strapped around his neck, transform the dog into the 'ultimate warrior'.

On this occasion, the animal was stopped with just two bullets. During other search warrants, dogs were so hyped up on methamphetamine that officers were forced to expend six to seven rounds into the animals to stop them. This indeed was a sad and dangerous abuse of man's best friend.

Investigator James was born a dog lover; therefore, for a short time he stood by the animal, feeling sympathy for the dog. When seeing his partner's dilemma, Investigator Bays walked over to his fellow officer.

"Too bad we couldn't have shot the bastard who abused the pooch," Bays said with an unusual note of sympathy in his voice

Robert slowly shook his head and walked away from the dead animal.

The house was a two-story structure. The first floor had a living room, kitchen and master bedroom. The main prize was upstairs, but the lower level would surely produce some useful evidence.

A search warrant was always intriguing to a law enforcement officer. Being able to tap into one's private lives was unique and

141

accessible to very few. A person tells friends and family members the part of life they choose to reveal. Being able to rifle though every inch of someone's home, revealed unknown secrets to the searcher, was at times as exciting as finding illegal contraband.

Investigators knew immediately they had hit the jackpot just by the foul odor that filled the air in the house. The smell was enough to turn a man's stomach. The best way to describe the odor in the residence is to compare it to a rotten egg frying on a car's catalytic converter.

The odor was definitely P2P. A pungent smell that soon turned to one of sweet victory. All their hard work was about to pay off; a slight smile was detected on Robert's face.

"Boys, it's time to go to work," Robert said as he stepped into the house.

The living room looked like a second-rate movie theater-food and drinks were mixed in with mounds of videotapes. Homemade movies lay beside other tapes that were probably rented and never returned to the store. Most of the video collection consisted of pornographic material. Some of the tapes were commercially made, and others consisting of sex scenes of the occupant's wife and her female friends, which had been filmed in their house.

As Investigator James rushed by the coffee table where most of these items lay, something caught his eye.

"What the hell?" Investigator James mumbled as he reached down to recover two Polaroid snapshots on the table.

The photos were of two women, possibly of Central American descent, and their stomachs protruding.

"Both pregnant?"

Investigator James has seen stranger things but for some reason, this just did not fit. This was no time to ponder on pictures. The real interest awaited upstairs.

142

As the investigators proceeded up the stairs, the pungent odor of P2P became almost unbearable. It was beyond them how someone could remain in an environment for hours and days smelling this.

"Just another reason why these people are so brain dead. This crap eats up the gray matter."

As the JDLST team reached the top of the steps, they observed two men and a woman sitting on the bedroom floor in handcuffs.

Standing guard over the group was the SWAT team leader. A muscular man, about six feet tall and weighing around two-hundred and forty pounds, with shirtsleeves rolled up past his elbows. The officer's forearms were massive and the grip on the MP5 was firm. The glare from his eyes made words pointless. He hungered for that adrenaline rush, almost to the point of daring these people to test him. This man was energized by something much more potent than methamphetamine, which was obvious to everyone. To test him would be futile. These criminals were going nowhere.

A substance on the SWAT officers pant leg caught the attention of Investigator James. Splattered on his black trousers was a red liquid. It then became obvious who had shot the pit bull. At this point, the detective almost wished the suspects would try to escape. Their demise might just be welcomed.

"Pieces of crap," were the words uttered toward the suspects by one of the officers as the cop checked on his sergeant. This adjective was commonly used by officers when dealing with such captives.

On the opposite side of the room was a door which allowed entry into a walk-in attic. The JDLST members moved forward in anticipation. As usual, Ronnie Bays was the first man through the door.

Just before the raid, the team was briefed and was sitting around bullshitting. It was the "quiet before the storm." During this time, Ronnie relayed a story about a visit to McDonald's earlier that day with his three-year-old daughter. Either a possible sexual predator, or an over-zealous child lover, made the mistake of striking up a conversation with Ronnie's daughter. No one would get the benefit of doubt from Ronnie Bays. Striking like a cobra, Ronnie physically took hold of the man while he was in mid-sentence with the child.

After quickly finding a pressure point on the man's hand, the suspect was immobilized with both pain and terror as Ronnie whispered words of advice to him. When Ronnie finally relieved the pressure, the man left as rapidly as his trembling legs could carry him from the restaurant. All were curious to hear the words that were said, as they listened intensely.

"My fantasy for serving justice to a child molester is this," Ron stated while his face and eyes reflected the look of a rabies-infected dog.

"I would offer the scumbag a cigarette, but only after I ram a gas hose down his throat and pump about five-gallons of fuel into him. After watching the shit-head suffer for a few minutes, I would politely offer him the cigarette and match, which I am sure he would use to end the pain."

"BOOM! Now that's justice!" Ronnie's eyes and face reflected crazed excitement while reciting these words.

No one could reply as Investigator Bays walked away smiling. There was no doubt in their minds Ronnie had relayed the exact words to the intruder.

Robert began to realize he was not the only man in the law enforcement arena that was affected by the job.

CHAPTER 34

The door to the attic swung open to reveal the proverbial pot of gold. In full operation was a very large methamphetamine lab boiling away. Huge beakers, flasks, heating elements and condensers lined the room. Gallons of liquid speed were boiling away, enough to manufacture close to fifty-pounds of meth. This product would have produced approximately one million dollars' worth of dope on the street, if processed properly. In reality, this rarely occurred. Often, the meth cook would be so stoned and sleep deprived that he would begin making mistakes and ruin over half the product before it was finished. There were a few exceptions to this common scenario, but only a few.

The collection process was slow and meticulous. When a speed lab is in this stage of cooking, an uncontrolled or rapid cooling process could produce an explosion or fire. These unplanned mishaps had resulted in the detection and seizure of numerous drug labs in the past. The investigators were thankful that the powdering stage had not yet begun. This stage required the use of extremely volatile substances, such as ether, to complete the process.

About a year before this operation, the JDLST team was dispatched to a rural, central Texas town where a large lab had just exploded. One fatality was reported, and the second suspect was airlifted to Brooks Medical Center's Burn Unit in San Antonio. Once the team arrived, they determined that the meth cook had been in the process of powdering a large batch of methamphetamine. He used a body shops' paint booth as his processing lab for turning the liquid into a white powder. The booth allowed the trapping and filtering of vapors to prevent detection.

After being sleep deprived for several days, one of the first senses a person begins to lose is their mental alertness. The meth cook, apparently satisfied with his product, decided it was time to light up a cigarette. A flick of the lighter was all it took. A person not familiar with a paint booth can visualize it as a large, self-contained metal box, large enough to house most vehicles. For this individual, a more fitting description would be an oversized tomb.

The ether vapors filled the air. Lighter than gas fumes but just as volatile, these vapors penetrate every substance or being that they touched. A spark from a light switch or even static electricity was enough to ignite the hazardous vapors. A match and cigarette would always prove to be a deadly combination with ether, just as it was in this case.

The explosion could be heard for miles. The paint booth no longer existed. The steel sides, ripped loose by the blast, were propelled through the metal walls of the building and into a field outside. The blast was so intense it tore the entire building from its foundation and pushed the walls out ten feet from the foundation. The smoker's body was torn to pieces, which was a Godsend compared to his partner.

The second meth cook happened to be returning to the lab after making a quick trip to town. As he was exiting his car, an explosion occurred. Unfortunately for this suspect, he had just spent two days in the building prior to leaving, causing him to be saturated, both externally and internally, with ether. As the explosion ripped through the building, flames followed all trails of the thin gas and set fire to everything exposed to it, including the second suspect outside. The man was immediately transformed into a living torch.

Running from the scene, the man knew a cattle water tank was located right behind the shop, so he ran and dived into the water. While racing to the pond, he left behind a trail of flesh and singe marks. Every piece of living vegetation he touched immediately died and turned brown.

The water saturated his body to the point of extinguishing the fire, but the damage was irreversible. A huge amount of flesh had already melted from his body. The man had ingested so much of the gas, when he arrived at Brooks Medical Center, his intestines were still boiling from the heat.

The man experienced a slow death that no one wished on any living creature. This was a judgment with a sentencing of Hell before life's painful conclusion; dying was a welcome relief.

Obviously, Investigator Bays was not present to witness this death. If so, his prior thoughts for the demise of sexual offenders might have changed; or maybe not.

This incident was another grotesque memory for Investigator James. It was, yet, another moment to ask himself, *"why did I make this job a part of my life."*

CHAPTER 35

The breakdown of the lab and booking of evidence took over twelve hours. Luckily, no one was injured, no fires or explosion occurred. Now, it was time for Investigator James to work his magic. Robert possessed a talent most law enforcement officers consider a gift. This investigator was able to communicate effectively with just about anyone. Robert immediately made the suspect feel at ease. He seemed to transform into a friend rather than someone about to file a criminal case, an approach that cultivated confessions from many criminals. This talent could not be learned in any police academy. Investigator James' personality, along with his training and working the streets, provided him this gift.

Looking at the three subjects in custody, it was obvious which one was the dope cook. One wild-eyed suspect was thin, and he was only five-foot, six-inches tall-not what one would picture as a powerful icon of the methamphetamine world-but without a doubt, he was the cook. Investigator Waterman approached Robert and offered his assistance with the interrogation of the other two subjects. Robert accepted with a nod of the head.

After coming to the unit, Blake and Robert quickly earned each other's respect, trust and confidence. Each could almost read the other's mind, allowing a well-tuned working relationship, which was necessary for such an assignment.

The meth cook's identification reflected that he was Albert Payne. Albert had been a meth abuser for years. His pale and pitted skin, thin body and flesh covered with fresh, oozing blisters told the story.

As the interrogation began, it was obvious to Investigator James that Albert would be difficult to break; the suspect was devoted to his lifestyle. Albert also had an additional concern. In addition to cooking the dope, he was tasked with making sure the lab was secure during the process. Albert was the cook, but it was someone else's money funding the lab. With the JDLST team confiscating the lab, Albert now had a larger fear-the moneyman.

With a one-hundred and ten-thousand-dollar investment being confiscated, Albert had to protect the identity of his boss in order to maintain his life. The only way for this to occur was for him to remain silent and spend significant time in jail. Cooperating and being released from custody would result in his demise.

The initial interrogation of Albert by Blake Waterman did not result in a confession. The only information Blake got from the meth cook was that this was his lab and no one else was involved. The other two who accompanied him were insignificant and served as assistants. Regarding the man who fled the scene, Albert had no idea who he was. Investigator Waterman discontinued his interrogation of Albert and led the two assistants off to an adjoining room.

With a lab of this magnitude, it was doubtful anyone would snitch out the moneyman, but the investigators would certainly try to get this information from him or her. One commonly used interrogation tactic was to separate the suspects. If kept apart long enough, each individual would wonder if the other had ratted them out. Blake took Albert's two assistants out of the room, so Robert could have his time alone with the meth cook.

It soon became apparent to Investigator James that Albert was not going to divulge any information about the lab's money man. After speaking with Blake about his interviews, he conveyed to Robert that one of the women in the room with Albert wanted to talk, but it would have to be later. It was time to transport their suspects to a jail cell.

As Investigator James escorted his prisoner through the house to the awaiting patrol car, they passed the table containing the photos of the two pregnant women. Still curious, Investigator James bent down and seized the two pictures.

"Who are your pregnant friends here, Albert," Robert asked.

The look on Albert's face soon changed to reveal one of shock and fear. Albert's choice of silence was no surprise to Robert. Something was significant about these photos and Albert's reaction just helped confirm this. The investigator quietly slipped the photos into his pocket as Albert was released to a waiting patrolman.

Four suspects in jail, the seizure of fifty pounds of liquid P2P and over seventy-five thousand dollars in cash. *"Not a bad day. No sir, not a bad day."*

"One of Sergeant Park's cigars would definitely taste good right about now," Robert thought. *"Indeed, it would."*

CHAPTER 36

7.35 A.M.

The search warrant was a success, with one dog shot and a suspect injured after experiencing the wrath of Investigator Ronnie Bays. These were the only setbacks in Robert's mind that occurred, but Ronnie disagreed. The fact that he had the opportunity to kick some ass after being a gun's target, gave pleasure to this investigator.

Two females were taken into custody from the house where meth cook Payne was operating. One appeared to fit the typical doper type profile, but the other had the appearance of a professional businesswoman. The second female was soon identified as Lori Sims. Now, it was time for Robert to work his magic on Lori and see what information he could obtain from her.

Many deals promising minimal or no prosecution, have been made in the interrogation rooms of police stations. This night would soon follow protocol.

Lori was a pharmaceutical representative with one of the nation's largest drug manufacturers. In Robert's mind, a meth lab with a businesswoman who makes over one-hundred thousand dollars a year, is abnormal. Robert's interrogation of the suspect soon revealed the answers to his curiosity.

Lori Sims was a college graduate who had been working in her position for the past six years. She enjoyed her job and Lori had a desire to climb the corporate ladder, which gave Robert additional leverage against her. An arrest and conviction for manufacturing methamphetamine would surely end her career, and Lori knew it.

Lori Sims' story was one somewhat familiar to Robert. Once the money started flowing in after college, she became entangled in the fast crowd of Dallas and started hitting the party scene hard. Being an attractive, well-built woman, Lori was never deprived of invitations to attend social gatherings.

Lori's is a textbook case; she initially began using marijuana, followed by cocaine and then Ecstasy. Now, Lori could not make it through one day without putting a chemical into her body. She had become an addict.

Information from Lori flowed without much prodding from Robert. She knew the only way to help her cause was to give Investigator James something of substance. Lori acknowledged the fact she had an addiction problem, several of them, and this may be the best way out.

"Investigator James, I got involved with the wrong guy; who is the reason I am here."

She told Robert how she met a wealthy businessman in a local bar, who possessed charm and B.S. like no one she had ever met. They began dating, with trips to the Mexican Rivera on a private jet occurring monthly. One thing soon led to another and before she knew it, this man had her addicted to coke and meth. Lori's financial security soon dwindled to nothing, and she traded her home for a five-hundred and fifty-dollar a month, one-bedroom apartment. By reducing her lifestyle, Lori had more money to support her habit. By the grace of God, Lori managed to maintain her job.

Lori Sims continued to tell how she and this individual quit dating, but their friendship continued. Lori needed his dope and he needed Lori's talents. In some strange way, she still wanted to be his woman, and he knew this. To diminish her mentally, this man would have Lori come to his home during the evening. After wining and dining her, a second woman appeared, quickly becoming involved in the sexual atmosphere. Soon, the clothes fell, and Lori knew what she had to do. For the drugs to flow, she was required to become involved in a threesome with the two. As playtime progressed, portions of powder were given to Lori until her hunger was satisfied.

As Lori's drug problem worsened, her ex-lover began using her to help with his operation, such as the drug lab she was in tonight. It was Lori's duty to watch over the process, and to make sure all the finished product was delivered to the boss. A constant problem with meth cooks was that usually a large chunk of the powder would not make it to the financer of the lab. Using Lori, the cook was not intimidated by her presence, but knew of and respected Lori's role well.

"Okay, Lori. This is all fine and dandy, but I need a name."

"He is big Investigator James, real big. This man is involved in more than you ever imagine."

"Drugs, prostitution and… We have to be very careful. If he suspicions that we spoke, I am dead!"

"A name Lori, I want a name," demanded, Robert.

"His name is Gene King, or as many know him; 'The King'."

Silence immediately filled the room. Ms. Sims had Robert James' undivided attention.

CHAPTER 37

Back in the Atlantic, Gene King was aboard his ship. This time there was no gambling, no women and no special guests. Gene had made the trip down a few days prior, accompanied by his lieutenant. On board the ship, awaiting Gene's arrival was Doctor Robert 'Bob' Perez.

The doctor was still a young man for his profession. Barely breaking the forty-year-old mark, he fit in very well with the rest of Gene's faction.

Dr. Perez first became acquainted with Gene a few years earlier, during his first visit to the King's floating palace of pleasure. The initial twenty-thousand he paid to board the ship was affordable, but what came afterwards was not. Bob, an OBGYN specialist, just graduated from medical school five years prior to meeting Gene. He was still burdened with excessive loan repayments required each month for his education loans. In addition, setting up shop was not a financial walk in the park either. Granted, Dr. Perez was making good money, but not enough to afford all the vices on Gene's ship. The obligations of being a married man with two children loomed over his head.

Bob Perez was coerced by some colleagues to make a trip to the 'Love Boat', as they called it. This was only after a year of attempts to get him to make the investment. Once the good doctor boarded the ship, common sense quickly eluded him. With plenty of cocaine up the nose, two of the ship's vixens guided this high flyer to a black jack table. Things went down-hill from there. Being in the hole for over seventy-five thousand dollars, Bob thought lady-luck would come to his rescue; lady luck never arrived but he continued to play.

"Gene, the pit boss just called me over. There is a problem at one of the tables. A guest is signing markers that we don't think his ass can cash," Bradley advised his boss.

"Tell me about this guy Bradley. Who, where and what is he all about?"

"He's a young doctor, OB/GYN specialist."

This brought a smile to Gene's face.

"Let him play, Bradley. Keep giving him the powder and cut him off when he hits the three-hundred-thousand-dollar mark. I can use this guy."

"You got it boss," relied Bradley as he exited the room.

As predicted, Dr. Perez hit that magic mark. Upon doing so, Gene instructed his lieutenant to escort the good doctor to an adjoining room, where he awaited. Once Bob Perez was in Gene's presence, the "prayer meeting" began. The conversation was brief and to the point. Gene King had the winning ace in hand in this game. With too much at stake to lose, the good doctor succumbed to the King. Gene added a much-needed physician to his flock.

Now, two years later, Dr. Perez was one of Genes most trusted employees. The King knew that his good doctor would never betray him. Dr. Perez had way too much to lose, and over the past few years Gene had collected additional ammunition that could be used against him.

Gene always preferred to be on board during the surgeries. In the bowels of the ship, Gene had converted a room into a small surgery center. It contained all the equipment that Dr. Perez needed to perform his procedures. Only one surgery had ever gone wrong. The ocean, fifty miles from shore, assured Gene that the body would never be found.

Only thirty minutes until the first procedure. Gene and Bradley were downing a cocktail when Gene's phone rang. Only a few had this number, so it was certain that he would answer if anyone called.

"Hello," was the only word spoken by Gene for almost a minute. The look on his face conveyed to Bradley that something was wrong.

"Who the hell is this Investigator Robert James, and what is the JDLST?" I want answers Bill and I want them now. That's why I pay you the big-bucks, damnit,"* Gene shouted into the phone.

155

"You're a lawyer, so handle it. Get the bitch out of jail, but leave the others there to rot!" The King was pissed.

Gene slammed the phone down.

"What's up, Boss Man?"

"It appears that one of our labs in Ft. Worth was hit. Our cook, Albert Payne was arrested in the middle of a process, along with Lori Sims. Some dumbass that Albert brought in as a lookout sentry took a few shots at the police too."

"Is he dead, Gene?"

"Unfortunately, no, but he should be and WILL BE! Some cowboy cop gave him a good ass kicking and he is in jail, but that is his own problem now. That punk does not know any of us, so screw him. I want Lori out ASAP before she gets jail-phobia and starts singing. Bill is all over this one, but it appears that a federal task force made the hit. This makes things a little tougher, but nothing that we can't handle."

Bradley watched as the King slid over to a small table and pulled out a packet of white powder. No doubt, it was cocaine. This event was becoming more familiar with Gene these days. What was once a well-oiled machine was now beginning to squeak, and Bradley was looking at the reasons why. When you're using what you're selling, the brain's common sense well goes dry. None of Gene's labs were ever raided, he was just too careful. It was obvious someone was running his or her mouth. Maybe not purposely, but it was happening.

Bradley's confidence in his boss was starting to diminish.

"Hey asshole," Gene said in a boisterous laugh. *"Let's get down below. We have some surgeries to attend."*

CHAPTER 38

It was almost 2 P.M., which marked two days straight that Robert and several other members of the JDLST had been without sleep. By all logic, Robert should be tired, but right now, he was experiencing one of the largest adrenaline rushes of his life. Finally, the team had a break. One investigator had a source who knew Gene King better than most, and this source was willing to cooperate.

During the four and one-half hour interrogation of Lori Sims, Robert learned a lot about the demonic drug dealer. Lori told him all about the meth labs and coke runs from Mexico, along with his new drug, Formula-X. Now, keeping her alive would be a project in itself. Normally in these situations, Lori would have immediately entered into a witness protection program, but she refused. All Lori requested was for her criminal charges to be eventually dropped, along with some assistance in relocating. With Lori's position at a national corporation, this could probably be handled without much problem, but only after she fulfilled her obligation with the JDLST.

After Robert had clearance from Special Agent Michaels and the Federal Prosecutor, he could offer Lori a deal. She was to continue her relationship with Gene King, but only long enough for the team to gather significant evidence against him. Lori knew that if she did not follow through with her end of the bargain she would look at twenty-plus years in a remote, hot Texas prison. Reluctantly, Lori agreed.

The plan was simple. Robert would take Lori to the Tarrant County Jail, where a high bail-bond would be set. Under the authority of the JDLST, Lori would be released without having to pay a dime. Gene knew everything about Lori, including the salary that she could make at her day job. It would be no surprise when Lori told the King that she bonded herself out of jail by tapping into her personal 401k plan.

Lori's bail-bond records would reflect the name of an attorney who was supposedly representing her. When the JDLST was initially organized, the Federal Prosecutor's office sought out several local attorneys, whom they knew were beyond approach. All were reputable, established attorneys in their community, who focused on criminal defense work. The work would be easy for these selected attorneys. All they had to do was keep an oath of secrecy and for everyone they were assigned, Uncle Sam would slide ten thousand dollars their way.

These steps were extremely important when working organized crime cases, especially when they involved the rich and powerful, such as Gene King. Money can buy about anything, which includes cops, politicians and even some judges. It was imperative that all adhere to the guidelines of this protection plan; otherwise, witnesses would begin to disappear, and their sources would dry up.

"Take her to Tarrant County, walk her through and then get your ass home, Robert," ordered SA Michaels.

"Will do. We're gonna get this guy, Boss Man."

"That we will, Robert. I will have the team ready for your briefing at 11:00 A.M. sharp tomorrow. Now get Ms. Sims taken care of so you can go home and get some rest."

The trip from Dallas to Ft. Worth was quiet for Robert and Lori. Both were exhausted from the events from the past twenty-four hours. Lori asked that Robert drive through any fast food restaurant, so she could grab something to eat. Not a bad idea for Robert either. The excitement of the day seemed to drown out the signals of hunger that his empty stomach was sending.

Upon arriving at the jail, Robert was met by an assistant prosecutor from the Federal Prosecutors Special Crimes Unit.

"I will take it from here, Investigator James. I have direct orders from SA Michaels to send you home as soon as you delivered Ms. Sims."

"I will just hang around until she is released," replied Robert.

"She is in good hands Mr. James; this is not my first rodeo. Now go home before I have to call your boss," the attorney said with a light-hearted smile.

An air of relief and trust soon encompassed Robert's mind as he handed Lori over to the prosecutor. Lori was a long-awaited prize in his endeavor against Gene King, and Robert wanted to make sure his valued witness was secure and protected. For Robert, this was comparable to possessing a million-dollar lotto ticket you can't take your eyes from until it is cashed. The Special Crimes Unit was composed of the 'best of the best', where integrity issues never arose. Without knowing the man, for some reason Robert felt no anxieties. His new informant would be safe.

"Lori, page me tomorrow at noon, and not a minute later!"

"I certainly will Robert, and, thank you."

"It's bed time," thought Robert as he set his car in motion toward Dallas.

CHAPTER 39

Off the coast of Florida, things had gone well--four patients and four successful surgeries. One day of recuperation and it would be time for the women to earn their pay. The King was pleased but Bradley's thoughts were more about the concerns he now had for his boss, and not as much on the four women.

It was time for Gene and Bradley to head back to Ft. Worth. The lieutenant had given orders to several of his men aboard the ship regarding the women. It was important that both he and Gene be removed from this part of the plan, in the remote event the women would be detected and apprehended.

A helicopter waiting on deck soon whisked the men back to the mainland.

CHAPTER 40

At 11:00 A.M. sharp in the JDLST office, Investigator Robert James began his briefing. The next thirty minutes were like listening to a crime drama for the other investigators. Robert recited details concerning drugs, sex, money and murder. Movies were not as exciting as the true-to-life crime drama that was beginning to unfold in front of them.

Investigator James told the others about Lori being part of Gene's life for the past couple of years, and that she knows a little about much of his operation.

Robert's plan to have Lori infiltrate Gene's organization seemed simple, but most likely would get complicated. First, Lori was to continue her association with Gene and feed information to Robert. The other members of JDLST were to split into two-man teams and focus on Gene's associates, especially his lieutenant, Bradley Dean. Traffic stops, search warrants, arrests and seizures were all part of the plan. Robert knew they couldn't totally rely on Lori for all their information, so other informants would be sought. It was important to have numerous avenues of information, but more importantly to Robert was that others would be blamed for Gene's unfortunate circumstances rather than Lori.

As with previous assignments, Robert would work with Investigator Blake Waterman, and Robert would be the only contact with Lori. However, once information was obtained from her, Robert would pass it along to Blake. Investigator Waterman was relentless. Once he had settled on an objective, he refused to accept defeat. When those in the office heard Blake announce, "I'm on a mission from God," all knew some crook was going to suffer the legal wrath of this man. Without a doubt, Blake was damn good at his job.

For the JDLST unit, the remainder of the day was spent on planning strategy and identifying targets. At noon, Robert received the promised telephone call from Lori. Today though, he would be too busy to meet with his informant. There were too many loose ends to tie up at the office, and Investigator James put his new informant off until the following day.

It was almost 8:00 P.M. before Robert took a break. The excitement of the job had kept him running on all eight cylinders, but fatigue finally set in. The boss ordered pizza earlier that day, and the remainders were now cold.

"Ahhh," Robert mumbled. *"A cold pizza, diet cola and chocolate chips cookies: the perfect meal for a bachelor."*

It was time to take a food break. In his office, Robert had a small portable television placed there to view evidence and training tapes.

"Not tonight though," as Robert began to thumb through the channels, knowing that his favorite television show, "Miami Vice," would soon be airing. This break was strategically planned.

For an hour, Robert relaxed while watching Don and Rico cruising around in their cigarette boat, partying down and chasing crooks. Being a cop, Robert filtered reality from fiction, but the purpose of watching this show was for entertainment and diversion, and the hour-long escape from reality was welcomed.

An hour later "Miami Vice" was over and Robert knew it was time to shut down shop and go home. Tomorrow would be another busy day. Knowing that he had a lead on a crook he had wanted for several years, gave him satisfaction. Robert knew the road to bringing Gene King to justice would be long and hard, but at least he could embark on the journey.

The two women who were murdered in Springdale were still on Robert's mind constantly. In occasional silent prayers, Robert asked God to let the women know that someday he will avenge their murders. One day, he would silence the voices in his head asking for this to be done.

As Robert rose to leave, he looked at the Polaroid picture of the two pregnant Spanish women he retrieved from Gene's lab a few days ago. Curiously, Robert stopped and began analyzing the photos. He went quickly to his file cabinet and pulled out a large binder that housed reports and photos from the Springdale murder.

"There are some differences but many similarities. All four women look like they could be sisters, or at least from the same country."

"There has to be some connection here," Robert thought, as he turned out the lights and locked the office door behind him.

Tomorrow would be another day; maybe the answers would be found. It was time for this weary law officer to go home. The excitement and adrenaline rush that had kept Robert going for the past few days subsided, leaving an exhausted man behind.

CHAPTER 41

For the next two weeks, Robert and his new informant spent hours each day, traveling through many cities and towns in North Texas. Addresses, names, descriptions, vehicles and properties - they are all part of the immense diary of intelligence he was collecting with Lori's help.

After each day, Robert passed the information to Investigator Waterman, who started the paper trail for the new chapters of the Gene King crime saga. This process involved hours of computer checks and visiting courthouses for research. He also conducted meetings with law enforcement officials throughout the South to gather information about the King crime family.

This part of the job was not glamorous, but necessary in working organized crime cases. To make such a case, a law officer must prove an organization of four or more individuals exist for the common cause of committing crimes. In Gene's case, Robert knew it would take numerous cases against this man to send him into retirement at a federal prison.

During the day, Lori continued her normal routine of working her job as a pharmaceutical representative. At night, she belonged to Robert. For Lori, this had evolved from a burdensome task to one of pleasure. This was somewhat comparable to the Stockholm syndrome as Lori was becoming dependent on her badge-toting captor. Not exactly a prisoner, but developing an obligation to a man that she only recently met.

Without a doubt Lori knew that she belonged to Robert James. At first, she would constantly wonder how long this process would take. After spending two weeks with Robert, now she was beginning to dread the day that it would end. The informant was developing an emotional tie to her young investigator.

164

Week two had come to an end at 2:15 A.M. on a Saturday morning. Robert had just pulled into the parking lot at Lori's apartment.

"Let's say Monday, around six," Robert asked.

"Certainly."

A moment of silence engulfed the car as Lori had fixated on two men walking through the parking lot. She then seized the opportunity to test the waters.

"Robert, those guys are kind of creepy. Would you mind walking me to the door?"

"Sure," Robert replied as he took the pistol from his console and stuck the auto into his pants.

"Just like my credit cards; I never leave home without it," he snickered.

At the door, Lori paused again. A well-lit night and the rays of the full moon had highlighted her captor's face. Not only was Robert her emotional crutch, but Lori was also attracted to his physique and good looks.

Robert also felt the awkwardness that filled the air, and he stood motionless, staring back at the attractive woman standing in front of him.

"A hug goodnight, Robert," she asked.

Without a word, the investigator walked closer and wrapped his arms around her curvaceous and toned body. Robert loved women anyway, but his job was depriving him of this pleasure. Robert enjoyed this moment, but he quickly released her and took a few steps away; obviously both were consumed by the moment.

With little nerve that she could muster, Lori managed to ask, *"Robert, would you like to come in for a nightcap?"*

165

Hesitantly, Robert rejected Lori's invitation; both were disappointed this was the answer.

"See you Monday, Lori; enjoy the remainder of your weekend."

Robert then returned to his car, rolled the windows down and drove home. Silence filled the car; usually seconds after he turned the ignition, the on-button to the stereo shortly followed. Not tonight; Robert had something different on his mind. He could not deny that over the past couple of weeks, something was going on between him and Lori-not job related, but personal and emotional.

Robert was attracted to Lori, and his desire for a sexual encounter with her was intense. He must be strong, though; he could not commit the Cardinal Sin by having a relationship with a woman in Lori's position. This sin could cost his position on the task force, and possibly his job.

Robert knew he must keep this relationship strictly professional. He had to fight this feeling. If Lori decided to back out of their deal, Robert would be responsible for her incarceration.

"Keep it professional dude, keep it professional," Robert told his reflection in the car mirror as he accelerated toward the interstate.

Inside her apartment, Lori sat watching out the window, gazing down at her prince as he drove from the parking lot.

"Oh God. Monday evening, hurry up and get here."

Lori could not bear to gaze out the window any longer; at this point, Monday was light years away.

CHAPTER 42

At 6:00 P.M. on a Monday evening. Robert picked up Lori and it was time to work.

After gathering intelligence for two weeks, the time arrived to hit the streets. Lori would actually take the young investigator to meet members of the criminal underworld who were involved with Gene King. It was crucial that Lori's identity be protected; therefore, the CI had to introduce Robert to several of her associates, who would assist him in infiltrating the homes of Gene's associates.

"Ready to get to work, Ms. Lori," Robert asked.

As each spoke and looked at the other, both realized things were different between them. For Lori, the romantic feelings toward Robert consumed her. For the young detective, a yellow caution flag was attempting to beat down his feelings for her. Both knew the feelings must be set aside for the work to be done. Lori's freedom and Robert's job depended on this case being a law enforcement success.

"Okay, Mr. Robert, take me to Cooper Street in Arlington. I will introduce you to my step-brother, Rusty."

"Your step-brother," Robert asked her. *"I never knew."*

"Well, once you meet him you will understand why I never told you," Lori replied. *"This is my test for you, Robert; before I put my life on the line, I want you and Rusty to make one meth buy, so I can see how you perform. Rusty does not know Gene King but I am sure wherever he takes you, Mr. King will not be associated. The evening could be interesting and educational for you, Robert. You will be running with the street scum,"* she snickered.

A cop never allows informants to direct an investigation or to give orders. Normally, Robert would have been all over any crook or CI that even thought of doing this. Lori was different, and with all she had to risk, the investigator understood her concern.

"To Cooper Street it is then," Robert replied.

Lori's stepbrother Rusty was completely opposite from his sister with whom he grew up. He was a blue-collar worker, with a streetwise look and demeanor. As a juvenile, Rusty was in and out of about every juvenile facility in the Dallas-Ft. Worth area. He never committed a crime of violence, just petty thefts with an occasional car-theft. Obviously, the crimes were committed to support his early addiction to methamphetamines.

Robert navigated his car into an apartment complex, which was just a step above the status of a ghetto. Once Rusty and Robert were introduced, Lori would return home before the games began.

"Robert, I will not tell Rusty much about you except that you are a friend who needs a fix. Rusty's only question will be how much powder will he get from the deal. Thoughts of going back to jail are practically non-existent from this idiot, Robert. He just wants his meth."

"Got it."

"I will be right back, Robert," Lori said as she exited the car.

As she walked from the car, Robert admired the looks and physique of his captive CI. Her graceful gait and form-fitting clothes made Robert's mind drift from the subject at hand.

"Snap out of it Dude; keep your mind on the job!"

For a moment, Robert realized how all-consuming his job was, which left no time for female companionship. This was abnormal for Robert to ignore the pleasures of adding names to his little black book. The Gene King case derailed any recent romantic endeavors. Lori's presence added to this case, in more ways than Robert allowed himself to admit.

168

"Focus, Mr. Police Officer, focus!"

A few minutes later, the CI reappeared from a hallway with her brother in tow. Rusty looked exactly as the visual picture Lori painted for Robert. Lori was correct; there was no family resemblance between the two half-siblings.

"What's up, bro? Rusty's my name and meth is my game," Rusty boasted as he entered the car.

"Not much, guy. Let's take your sister home and go find some 'go-fast'."

"Game on, Dude!"

During the fifteen-minute drive back to Lori's apartment, Robert debated if he had made the right decision. Apparently, drugs had devoured part of Rusty's brain, at least the common-sense portion.

For Robert, the drive back to Lori's apartment seemed to take forever. Rusty rambled continuously, engaging himself in many topics that made little sense to anyone listening-a common trait for a meth user.

"This night is going to be a long one. Help me Lord!"

"Have fun, boys," Lori said as she left the car.

There were no hugs tonight, just a sheepish smile and wink to Robert as Lori walked away.

"Robert, you know where the Slumber Inn is in Haltom City?" Rusty asked.

"Nope, but I am sure you can get me there," Robert replied.

"And by the way Rusty, just call me "Mad Dog." This 'Robert' shit is how women talk to men; not bros like us."

"Got it, MAD DOG!"

169

"What an asshole," Robert thought. *"Maybe I should do the world a favor and shoot Rusty now."*

A few minutes later, Robert pulled his car into the parking lot of the Slumber Inn and parked in the rear lot.

"How much cash-ola you have on you, Mad Dog?"

"I have enough money to make us both happy, Rusty. I want to go home with nothing less than two eight-balls of powder tonight."

"Whoa, Dude! Wait here for a few minutes, Mr. Big Spender; I will be right back."

Five minutes soon turned into thirty. Robert waited in the car and observed all the addicts looking out their windows for cops, while others trolled the parking lot looking for dope. Robert assumed Rusty had scored and was sampling the product before bringing it out. Like most other speed freaks, Rusty lost track of time.

Forty-five minutes later, Rusty finally appeared.

"I made a connect Mad Dog. Un-ass that seat and let's go!"

Reaching down to make sure his Sig. 45 was secure and hidden; Robert followed Rusty into Room #125.

"Carol, this is Mad Dog."

"You a cop, Mad Dog?" she asked.

"If you are, Dude, and don't tell me, and if I do anything wrong, that's entrapment," Carol instructed her new friend. *"I can't be arrested, then."*

"You're about to insult me, Baby," he replied.

"Sorry, Dude, but a person has to be careful these days."

Carol produced a small, plastic baggie containing approximately a gram of a yellowish-white powder, definitely not the finest dope in the land. The yellow tint revealed to Robert that the meth was not pure; either dirty in the powdering process or the cook ran short of his chemicals and had to make a substitution. Knowing meth was composed of and processed with acids, lye, and aluminum crystals, along with the process of converting the liquid to powder by using toxic gases; turned Robert's stomach.

"No wonder these people look like shit," Robert thought.

Carol was no exception. Her thirty-one-year-old body resembled the body of a person twenty years her senior, who drank and smoked her entire life. Carol was as skinny as a rail, her hair was uncombed, and speed sores and scars covered most of her exposed skin.

Robert and Rusty watched as she took some powder from the baggie and placed it into a spoon. After carefully adding a small amount of water to it, Carol mixed the potion with the tip of a syringe. Once the potion met the desired consistency, the poison was drawn up into the syringe.

"Hold me off, Mad Dog," Carol yelled. *"Let me run this stuff, and then we will find your eight-ball."*

Then, Carol produced a small strand of cloth and began to wrap it around her upper arm.

"Pull tightly, and I will tell you when to release it."

Robert grabbed both ends and pulled them together, causing the skin to fold. With most people, veins protrude, exposing a target for the incoming syringe. This was not true in Carol's case, because she had shot dope so long that scars highlighted each vein.

"Damn it! Hand me that razor on the coffee table."

Robert followed Carol's orders and handed her the blade.

Had she taken the time to watch his face, Carol would have known at this moment that Robert was a cop.

The investigator's face turned pale, as Carol pushed down on the razor and forced it into her arm, making a four-inch long cut. Her arm began to bleed profusely. She had to quickly wipe blood away before it covered the interior of the wound.

"Found you, Bitch!"

Carol rejoiced as she slid the syringe into a vein exposed by the open wound. Her face changed instantly; Carol was in her place of pleasure.

"My turn," Rusty said as he grabbed the bloodstained syringe from Carol. Robert watched as Rusty reloaded the syringe and injected the meth, along with some of Carol's blood, into his arm. The possibility of AIDS or Hepatitis being transmitted from Carol's dirty syringe was apparently not a concern for Rusty.

"Ok, Baby, let's go find your stuff, Mad Dog. Let's see, you wanted a couple of eight balls, right?"

"At least."

Carol showed a baggie containing one eight-ball.

"That will be three-hundred and fifty bucks, Dude."

"Bullshit, Carol – Two-hundred and seventy-five. This stuff is dirty, and it has been cut," Robert replied.

Carol reached over, grabbed the money, and handed the baggie of meth to Robert.

"I can get the rest of the meth for you, but it is a few miles away. Let's ride boys."

By this time, Rusty's actions were similar a ping-pong ball caught in a wind tunnel. He was chewing his gum at a such rapid pace,

Robert expected it to burst into flames at any moment; the meth was doing its job.

"Over here, we are taking my car."

Carol pointed toward a nineteen-seventy-eight, mid-sized Dodge Station Wagon.

"Hey, it's not the best car in the world but it gets me there," Carol informed the men as she pointed toward her prized chariot.

"Rusty, sit by your woman up front there; I will take the back seat."

Robert's offer was not made out of courtesy, but rather out of caution. He knew if anything went wrong, being in the back seat would be to his advantage.

Carol put the car into motion and shot out of the parking lot like a rocket.

"This puppy has a three-sixty in it boys. Looks are deceiving, aren't they?"

Haltom Road, a forty-five mile-per-hour speed zoned city street, was supporting Carol's vehicle charging down at eighty-five MPH.

"Hey, Baby, I want to get there in one piece," Robert shouted toward the maniac driver.

"Just sit back and enjoy the ride," Carol replied, as she continued her reckless driving.

Robert was not the only one that Carol was making nervous. After a couple of close calls, Rusty was obviously scared, despite his state of mental euphoria.

"Slow down Bitch, or I am gonna beat your ass!" Rusty was not hiding the fact he was not enjoying the ride either.

Carol continued without yielding to either of her passenger's request.

Ahead was a stoplight.

"Hopefully, we can hit the red and escape this hunk of doom," Robert thought.

The light was red and finally Carol began to slow down, but as she approached, it turned green. Since it was 3:00 A.M., there was not a single car in front of Carol to cause her to slow down. As she began to accelerate again, Rusty made good on his promise.

The car was about to hit forty-five mph when suddenly, Rusty hit Carol mid-face with his closed fist. In an instant, the Dodge was being piloted by an unconscious driver.

The car slowed as it ran off the road and onto the parking lot of a fast food restaurant. Only a slight impact was felt as the car struck a light pole in the parking lot.

"You dumbass, you could have killed us both!" Robert was furious with Rusty.

Without another word, Robert's clenched fist, with his one-hundred and ninety-five-pound body propelling it, landed a punch onto Rusty's face.

With an eight-ball of meth in hand, Robert escaped the car. Not once did he look back at the two unconscious bodies lying in the front seat.

"You two can rot in Hell!"

Robert walked briskly from the accident scene, knowing the police would soon arrive, which could compromise his undercover status. At this rapid pace, it did not take long for Rusty and Carol to disappear into the darkness of night.

174

CHAPTER 43

Sunday afternoons were lazy on the eastern beaches of Florida. Summer months had come and gone, allowing the locals to repossess their esteemed sandy beaches. Most families and young beachgoers abandoned the warm beaches and returned to their native states further north. Florida citizens wreak wealth, which allows most to escape during the summer months. Many millionaires jetted off to other states and countries, with the sole intention of eluding the northern evaders.

Unfortunately, the U.S. Coast Guard's business was not seasonal. Ocean rescues are only one of the main duties of these elite aquatic soldiers. While patrolling the eastern and southern waters around Florida, the Coast Guard can expect anything. From the interception of Cuban refugees to the interdiction of drug-running powerboats, nothing was out of the normal for them.

"Coast Guard Unit 42 to Base."

"Go ahead Unit 42," the dispatcher replied.

"We will be boarding a 42 Foot Scarab, Florida registration number A42165," the boats communications officer broadcasted.

"10-4 on your information Unit 42; will be standing by."

Coast Guard Unit 42 was an interceptor boat with a primary function to intercept board and inspect watercraft coming in from international waters that may carry illegal cargo. Their boat was equipped with two 62-millimeter machine guns and a crew of eight that could send chills down the spine of Captain Hook.

As soon as Unit 42 activated its lights and siren, it was obvious that the Scarab would be yielding to them. The Scarab was a boat of choice for drug runners because of its speed and ability to outrun most of the Coast Guard's fleet. Occasionally, sea smugglers tried to elude the Coast Guard during interdiction attempts, but soon met the wrath of the long-range weapons and the devastation from the air support.

The Scarab's skipper immediately shut down the three engines propelling the boat; the Coast Guard expected this to be a routine boarding.

"State the purpose of your entry into the United States of American," the Captain commanded from the boat's skipper.

"We are American Citizens. This boat is registered in the State of Florida, and is occupied by U.S. Citizens," he replied.

"We will be boarding for inspection."

Four Coast Guard officers made entry onto the Scarab and conducted a quick search of its premises. There were three people on board—the skipper, Dr. Perez and his pregnant wife. Nothing of a suspicious nature was discovered during this brief inspection.

"We appreciate your compliance; you are now free to go," the Captain said.

"And, Doctor, good luck with junior there," he nodded and smiled at the pregnant wife.

Coast Guard Unit 42 then made a U-turn and veered north, away from Miami.

"Wish they were all that easy," the Captain thought as the distance between them and the Scarab began to widen.

"Let's get to Miami," the Doctor ordered the skipper.

Most people in their position would have been relieved that the Coast Guard left without taking possession of the valued-illegal cargo the Scarab contained. For Dr. Perez, this was not much of a concern. He

176

knew the cargo was too secure to be detected by a visual inspection. Fortunately for the boat's skipper, he had no idea what cargo he was transporting.

"Just a doctor and his pregnant wife," the skipper thought. *"Illegal substances will never be a part of any cargo I am hauling."*

The skipper silently boasted as he steered the Scarab toward Miami.

CHAPTER 44

Bradley Dean just reached the Austin area and directed his vehicle to the secluded hills around Lake Travis. Several years back, Bradley made a connection in the area where some meth products were taken for distribution. This connection, as with many others, was not known by Gene King. A part of the King's strategy was that a buffer be placed between him and most distributors. Gene trusted Bradley enough, so distributors were spoken of only if a problem developed.

Through his connection, Bradley rented a small house in the Hill Country, a maneuver kept hidden from Gene. For the first time since the men became friends, Bradley was beginning to question his boss. Obviously, Gene had an addiction to cocaine, which was beginning to interfere with the business. The secret became obvious during one of Gene's cocaine highs when he started running his mouth to a female friend, Lori Sims. Lori was under Bradley's scrutiny, and he no longer trusted her. Gene appeared not to be the wiser.

A major meth lab was raided in Ft. Worth and the JDLST had one of Gene's prized pupils in their possession. Gene believed Lori's story about how she got out of jail, but Bradley was apprehensive. Being in the drug business his entire adult life, Bradley knew the bail for this type of arrest was extremely high, unless of course, the prisoner cooperated with the cops. Even though Lori had a decent job, the possibility of her coming up with the needed cash in one day was improbable. A year ago, Gene, too, would have questioned Lori, and had her attend one of his 'prayer meetings'; which was not the case this time. The King was getting careless.

Gene's lieutenant spent the remaining five days in Austin. Reporting in each day to Gene, Bradley told the boss he was in Houston, enjoying a few days with a woman. This was out of the norm for this lieutenant, but Gene gave him the benefit of the doubt.

The remote house was perfect for Bradley Dean. The entire process would only take a few days and the yield would be large. Fortunately, the processing of Formula-X did not emit the horrid odors that came from meth. This house was located about one mile from a paved road, and any vehicle coming down the private drive was noticed immediately. It also helped that a family member of a biker friend that Bradley knew owned the property. He relied on the bikers to guard the location while he was cooking Formula-X. Bradley, indeed, found a safe place to process his retirement fund.

Bradley Dean also knew that making Formula-X without Gene's blessing was risky. The risk was not from being detected by the police, but from Gene. The boss knew Formula-X was unique, and only his lieutenant could manufacture it. If Gene found out what Bradley was doing, the consequences would be grave!

CHAPTER 45

Another week passed; it was time for the Monday briefing at the JDLST office in Las Colinas, Texas. During this time, investigators would give a progress report on their segment of the investigation, along with other projects they may be working on. Lately, Gene King consumed most of the unit's time. With the information Robert was able to pass along to Blake Waterman, criminal cases against Gene's organization were being made. Investigator Waterman was a master at turning sand into crystal. Working with names and locations, Blake made things happen.

As Special Agent Michaels called upon each to report, pens were rolling and notebooks filling. Investigator Waterman was stacking numbers for raids run and criminals incarcerated. Ronnie Bays pulled in intelligence from the biker gangs, one of the main line suppliers for Gene's meth-operation. Mike Bales, another excellent investigator, was gathering information and coordinating operations with other law enforcement agencies regarding Gene's operations. Investigator Bales, a prior homicide investigator, was looking at several murders in Texas and Missouri that fit the profile of the King's method of operation.

With each raid, evidence was gathered. Most pieces alone would not lead to Gene's indictment, but combined with evidence of other cases, he would implicate Mr. King and his organization. Without a doubt, each seizure pissed Gene off. He grew to hate the words 'JDLST' and 'Investigator Robert James'. However, Gene was still under the illusion that he was untouchable.

Being a mastermind, for years Gene King had stashed money in offshore and overseas accounts. The Grand Cayman Islands and Switzerland seemed to be his favorites. If the unimaginable did happen, the King would flee the U.S. and live abroad from the millions he had saved, and he would live comfortably.

180

By plane, boat or car, if necessary, Gene could escape to a country that had not entered into an extradition treaty with the United States-most likely a country with government officials owned by the Cartel. Over the years, Gene had befriended many of the Cartel, while supplying them with a major drug artery into the U.S. Friends for life they were, but friendship did not necessarily mean that one in this environment would ever live to see his hair gray.

Robert's pager began vibrating; looking at the display, he noticed it was Lori. The call was earlier than most working nights, but she was ready to go. Apparently working from one's home gives additional freedom at times. It was two days since Lori had seen her favorite investigator, whom she had missed.

The last time Lori saw Robert was on Friday evening, when she introduced Robert to her stepbrother, Rusty. She was anxious to hear how their night went, especially since Lori had not been able to contact Rusty all weekend to inquire. Lori was also anxious to see if Robert passed her little test. Tolerating Rusty was a chore for anyone, especially a person as disciplined as Robert.

The curiosity was eating at her, until she was almost becoming nauseous. On the other hand, maybe her stomach twisted only when thinking of Robert James.

It was early afternoon when Robert arrived at Lori's apartment. He was reluctant to go to her door, unsure if he could resist if another invitation were extended to him. Robert knew the temptation was inevitable but, he was doing all he could to delay it. Since the moonlit encounter at her door several weeks ago, Lori had displayed herself to Robert as a woman being picked up for her first date. With hair and makeup done perfectly, and clothes revealing her toned body, she was trying her best to capture Robert's attention. Robert was putting his best effort forward to resist this temptation, which in turn caused Lori's efforts to intensify. Robert slowly made his way to Lori's door.

"Where to today, my dear," Robert asked as Lori entered his car.

"We're going to stay in Dallas tonight. But first I want to hear about Friday evening with Rusty."

"Oh, God," Robert sighed, *"must we?"*

181

"Yes sir, and before we even leave this driveway. So start talking, Mr. Cop Man," Lori said with an eager voice and smile.

Robert did not know how Lori would handle the truth, but he knew she would rather hear it from him than Rusty. After a five-minute dissertation, Robert ended his rendition of the evening.

Lori was silent for only a few moments when she erupted into a loud, lengthy laugh.

"So, you survived my brother and made a drug delivery case on a crook. Sounds like an eventful evening to me, Robert," remarked Lori.

"And Robert, I am glad you're okay. Now, head east, young man."

Robert sat in silence, but by the look on his face, Lori had given the perfect response.

"And our initial stop will be the first men's clothing store you can find," she ordered.

Robert noticed that Lori was dressed to kill, but he did not have a chance to ask before she gave her orders. Unsure at first, and a little reluctant to ask, Robert thought that maybe she had dressed this way to impress him. After receiving Lori's instructions, a silent sigh swept over Robert, knowing that keeping his mouth shut spared his ego.

Soon, a mall was in their sights, so Robert maneuvered his car through traffic, onto the entrance drive and into the parking lot. Once inside the mall, Lori was in command.

Law enforcement work was Robert's forte', but the mall belonged to Lori. Seeing a store of her liking, she grabbed Robert's hand.

"This store should do. Hope you have a high credit limit on that little gold card in your pocket."

"Please make this as painless as possible, Lori. I am a public servant you know."

With a schoolgirl grin, Lori pulled her captive into the store.

182

Thirty minutes later, the shopping venture was complete.

"Here's my card, and I would like to wear the new clothes out," Robert told the gentleman who assisted him.

Robert had traded blue jeans and polo shirt for an outfit made for the nightlife of Dallas. No one would argue that Robert and Lori made the perfect-looking couple, and certainly, Lori agreed.

Back in the car, Robert followed Lori's directions, which guided him into the parking lot of a large building just north of downtown Dallas. The lot was full of cars and a small army of young men working valet parking in front of the establishment. This place was far removed from "Scooters" in Ft. Worth. The outside looked like a converted warehouse, but the expensive cars lining the parking lot gave a person instant knowledge that this was a playground for the young movers and shakers of Dallas.

Feeling somewhat embarrassed by his modest vehicle, Robert self-parked in a space about as far from the front door as he could. Lori did not seem to mind, probably knowing what was running through his mind.

At this point, Robert asked Lori to brief him about the club. She began her dissertation about Gene King and a young female movie star buying this place last year and transforming it into one of the hippest clubs in the Dallas area. At times, lines consisted of several hundred-people waiting outside to enter. Lori had never been here, but knew this was a place one could score on the much sought-after drug, Ecstasy. With Gene King being one of the club's owners, this drug of choice would not be Ecstasy, it was Formula-X-music to the investigator's ears.

Before exiting the car, Robert pulled his pistol from beneath the seat and hid it under his shirt.

"I know," Lori instantly relied, *"you never leave home without it."*

"You know me well; you know me well."

A twenty-dollar per-person cover charge was the first indication this place was not for the financial meek-of-heart. The entry lines had yet to form, but most likely this was due to the Cowboys playing in Dallas tonight. Once the game ended, the lines would begin.

"They don't have anything like this in Springdale," Robert thought as he entered the building.

The modest looking exterior was quite different from the inside. Once entering through the main doors, a huge room revealed portable bars and couches. About every twenty feet, large white cloth drapes divided several sofas, appearing to be an inexpensive attempt to allow some semblance of privacy for the patrons. Upon looking closer, the drapes were not just privacy dividers, but also projector screens. The screens displayed pieces of art that changed every three to four minutes to match the mood of the music.

Located directly in the middle of the club was a large dance floor, surrounded by numerous large white pillars, reaching from the floor to the ceiling. Draped around each pillar was a small bench seat, which initially made a person question the benches' existence.

The room was lined with people, mostly beautiful women, dressed in the sexiest, revealing clothes Robert had ever seen in person. Cleavage and short skirts were everywhere-enough to make Robert ask himself if he were really being paid to be there.

Lori watched as Robert took in the surroundings. Obviously, her young investigator was mesmerized.

"How about a drink," Lori asked.

"Sure. A glass of Chardonnay for the both of us," Robert responded as a huge smile broke the schoolboy look on his face.

"There is a story behind that smile, isn't there."

"Bring me my wine and I will tell you," Robert responded as he passed Lori a ten-dollar bill.

"I thought you were buying me a glass, too. You need to fork over more money, big spender. We're in Dallas tonight."

Robert handed Lori some more cash, knowing that this would probably be an expensive evening for the federal government.

184

As Robert awaited Lori's return, he maneuvered closer to the dance floor, watching in a manner reflecting his eagerness to adapt. One talent an undercover cop possesses is his or her ability to familiarize themselves quickly to the environment. Whether in a biker bar, meth-lab, or a plush Dallas nightclub, adapting as soon as possible could save a cop's ass.

The dance floor was occupied mostly by women, floating around as if they were dancing on a cloud. They were engaged in motions and movements reflecting their sensuality, for which the drug Ecstasy is well-known. The men were standing around watching, like a hungry pack of wolves. Before the sun's light is seen again, many of the onlookers will have captured their prey.

In one corner of the building were concrete stairs leading down into a lower level. A red light emitted from the area, which brought out the curiosity in Robert. Why and what, were two questions to which he would soon seek answers to.

"Here you go, Big Boy." Lori returned with two glasses of wine and handed a small amount of change to Robert.

"Gee, thanks," Robert snickered as he slid the money back into his pocket.

For the next two hours, the couple watched and mingled among the crowd. Lori brought Robert here for a reason; the investigator trusted the reason would be revealed in due time. Working undercover required a large amount of patience. Rushing into anything could point toward detection, and this case was one that would cost the lives of Robert's and his informant.

After two glasses of wine, Lori noticed that Robert was transforming into a normal person, allowing his cop persona to diminish. Recognizing this weakness, Lori made sure his glass never ran dry.

"Robert, you do dance, don't you?"

"Well..."

Before Robert could say another word, Lori's hand reached down and grabbed his hand and they were off to the dance floor.

After the first dance, Robert began to ignore the fact that he was on business with a criminal informant. Robert intently watched his attractive dance partner move in ways that revealed her seductive form. It was clear Lori was mapping her moves with the intention of attracting this man! Her plan was working. Robert James was being drawn into her trap.

After their fifth-dance, Robert was ready to rest and rehydrate.

"I will make you a deal, Lori. I will pay if you will fetch us another glass of wine. I need to make a quick trip to the men's room."

"Deal," she responded. The two then went their separate ways.

Restrooms to the right, the sign and arrows indicated. Robert followed the signs down the hallway to the point of two doors that were separated by a set of water fountains. Robert stood looking at the first door, searching for the sign indicating male or female. There was none. Before he began to walk toward the second door, a man exited.

"Restrooms," Robert asked.

The man nodded, indicating his guess was correct. Robert then opened the door, entering first into a large lavatory area where two women were standing, inspecting themselves in the mirror.

"Oh, excuse me," Robert said in an embarrassed manner as he rushed out the door.

"That guy that came out of here must have been drunk."

Robert marched to the next restroom and entered. Upon doing so, he found a similar room. The lavatory area was occupied by three women and one man. One of the women was shirtless, and wiping her chest and neck with a wet towel. Robert stood gazing, a similar look to that of a deer caught in a car's headlights. One of the women in the lavatory immediately sensed Robert's dilemma and told him that all restrooms were unisex.

"Nothing like this in Springdale," Robert muttered aloud.

As he walked toward a stall, Robert noticed there were no doors, just glass dividers; obviously one's privacy did not exist in this establishment.

After taking care of business, Robert returned to the main floor and found Lori waiting for him, with two glasses filled with wine. After recapping his restroom ordeal to her, Lori laughed so hard she forgot to ask about his earlier promise to tell the story about ordering the wine.

Lori and Robert then took a set on a bench seat that encompassed one of the pillars. Almost immediately upon doing so, two attractive females approached them. Without a word being said, the women began to dance in a manner that would have seduced any man. Lori seemed to be undaunted by this behavior, and watched intently with her man. When the song ended, the two faded away and disappeared among the crowd.

"Ecstasy, the drug of seduction, and of choice in Dallas," Lori responded.

Still thinking about what just happened, Robert did not reply.

"Ready to go to work, Robert," Lori asked.

"You bet."

The two then left their seats and Lori led Robert toward the distant set off stairs that descended into the red-lit basement. As they approached the area, Robert noted that the red lights highlighted another dance floor.

"The Devil's Pit, they call it," Lori said as she led Robert down the stairs.

Upon descending, the sixth sense that many law enforcement officers possess began to signal Investigator Robert James that something was abnormal. A dark stale air seemed to loom, and the people dancing in the Devil's Pit were different from the ones upstairs. Pale, hollow and seemingly un-attentive to any of their surroundings, they all seemed to move just enough to signal the others that they were still alive. It did not take a dope cop to assume that all were stoned on their drug of choice.

Robert and Lori worked their way through the dancing couples, and toward a door that was located at the backside of the floor. As they entered, another bar was revealed. This one was different. There were no white drapes and no projected artwork. Just small lamps hanging on the wall that gave out less light than a candle. The room was dark and cold, and so were its occupants.

The bar was lined with about twenty barstools, with all being occupied. Crowding around the chairs were numerous people standing and barking out their orders to the bartender.

Several other tables surrounded the room, which were just barely illuminated from the dim lights. At one table, a couple was seen taking turns sliding the needle of a syringe into their arm. At another, a razor was being used to divide and line up a white powdery substance that was probably cocaine. This place was indeed dark for a reason.

Robert watched the bartender approach each customer, asking for orders. To his amazement, with an exchange of cash, most were being handed their drug of choice. There was powder in baggies, an assortment of pills and of course, Ecstasy.

"*What do you need*," the bartender asked, Robert.

"How about some X, and how much for each?"

"*Ten bucks and this is the best shit that money can buy.*"

"*Then load me up*," Robert ordered. "*Give me twenty-five of those babies.*"

The money and pills exchanged hands.

"*You know buddy*," Robert said to the bartender, "*I am headed out of town tomorrow and could use a little 'go-fast'. Got some?*"

"*I have just about anything you want*," he replied.

"*Then an eight-ball will do.*"

Another exchange of money and drugs transpired, after which Robert took the hand of his informant and quickly left the bowels of the dark dungeon.

Despite being a cop and witnessing many horrid situations in his life, this place gave Robert the creeps and he was glad to be out of it.

Lori had once again come through for her investigator. Before leaving the club, Robert wanted one more glass of wine to ward off the thoughts of the evil pit from where he just escaped.

"Should we have one more before we hit the road, Lori?"

Her reply was expected. Lori would do about anything Robert asked, especially if it meant extending her time with him.

Again, the two were caught up in the festive and sensual atmosphere of the main level. The music was great, the white-theme decorations amplified the club, and people practically floating on the dance floor, most of whom were under the influence of either alcohol or Ecstasy.

It was almost 1 A.M. and Robert was feeling no pain. The effects of the alcohol, accompanied by the mental high of buying illegal drugs from one of Gene King's businesses, took Robert to a comfortable place. Adding to his state of euphoria, a young, attractive maiden stood next to him. Thinking of Lori as an informant was beginning to escape him.

The lights grew dim as the music system in the club began to blare out the Guns and Roses tune, Sweet Child of Mine-one of Robert's favorite songs; and apparently, Lori felt the same. Without saying a word to Robert, she moved to the dance floor and broke into a solo dance routine, swaying in ways which were hidden earlier. Robert saw a seductive woman who projected sex with every move.

The club's sound and light man soon noticed Lori and focused a spotlight directly on her. Others around either stopped the dancing or moved back to give Lori the limelight. She continued, dancing as if she were unable to break the hypnotic rhythm of the song.

"Good. It's not just me. Everyone in here thinks she is hot!"

For now, Lori was the star of the club. Except for those still in the Devil's Pit, all eyes were on her.

189

The song ended, and Lori returned to her seat. Awaiting her was a man much different from the one who escorted her into the club earlier in the evening. The lustful eyes of Robert James were sending a message that words need not to accompany. At this point, Lori knew that Robert was hers for the night.

"Let's get out of here." Robert then pulled Lori toward the door.

Lori's seductive dance worked, as the two left the club, Robert led her in a direction away from the car. Behind the club was a hotel, which was their destination for the night.

When Lori displayed her solo dance routine, the spotlight drew the attention of many in the club, including the host of what appeared to be a small private party in one corner of the club. This admirer was a man, accompanied by numerous women and a table decorated with bottles of fine wines.

After watching Lori work her magic on the dance floor, Gene came to a quick decision to remain obscure to the woman.

"My dear Lori," he thought, *"tonight is your night but someday soon, you will deal with the King, again."*

Since Lori's arrest, Gene decided that it would be best if she remained at a distance until she was no longer an item of interest to the Feds. A few occasional phone calls was the extent of their contact with each other since Lori's incarceration.

As the song ended, Gene watched attentively as Lori returned to her companion.

"I know that guy," he thought.

"Hey girls, do any of you know him," Gene asked while pointing to Lori's escort.

The women with Gene were so intoxicated they could barely see three feet in front of them. Even if this were not the case, all would have denied knowing Lori's date.

"No," they each replied.

190

"In due time, I will figure it out. I never forget a face and you, my friend, look familiar."

The King assured himself before returning his attention to his harem.

Tonight, Lori's wish was finally fulfilled. Upon arriving at the hotel, the young investigator and his informant engaged in a night of carnal pleasures, and Investigator Robert James had committed the Cardinal Sin of his profession.

CHAPTER 46

The morning rays penetrated the hotel room that Robert and Lori rented. The sun highlighted the nude, toned body of the informant that lay next to him. Her body, smooth and soft, was again a temptation to Robert.

They only slept a couple of hours, but this short nap allowed some of the wine to dissipate from their systems. As common sense began to seep back into his brain, Robert began to regret what happened. Knowing that if anyone from the JDLST ever discovered this, he would be removed from the unit and possibly fired.

Lori was awakened by the restlessness of her mate. As her eyes opened, she noticed Robert was staring at the ceiling, in deep thought. Instantly, she knew what he was thinking.

Lori moved close to Robert and embraced him again.

"Robert, let's make this simple. What just happened between us will forever be our little secret; but under one condition."

"And what is that, Lori?" Robert responded in a concerned way.

"Make love to me one more time before we leave."

The two entwined; soon Robert's haunting thoughts faded to pleasure.

Not more than ten miles away, Gene King was inspecting the fruits of his night's labor. In his king-sized bed lay three naked women. The odor of alcohol, pot and sex filled the air. On the bedroom bar-top, white powder clouded the dark marble surface that supported it.

192

Cocaine was abundant to anyone wishing to partake. The crusted nose of Gene King left no guessing which poison he had chosen.

"It was morning and time for these wenches to leave," Gene thought as he looked at the passed-out brood.

What a fun night it had been for the King, but the evening missed one thing. Usually these orgies included Gene's friend, his lieutenant and personal photographer. Once again, Bradley was gone.

"Where was his lieutenant and exactly what was he doing?" These were thoughts that raced through Gene's mind.

The King was beginning to become suspicious of his once close and most trusted comrade.

CHAPTER 47

Bradley Dean was back in Austin's Hill Country. He was in day three of another cook, which would be the largest one he had produced. Chalking up another cook for the retirement fund was his purpose. As odd as it might sound, Bradley had never sampled his product. As a chemist, he knew that if he did not properly mix or process the chemicals, the results would be mentally or physically devastating.

Once the dope-cook was complete, Bradley would go into Austin to seek a few human lab rats. The notorious downtown Sixth Street would be his target. Bradley grabbed a handful of Formula-X and off to Austin he went.

This Saturday night on Sixth-Street appeared to be status quo for its famed reputation. The street was blocked off with police barricades, which would allow those in attendance the freedom to roam from bar to bar. Every weekend this location transformed from a place of historical hotels and restaurants during the day, to that of a New Orleans Mardi-Gras scene at night. This evening would be no different.

Female co-eds were his target. Bradley knew that Austin was the city to numerous colleges, with the University of Texas being the largest in the nation. The sixty-thousand plus college kids in town also attracted people from other parts of the state. Looking around, Bradley could tell that he was in a target rich environment and that finding someone to sample his product would not take much effort.

The circus was again on Sixth-Street, with wall-to-wall people stretching for blocks. The crowd consisted of thousands of women, of which most were under the influence of alcohol, drugs or both.

"What the hell?"

While scanning the crowd, Bradley noticed a bicycle that was being driven down the street with a small, homemade trailer in tow. When the vessel stopped, a male subject in his early fifties unsaddled the bike seat. This bearded man, who was wearing nothing but a thong, seemed to be a local celebrity. Many in the crowd began shouting his name and crowded around for photos and autographs. The "Keep Austin Weird" adage was definitely making sense. Bradley knew he had come to the right town.

Keeping an eye on the partygoers were dozens of police officers and sheriff deputies. Cops on horseback, bikes, motorcycles and foot mingled among the crowd. For Bradley, this was no threat. He knew the odds of him being singled out and searched were close to that of winning the lottery. The streets of Austin were a sure bet and safe place for his experiment.

During the evening, Bradley was able to attract two girls from the crowd, simply by making the promise of a hotel party with plenty of free drugs. Just the mention of Ecstasy to young women who liked to party was the right bait for his catch.

The chemist took the two women to a nearby hotel room and the festivities began. Soon Bradley began reaping the benefits of the Formula-X. The drug was working, and more effective than ever. Just minutes after both girls choked down the pills, their entire demeanor changed; their clothes were quickly shed. The party had begun, but this time without his boss and friend, Gene King.

CHAPTER 48

Sunday morning rolled around; Bradley was pleased with the results-a night in a hotel having sex with two women ranked second on his list of accomplishments that morning! The fact that the Formula-X achieved desired results ranked number one.

Bradley awakened the two women who were in his room and took them to their cars. Before parting, the two were begging for more of the magical pills. They were willing to pay about any price for the X. Bradley refused the money, but gave both some drugs as a parting gift.

"I am a chemist, not a petty street level drug pusher," Bradley thought as he handed the pills to the excited women-without a doubt, his latest batch of Formula-X was another success.

The thrilled women left in a rush, hardly saying goodbye to Bradley. Little did the girls know they had just been in the presence of the mastermind of Formula-X.

Feeling his lab was secure, Bradley decided to stay in Austin for a few hours, to roam downtown and find a decent restaurant, which was accomplished easily. This day of leisure found him driving back to his rental house shortly after dark.

The drive to the lab took about forty-five minutes, not because of the distance, but one had to drive slowly to negotiate the winding, deer-lined roads around Lake Travis. It was a pleasurable drive for anyone because of the beautiful scenery surrounding the lake. Bradley was not a religious man by any means, but on this day, he felt that only a supreme being could create such a magnificent place in the middle of Texas.

Bradley just left the Lake Travis County lake road and turned onto the gravel road leading up to the lab. As he rounded the last turn, the headlights caught a reflection in front of the house where three motorcycles were sitting, all unoccupied. For most individuals, this would have been a concern but not to him. Bradley told his local distributor he was cooking another batch and it would be ready after Sunday. Moving drugs by the cover of night was a common practice, so Bradley felt assured that he knew who his visitors were. As Bradley approached the house, he found the front door unlocked; in entering, three men were in the living room.

Bradley froze in his tracks:

"Hello, Gene."

CHAPTER 49

On Monday morning at approximately 7:45 A.M. Robert's pager begun to beep; the office was calling. Seeing the number, his mind began immediately to race.

"They know!"

Fearful Lori had already gone to Special Agent Michaels about their weekend fling, Robert was apprehensive about calling the office. With the pager notification being made almost four hours before his workday officially began, this was most likely an important call. Robert knew he had to call the office ASAP.

The investigator's fingers shook as he dialed the number. The phone began to ring.

"Mike Bales," the voice identified himself.

"Hey, this is, Robert."

"I have some bad news, Buddy. You need to be in route to Lake Travis in Austin. I am leaving now from the office. We have a floater who will be of interest to you," Mike advised.

"Bradley Dean is dead, Robert," Mike said hesitantly.

A moment of silence prevailed; Robert was stunned.

"Okay, how long of a drive is it, Mike?"

"About two-hundred miles," he said. *"But for me today, that should only take about two and a half hours.*

"I will be there a short time after you arrive, Mike. See you there."

"When you get close, go to the intersection of Highway 620 and County Road 2222. When you arrive, call for a Lake Travis Sheriff's Unit to meet you there. I was advised they will need to guide us in."

"Will do; see you soon, Mike."

Investigator Bales went to work early that day to prepare some intelligence information for their Monday briefing when he received the call. The Lake Travis Sheriff's Lake Patrol had just pulled a body ashore at Windy Hollow Park.

Bales was working with the Lake Travis County Narcotics and Intelligence Units because of associations between Gene King and their local biker gangs. Since the body was a 'fresh kill,' detectives rapidly identified it through the national AFIS system.

The deceased was identified as Bradley Dean. Lake Travis County knew he was a person of interest to the JDLST; therefore, the call was placed.

Drowning was common in this portion of the lake because of the swift undertows accompanied by a sharp drop-off located fifty feet from shore. The mixture of alcohol and lacking the ability to swim resulted in several deaths a year at Windy Hollow Park, which required frequent patrolling.

A park department employee was out removing trash from the park's beaches, when she observed a body floating off shore. An immediate call to dispatch resulted in a patrol boat arriving on scene minutes later.

This recovery attempt was simple compared to most. Lake Travis was one of the more dangerous lakes in the U.S., thus some recovery efforts meant several days of searching with scuba divers, nets and hooks. Numerous agencies patrol the waters of Lake Travis, but even with these multiple resources, finding a body in the deep lake sometimes took days. Some individuals who go down are never recovered.

When Lake Unit 30 arrived on scene, the two deputies occupying the vessel easily recovered the body from the waters. Not wanting to remove the dead male from the crime scene area, the deputies floated him to the nearest beach, and carefully laid his body on the sand. The deceased was slightly bloated, and decomposition had not set in. By some miracle, the body had snagged on a large piece of wood, preventing it from sinking to the bottom. It was clear that this was not a drowning. The massive bruises on the face and neck indicated his death was probably a murder.

In most cases, a dead body in a lake sinks to the bottom, where it may remain for several days, if not interfered with. Once the bloating and decomposition of the body begins, the more likely the carcass is to float to the top; this case was an exception.

Before leaving for Austin, Robert made a quick trip into the office to exchange his undercover vehicle for one of the unit's standard equipped detective cars. These units are equipped with a police radio, emergency lights and a siren, which allowed Robert to expedite his journey and communicate directly with other law enforcement agencies.

Fifteen minutes later, Robert was at the office, taking the keys to one of the Mercury Marquis detective cars. The vehicle was a typical detective car, easily identifiable to most citizens by the dark color, excessively tinted windows and black wall tires. One of the standard issue police vehicles to law enforcement is the Ford Crown Victoria, but the federal government had to be a step above standard issue; this Mercury was just that to the Crown Victoria.

Southbound on Interstate-35, Investigator James was speeding with lights flashing and siren blaring. Things had not changed much since he worked patrol. Most citizens still did not know how to react when approached by an emergency vehicle.

"Dumbass," Robert shouted, as he began to pass a vehicle that had come to a full stop right in the middle of the interstate when they saw him approaching.

"Some things never change."

At the two and one-half hour mark, Robert arrived in the area of Highways 620 and 2222, in the far west portion of Austin.

"Federal Unit 664 to Lake Travis County S.O.," Robert spoke into his police microphone.

"This is Lake Travis County, go ahead Federal 664."

"I have been called here for the deceased on Lake Travis. Can you have a unit in route to my location to direct me? I am at 620 and 2222."

"10-4, Federal 664. A unit will meet you there shortly."

A few minutes after Robert placed the microphone back on its hook, a sheriff's unit was pulling up to his car.

"You here for the floater," the deputy asked.

"Yes, sir, I am. Can you take me there," Robert asked.

"You bet, follow me."

This was the first time Robert had been to the Lake Travis area, which was nothing like anything he ever imagined to be in Texas. It was almost as if God had taken a chunk of the Ozarks and dropped it right in the middle of Texas. With rivers, creeks, hills and lakes, this place was gorgeous!

As Robert followed the deputy down a winding lake road, a road-sign suddenly captured his attention. 'Hippie Hollow Park Entrance — Warning: Nude Beach'.

"Only in Austin," Robert thought as he proceeded west from the location. "I might have to come back here for a vacation."

The Austin area was known for being a liberal city, but a county owned, nude beach was a surprise to this young Missourian.

The Lake Travis County patrol car began to slow as it turned into Windy Hollow Park. They arrived at the scene of the recovery.

The massive body of uniforms and suits at the beach left little to guess where the deceased lay. A thirty-foot, twin engine sheriff's patrol boat floated in the water next to the group of officers.

"Great," Robert thought. "I was hoping those guys would still be here."

As Robert parked his car, a familiar face emerged from the group. It was Investigator Mike Bales.

The two men greeted each other, and Mike gave Robert a quick briefing on what they knew, which was little. Apparently, Lake Travis County Detectives had already ruled the death a homicide, due to the massive amounts of trauma the body indicated. The deceased had trauma marks that would have required him to be alive when they were inflicted. To add to the suspicions, the victim's hands and legs were bound with ropes. This ruled out an accidental death or suicide; murder was the only possibility.

"Come on, Robert, let me introduce you to Bradley Dean," Mike said as the men began walking toward the corpse.

This was not the meeting Robert had hoped to have with Mr. Dean. Without a doubt, Gene had struck again.

CHAPTER 50

They had another body connected to Gene King, and yet not a bit of hard evidence to link him to the crimes. Special Agent Michaels recognizes and accepts the fact that organized crime cases cannot be made overnight. It takes months, and sometimes years, for the pegs to fall into place and to be able to indict and convict individuals involved in these cases. Agent Michaels displayed patience and tenacity concerning the Gene King case, knowing the hard work that was necessary to take down a major player in the drug arena.

Now, the JDLST was faced with more than an organized crime case. Standing by and adding up the body count was something that no law enforcement agency would accept, no matter how large of a case they were working. Robert knew time on his case against Gene King was going to be limited. With multiple murders on their books and with Gene King a prime suspect, SA Michaels would demand a timetable in which to conclude the case.

Robert and Investigator Mike Bales spent a few days in Austin, going over evidence and intelligence with Lake Travis County Detectives. The information was limited, but Lake Travis County did have a few items of interest. First, the narcotics unit had developed information via an informant that someone was manufacturing the drug Ecstasy in the area around Lake Travis. The detective had been trying to gather information for several weeks concerning this case, yet the only thing the narcotic detectives came up with was that the dope cook was a man from the Dallas-Ft. Worth area.

Not long after the "dope cook" information was gathered, a county patrol deputy engaged in a pursuit with a Bandera biker on County Road 2244. CR 2244 was located on the far side of Lake Travis, in an area the deep pockets of the Austin technology residents had not discovered. CR 2244 is also the route of entry to many small dirt roads where bikers live and manufacture meth. The pursuit resulted in the

Bandera wrecking his motorcycle and dying a short time later. His death prevented an interview, but a large amount of the drug Ecstasy was found in the man's possession. This fact was not normal for the Bandera due to their primary focus on methamphetamine; therefore, the deputy concluded that whoever the biker was running the dope for was probably heavily involved in the meth-world too.

Since the information the snitch gave was verified by the confiscation of evidence from the deceased biker, the narcotics unit coordinated efforts with the patrol division to stop and ID anyone who looked suspicious. When the suspects were stopped, a ticket or warning citation was issued. This was a routine procedure when searching for additional evidence or identifying suspects in a narcotic's investigation. Thus, Lake Travis County officials were able to locate a warning ticket that was issued to Bradley Dean on CR 2244, around the time of the biker's death.

Investigators James and Bales possibly had the answer to Bradley Dean's death. Also, the current investigation of Gene King revealed his association to the drug, Formula-X. According to information given by Lori Sims, Bradley Dean was the chemist who manufactured Formula-X for Gene. Lori also told Robert that the composition of this drug was unique from any other Ecstasy formula on the street. For that reason, Gene kept the formula a closely guarded secret. Only he and Bradley knew the chemical composition of Formula-X, and Gene left no one doubting that he owned it.

The investigators believed that Bradley Dean was cooking Formula-X without Gene's knowledge, therefore betraying his boss. In Gene King's world, disloyalty would certainly terminate a working relationship in more ways than one.

Bradley Dean was eternally fired.

CHAPTER 51

At 7:15 P.M., Robert walked through the doors of the hotel room, and his pager went off.

"A 512 number," Robert mumbled, *"must be the Lake Travis Sheriff's Office"*

Robert immediately called the number his pager reflected.

"Investigator James," the voice responded. Robert immediately recognized the voice to be that of Detective Bowers with Lake Travis Sheriff's Office.

"Robert, we have a break in the Bradley Dean case. I will come by and pick you guys up if you're still available."

"Hell, yes, we are available!" Robert responded. *"Mike and I will be ready."*

No more than ten minutes passed before Detective Bowers had Robert and Mike Bales in his car, speeding off toward Lake Travis. The twenty-five-minute drive gave Detective Bowers ample time to brief the two JDLST investigators. Apparently, an APB (all-points bulletin) had been broadcast to all of their patrol and air units, regarding Bradley Dean's vehicle. Late afternoon, one of the helicopter units spotted a vehicle in a remote area off CR 2244. The car was completely burned. When deputies ran the VIN (vehicle identification number), it was traced back to Bradley Dean as the owner.

After the vehicle was found, several patrol units began canvassing the area and knocking on doors of nearby residents, seeking information about the car fire. A local rancher noticed Bradley's vehicle a few days before the fire. The red sports car passed the rancher in a careless manner a few days ago and rapidly turned into a private drive. This pissed off the rancher to the point of remembering the vehicle, hoping for a future encounter. The rancher was able to lead deputies to the road the car was seen entering.

Upon arriving at the site described by the rancher, deputies located and subsequently approached a house at the road's end, but did not find anyone home. At times, cops are known to get their hands dirty and this time they did. A trashcan was behind the residence, stuffed with numerous garbage bags of waste. Upon digging through one of the bags, a credit card receipt was discovered reflecting Bradley Dean's name.

This was all that Detective Bower needed to secure a search warrant for the house. One murdered body, a burned sports car and a biker killed in a pursuit. Add some illegal drugs to this equation and this is a case any cop would love to investigate. Much to Robert's advantage, Detective Bower was hungry for this one.

Under strict orders from their senior detective, none of the Lake Travis County deputies had made entry into the house Bradley Dean was believed to have occupied. As Bower's car pulled up to the house, several detectives, along with a crime scene unit, were anxiously standing by.

As Detective Bower and his prestigious guests exited the black detective car, all of the by-stander's faces reflected an excitement similar to expectations at the kickoff of a football game. This game was about to begin.

The search of Bradley's residence took almost six hours, but the endeavor was fruitful for the cases of both Lake Travis County S.O. and the JDLST. Laboratory components, along with a few precursor chemicals, were discovered. There were also numerous items and documents reflecting that Bradley Dean definitely had possession of the house.

Crime scene investigators were busy swabbing, vacuuming and photographing evidence throughout the house. The law enforcement community was just beginning to enter the age where high tech crime scene investigations were supplementing the efforts of the detectives. As a result, these technicians were now a valued part of any complex case.

"Do you have any idea what they're doing over there, Robert?"

206

Investigator Mike Bales asked while pointing toward a crime scene officer vacuuming a couch.

"Not really," Robert responded.

Investigator Bales knew the answer and explained that the crime scene technician was looking for hair follicles and traces of human skin. These were pieces of evidence left behind in places where people sit or touch. Once the particles of evidence are located and collected, they may be analyzed.

"Analyzed for what?"

"Have you ever heard of DNA testing and the Ronald Trimboli case?" Mike asked.

"Just a little, but tell me about it."

Investigator Bales broke into a short summary about how an Arlington man was arrested and charged for the murder of three teenagers. All of the kids were killed in a home near Lake Arlington. Evidence involving bodily fluids was recovered during the investigation, which eventually led to Ronald Trimboli's demise.

After his arrest, Trimboli went on to be tried twice by prosecutors in Tarrant County. After two hung juries, many began to doubt that Ronald Trimboli would ever be convicted of this crime. This was when DNA testing was implemented into Trimboli's case. With DNA analysis, lab experts were able to conclude that a quantity of evidence left at the crime scene belonged to Trimboli. The DNA results reflected a greater than ninety-five percent conclusive rate that this evidence belonged to Trimboli. In the third trial, Trimboli was convicted of murdering all three teenagers, thanks to DNA testing.

"Tell me more about this DNA stuff Mike."

Due to his involvement in prior rape and homicide cases, Investigator Bales had the opportunity to solve several cold cases just by using DNA testing on blood and semen.

"In laymen terms, labs can take a sample of any part of the human body and break it down into components that are specific to only one person. This can be blood, saliva, semen, skin or hair. Blood typing is "old school" now. DNA testing will revolutionize law enforcement work, Robert; mark my word on it. It will be more powerful than any polygraph, blood typing or fingerprint evidence," Mike concluded.

"Oh, by the way Mr. Bachelor, any woman can now positively identify you as being the sire of their baby. So, be careful!" Mike laughed.

After hearing Investigator Bales' dissertation on DNA analysis, Robert became even more in tune as to what the crime scene investigators were collecting.

"Find anything we can pull some DNA from," the newly enlightened investigator asked one of the crime scene investigators.

"We have some hair strands, Boss Man, and they obviously belong to several individuals. All of the strands are probably of the male gender, due to the short length of the hairs. It will take about two weeks for the lab to get the results back, then we will know for sure."

The crime scene investigator seemed impressed by Robert's knowledge of this newly found science.

"And by the way Mr. James, you detectives have the toughest part of the DNA process. You have to find the person these hair strands belong to."

"We have just the person in mind, Mr. CSI guy," Robert replied with confidence.

"You, hot dog," Mike remarked and grinned as he walked away from Robert. "

Let's go home."

CHAPTER 52

The new week beginning, and Robert could barely control his anxieties over getting the results back from the crime lab. Usually, getting anything back from the lab could take weeks or months but this was a priority case. It also helped having the Lake Travis County Sheriff's office involved in this investigation, since the state crime lab was located only two miles from their office.

Robert's look of curiosity soon turned to a look of confusion, as he suddenly remembered what the crime scene investigator told him:

"It is your job to find who the strand of hair belongs to, Detective."

It had been years since Gene King was in police custody for anything. Robert then realized that somehow, someway, he would have to obtain a sample of Gene's DNA.

"Lori."

Several months passed since Robert had seen his informant, Lori. For the first few weeks after their evening of romance, Robert felt as if he were walking on pins and needles, waiting for Lori to notify Special Agent Michaels about him committing the Cardinal Sin. With the passing of time, the pressure regarding this incident began to release, as he learned that Lori was a person of her word.

Lori gave the JDLST almost more information than they could digest. Then search warrants were executed and multiple arrests made. The informant certainly helped to whittle down the King's empire. Lori was fulfilling her legal obligations to the JDLST and the Federal Prosecutor's office. Before taking time off, Robert advised Lori that she had fulfilled most of her obligations, but there could possibly be a few more requests down the road. Again, she was needed, for possibly the riskiest assignment of all.

Robert picked up the telephone and dialed the pager number that he had done so many times. The number was certainly one that will be embedded in his mind for years to come.

"Lori, we need to meet. Are you available?"

Without hesitation, Lori confirmed she was available. They agreed to meet at a location close to the JDLST office. Robert had a full-days' work left and did not want to venture far; the meeting with Lori would be brief. They decided to meet at a restaurant. A short time later, Robert arrived at the restaurant to find Lori there and anxiously awaiting his entrance.

"Is a hug out of the question, Mr. Investigator," Lori asked as Robert approached her.

"Not for you, my dear; come here."

Their embrace allowed both to know without saying a word, how much they had missed each other. Even though she was reluctant to tell him, Lori was in love with her investigator.

Robert's feelings were somewhat the same, but he refused to label his as love. This type of relationship was not allowed with an informant, especially one who may have criminal charges soon.

Neither could take their eyes off the other. Robert noticed that something was different about Lori. She looked vibrant and healthy, and had even put on a few pounds, which was good- reassuring him that Lori was keeping her distance from drugs, which was a concern of Roberts. However, seeing Lori so radiant helped alleviate these thoughts.

"You look great, Lori!"

"Thanks, Robert. I'm living right these days," Lori replied. *"And most of it I can thank you for."*

At this point, Robert had no idea how much he had contributed to Lori's change.

The two engaged in casual conversation, filling in the gaps for the past two months they had been apart. After indulging in a decent meal, Lori knew that Robert wanted to meet for a reason, and it was time to find out why.

"Okay, Robert. What's on your mind?"

Robert hesitated, giving Lori an indication she might not want to hear the words he had to say.

"Bradley Dean is dead. He was found floating in Lake Travis a few weeks ago." Lori fell silent, obviously in a mild state of shock.

During the time Lori was seeing Gene on a regular basis, she and Bradley became close friends. Being Gene's best friend meant that Bradley knew him better than anyone else. At times when Lori was confused or fearful of the King, Bradley was around to lend an ear. Despite him and Gene being best friends, Lori felt assured that most of what she told Bradley was held in confidence. A mutual friendship developed between the two, which oddly enough, was blessed by Gene.

"Keeping it in the family," was a motto Gene always conveyed to his clan.

The King felt if they relied on each other, the chance of anyone defying him was a little less. Gene believed that this factor, accompanied by his fear tactics, greatly lessened the odds of defiance.

Robert could see that Lori's mind was wandering-most likely to her memories of Bradley.

"Who killed him, Robert?"

Robert remained silent, and stared into Lori's eyes as if sending her an unspoken message.

"It was Gene, wasn't it?"

Robert did not say a word, but nodded his head in an affirmative motion.

"What do you want me to do, Robert? Bradley was a good friend of mine you know. Gene King; I hate that bastard! Tell me what you want me to do." Lori began to weep.

Silence filled the table for a few minutes, as Robert let his informant mourn the loss of her friend. After Lori regained composure, she apologized and gazed at Robert in a sober and serious way.

"My request is pretty simple. I just need a few hair strands, saliva or blood from Gene. Can you get that, Lori?" Robert asked. *"If so, this will fulfill your obligation to the JDLST and your criminal charges will be dropped."*

"Yes, but this is not for me; it's all about Bradley this time. You can consider it done," Lori responded.

Both knew this would be a risky assignment for Lori. Gene was progressively becoming more addicted to cocaine, which in turn made him very suspicious of everyone. Gene trusted Lori and never doubted her loyalty, but things were now different. His partner, Bradley, was dead and some of his drug operations were being seized. Knowing that the JDLST was after his ass, the King was on edge.

Lori and Gene had been separated for months now. Lori's attempt to come back into Gene's world after her arrest was a very risky one. Nevertheless, for Lori, the risk was worth taking. She owed this last favor to her friend, Bradley Dean.

The two stood beside Lori's car, not knowing how to end this meeting or what to say to each other. Robert knew that Lori was grieving Bradley's death, but he also felt that she did not want to part his company.

Lori knew she had things to do, and it would involve working on her own without the cherished investigator close by. Lori was also struggling with another topic that she wanted to discuss with Robert, but this item of importance would have to wait for another time.

"I will call you when I have the goods on him," Lori instructed Robert as she entered the car.

"Be careful, Lori. Feel free to call me, day or night, when you have what I need."

Lori smiled and nodded as she drove away.

It only took Robert a few minutes to drive back to the JDLST office, his thoughts consumed by the assignment he had given Lori, and the possibility of putting her in harm's way. Nevertheless, this was the only way. It was the icing on the cake to link Bradley's death to Gene King. Robert had convinced himself that Lori also knew the risk before she agreed to the assignment. For her, completing this could mean Bradley's death would be vindicated, along with all her criminal charges being dismissed. For Robert, it was a stake through the heart of this evil individual, Gene King.

As the investigator walked into his office, a FedEx package was lying on his desk. The package was addressed to Investigator Robert James, but there was no sender information listed. With curiosity, Robert picked it up and carefully opened one end. In a child-like manner, Robert peaked into the opening.

"A video tape. That's odd," he thought.

As Robert pulled the tape from the box, he noticed a label with writing on it. He immediately froze in his tracks and fell silent.

To: Investigator Robert James - JDSLT.

From: Bradley L. Dean.

The dead was about to speak!

CHAPTER 53

The third and final trip was here for Dr. Bob Perez. One encounter with the U.S. Coast Guard was enough for him. The Coast Guard fortunately misinterpreted the identity of the pregnant female with the good doctor. Dr. Perez's wife is fifteen years older than the female he was escorting when the Coast Guard stopped their boat after leaving Gene's ship east of Miami. This particular woman traveled to her destination in the states and then traveled back to Belize. A second woman did the same, and now Dr. Perez was in the process of completing an assignment with a third woman. She, too, was a native of Belize, and she appeared to be about seven months pregnant.

After leaving the powerboat in Miami again, a limo and driver awaited them at the dock. Once both were in the car, the driver drove off toward Miami International Airport. Dr. Perez and his young, pregnant companion boarded a plane to Los Angeles International Airport. This destination was three- thousand miles away from their prior trip to Florida.

The couple was greeted with smiles as they presented IDs to the security personnel at the gate.

"Dr. Perez, you are clear," the security officer notified him.

"And Mrs. Perez, it is not our policy to allow a pregnant woman to pass through our detectors. Please step around and you are free to continue to your plane," the officer announced.

Having a security officer lead his companion around, and not through, the X-Ray machine was indeed a blessing for both. Anything setting off the machine's alarm could possibly lead to a strip search of the female companion, which could have disastrous results.

Few words were spoken as the doctor and his "pseudo" wife spent the next four hours in route to Los Angeles. Both were somewhat nervous though for different reasons. Dr. Perez was in a situation that he did not want to be in, but there was no foreseeable end to his circumstances. Once this mission was accomplished, he would have only a few weeks rest before the next batch of women was delivered to the ship. This was a never-ending cycle.

This accomplice, on the other hand, knew her journey was coming to an end. In approximately eight-hours, she would be back in route to her homeland, with a purse full of one-hundred-dollar bills. There would be a price for this money, and a painful one at that. However, in her mind, it was worth the risk. The few days of agony that accompanied the assignment were an acceptable hardship for the easy money.

The plane landed on schedule at LAX. As with the Miami Airport, a chauffeur was awaiting the doctor and his accomplice. Both were whisked to their destination a short distance away. A remote warehouse in Los Angeles' vast shipping yard was their goal, as it was for several other individuals who were awaiting the arrival of Doctor Perez and his guest.

"I will return in about forty-five minutes; I don't want you moving until I return," Dr. Perez ordered the chauffer.

"Understand, boss. I will be here when you return."

As the doctor entered the building, he was met by three American males. No names were exchanged but each gave a minor impersonal greeting.

"This way doctor," one of the men indicated as he led Dr. Perez and the accompanying female into a room.

Once all were inside, the room was cleared, except for Dr. Perez and the female. The area was surprisingly clean considering its normal use. Only a few tools and bright lights, along with a metal bed, occupied the otherwise dismal place.

"This should only take a few minutes," Dr. Perez advised as he shut the door.

215

The men impatiently walked the floor, eagerly awaiting their prize.

Dr. Perez was now face to face with his nervous and wide-eyed accomplice. The one part of this assignment that she dreaded was now before her.

"Shall we get started?"

With a nodding of the head, the woman slowly removed her clothing and lay down on the cold, steel bed next to her.

A few muffled whimpers of agony could be heard in the cool, dark building as Dr. Perez began the procedure.

CHAPTER 54

With a videotape in hand, Robert remained motionless while an indescribable feeling of anxiety consumed his body. Without viewing one second of the tape, he assumed he knew what the contents may be. There was only one reason Bradley would have sent him a tape of anything. Robert assumed Bradley Dean anticipated his possible demise and wanted to be assured the revenge was sweet. A video made by Bradley and apparently given to a person unknown to Gene, in the event of his own sudden death.

The video was Robert's prize and he was not going to share it with anyone. The tape was delivered to Investigator Robert James, which in his opinion, gave Robert exclusive rights to be the first to view it.

With the package in hand, the investigator rushed to the break-room. This viewing would be special, deserving of a diet cola and chocolate chip cookies. The snacks in their break-room were set out and purchased through the honor system. Robert did not have the exact change, so he threw a five-dollar bill into the moneybox and rushed away with his prized possessions.

Upon returning to his office, Investigator James stared at the VCR, being almost powerless to hit the power button. Slowly, he touched the on-switch and slid in the VCR tape. The anticipation of viewing the contents was overwhelming.

"No Miami Vice tonight. This program will be much better than any episode they have yet to run."

Robert paused a few moments before making his next move. His finger soon found the play button.

"Now talk to me Bradley Dean!"

For the next thirty minutes, Investigator Robert James sat mesmerized, while the dead spoke. As the tape began, the corpse that Robert had seen at Lake Travis came to life. The introduction was as expected, with Bradley instructing Robert that the tape was made with him anticipating the possibility of his own death.

Bradley began by reciting a brief biography of his and Gene's life, beginning at high school age and working up to the present time.

Bradley did not leave out any important details. Robert sat and watched the most interesting crime drama he had ever seen or heard, either fact or fiction. Detailed descriptions were given of Gene's first involvement in the drug world and the satisfaction he felt after killing a man for revenge. The bundles of marijuana were a bonus to his first adventure. The saga continued. Murder and drugs, corrupt politicians, narcissistic behavior, sex parties, world travel; it was all there.

"The murders, the murders, get on with it," Robert shouted to the walls of his empty office. The impatient investigator soon got his wish.

The story was prefaced by a chance encounter that Gene had years back with the notorious killer, Luke Henry. This meeting occurred when Luke was introduced to Gene, while he was looking to score some meth. The encounter took place years ago when Luke was traveling though Dallas. For some odd reason, the two immediately bonded.

"The devil's children finally met," Bradley emphasized as he continued.

"Gene was so intrigued by Luke's stories of death and murder, that he retained the services of Mr. Henry to rid himself of one local competitor. Upon hiring Luke, Gene told the killer that he wanted to accompany him during the murder, to be assured that his death sentence was carried out. Once the men had their captor, the victim was slowly and painfully executed. Rumor has it that Gene became so involved with the killing that Luke barely earned his money. Each man found his soul mate, but in a non-sexual way - maybe "soul brothers" would be more appropriate."

"Needless to say, Luke Henry was, indeed, proud of his new pupil."

218

One by one, Bradley detailed the numerous murders he either witnessed or had knowledge of, in which Gene King could be held responsible.

In July of 1995, there was Jessica in Arlington. She was a drug mule who dated Gene at one time. Unfortunately, she decided to flee his flock, so the King killed her.

Then, there were the two females from Belize, who were killed in a city park in Springdale, Missouri. The women were tortured, and their stomachs set afire to "destroy evidence." The women were another pair of Gene's drug mules, but they made the mistake of attempting to extort additional money from him. Their attempts were met with horrific deaths; Gene sent a message for others with similar thoughts.

The list continued and concluded in a manner that sent chills up and down Robert's spine.

"And the last one murdered was me," Bradley said in a sober and soft voice.

Bradley Dean continued by outlining how he was the inventor of "Formula-X," and he initially swore to Gene that the drug would only be manufactured with his blessing and knowledge. Then, the King developed an addiction to cocaine, after which time his empire began to crumble.

"And this is mostly due to the efforts of you Robert, and the JDLST team," Bradley added.

Bradley continued by telling that when Gene's organization began to deteriorate, he rented a small home on the banks of Lake Travis and began to manufacture batches of Formula-X on his own. Bradley light-heartedly described this operation as his retirement fund.

"And I knew if Gene ever found out what I was doing; our history together would have no impact in determining the repercussions. Which means, Robert, since you have the video tape, I am dead. Gene killed me, and I want you to avenge my death."

"And one last thing, Investigator James; no life is sacred to Gene. He will stop at nothing. I never thought I would say this to a cop, but good luck and please send that bastard back to his daddy in hell!"

Bradley Dean grew silent as the tape faded to black.

Robert sat motionless. Time became insignificant as the investigator sat in silence, trying to digest what he witnessed. There was no need to replay the tape; to look for information that may have been passed over the first time. Every word on the tape was heard and comprehended. The biggest crime drama in Robert's career had just unfolded in front of him.

Investigator James had received a gift; and there was only one way to thank a dead man-to avenge his murder.

Bradley Dean had, indeed, come to the right man for the job. He knew that enlisting the assistance of Robert via this tape would eventually lead to Gene's worse nightmare, which was being arrested and sent to prison.

At this time and for this moment, Robert James had a new friend. The dead was no longer part of a recurring bad dream with pleas for help, but an important factor in solving the largest case in his law enforcement career. Indeed, the ghost and voice of Bradley Dean was an asset to this investigation.

"May God rest your soul. Goodbye, Bradley Dean."

CHAPTER 55

As with most telephone calls, the one that Gene just received from Lori was short. The King did not trust the old reliable landline, nor did he have much faith in the booming fad of the new cellular phone systems. In Gene's opinion, both were too susceptible to interception by a law enforcement agency. Gene knew he was hot right now, and caution must be exercised.

During their short conversation, they had arranged a dinner meeting at an old favorite Italian restaurant in West Ft. Worth. Normally, Gene would not have accepted such a short-notice meeting, but curiosity prevailed. The King questioned Lori's intentions. Lori had not seen Gene for months; their last encounter was two days before she was busted in the meth lab. Lori was not aware that Gene saw her with another man at a nightclub in Dallas a few months back.

"Assumption is the bitch of all mistakes," Gene thought as he recalled the night at the club where he saw Lori.

"I know that guy she was with, so I cannot believe he was just her date for the evening. That would be too much of a coincidence. There is something more to this. I just can't put my finger on it, yet."

Gene wanted to take his sighting at face value, believing that Lori was there with a date, but he could not accept this thought. Gene looked at things from different angles, which partially accounted for his survival in the crime jungle.

Gene did not have long. He knew what had to be done before meeting Lori.

"I need you over here ASAP," Gene said to the unidentified voice on the receiving end of his phone call.

"And I need everything that you have."

"You barely beat me to the call, Boss Man. Just today, we had an interesting development. Will 4:00 at your place work?"

"Yes, 4:00 will work," Gene replied as he hung up the telephone.

Lori was one of the few individuals in Gene's life whom he somewhat trusted, but no one was the recipient of this total confidence. Since Lori's arrest, Gene wanted to put a buffer zone between the two of them, in the event that she was the target of surveillance. He was no stranger to the tactics of law enforcement officers and enthusiastic prosecutors. The cops enjoy the game of making deals with people they arrest or investigate in crimes. This was especially prevalent in the drug world.

The reality of dopers turning on dopers was commonplace. When cops had a drug user in custody, their suspect would do or tell anything to be released, so their addiction could continue to be fed. No one was immune to this practice. The snitches would give up their mothers if it meant being back on the streets to pursue their addictions; Gene knew this. He wanted to exclude Lori from the list of possibly undevoted individuals, but no one was completely trustworthy.

Because of this type of disloyalty, Gene placed Lori under surveillance after she was released from jail. One of his henchmen was given the assignment to follow and photograph her activities at different periods during the past few months. Now, it was time to see what Ms. Lori had been up to. The parting words about a new development sparked Gene's interest.

It was exactly 4:00 P.M. when Gene observed through his security system's monitor, a car coming down the drive. He knew the vehicle and the man driving it. It was time to see if his feelings of anxiety were justified.

The visitor pulled his vehicle up to the front door and parked. As he exited, a thick manila envelope was evident.

Gene let the man in and guided him to a glassed-in patio overlooking the pool. Before they sat, the man handed the package to Gene. It contained numerous eight-by-ten photos, along with a couple of video tapes.

"*Look them over first, Boss Man, and then I have a story to tell you,*" the guest remarked.

Gene began examining each of the photos. He suddenly came to a stop-looking at one picture as though he were embedding a mental image of each detail the photo reflected.

His guest produced a second large envelope, which contained only a few photos.

"*Take a look at these, too, boss,*" the man said as he handed the packet to Gene.

As with the other photos, Gene examined each one carefully.

"*I took those at a restaurant in Las Colinas earlier today, Gene.*"

The pictures reflected Lori and a lunch date, who was familiar to him.

"*Keep going, Boss, it gets better,*" the visitor instructed.

Gene had a curious look on his face as he examined the numerous additional pictures. These were not photos of Lori, but of her lunch companion. They consisted of shots of his car, a parking lot and a large building. There were numerous close-ups photos of each.

"*What's the punch line,*" Gene asked.

"*Look closely boss. Lori's date parked in a reserved parking area. Look at the cars he parked next to.*"

"*They are cop cars, unmarked cop cars; detectives*" Gene exclaimed.

"**Damn it!**"

"*And, Boss Man, not long ago a pal of mine was pulled in by a federal task force cop, and questioned about your organization. He did not remember the exact location where their office was located, but he described this area to me.*"

223

"Was it possibly the JDLST," Gene asked.

"Yes sir, it was them. And look at the next picture, which is some guy Lori's date was talking to in the parking garage."

Gene sat quietly and closely examined the photo. Attached to the second man's belt, without a doubt, was a pistol. Gene looked back at the close-up of Lori's lunch date-this man looked familiar to him.

"I know this guy, this face. I know I have seen him before."

It only took a few more seconds before a smile broke the somber look on Gene's face.

"The club at the Lake of the Ozarks, right after I killed those two bitches in Springdale. And Lori's date at the club in Dallas."

The pieces of the puzzle had come together. Gene's near photographic memory paid off. It now made sense. Even though the two had never formally met, he finally knew the identity of this man.

"**He's a cop**," Gene said in a begrudged manner.

"I figured that, Boss, but any idea who?"

"Investigator Robert James; at last we meet," the King said with a smile.

"It looks like we have been on a little collision course over the past few years my friend."

Gene spoke to the photo of the cop as if its image were sitting next to him.

The King lowered the pictures; he was pleased with this new information, but now there was important business to tend to. It was time for his visitor to be rewarded and shown the door. Gene wished to be alone.

"You did well, my friend," Gene said to his guest.

Gene rose from his seat and disappeared from the room. The King returned a short time later with a large manila envelope in hand.

"Here is a modest reward for your good deeds. Now go and enjoy the fruits of your labor," Gene ordered.

There was no need to look in the packet. The large bulge depicted that his boss had been more than generous. The smile on his face, along with the visitor's quick, but firm parting handshake, affirmed that the reward was greatly appreciated.

Gene escorted his messenger to the door and watched as he drove away from the house. Obviously, Gene was consumed in thought.

"Lori, my dear, Lori. Tonight will definitely be a night for you to `remember. But a short memory it will be for you, my little traitor bitch!"

Gene closed the door as he re-entered his home. Only two hours before his dinner date. There was little time left to prepare for Lori's last supper.

CHAPTER 56

The small Italian restaurant was symbolic for the evening's dinner with Lori, as this was the place they went on their first date. This Italian restaurant was well-known among the elite of the Ft. Worth area. Located outside the gates of an esteemed college, the establishment had catered to local patrons over sixty years. Young men and women, along with their parents and grandparents, made up the ownership, wait-staff and chefs of this fine restaurant.

"The perfect place," Gene thought. *"This place is the alpha and omega of our relationship; the beginning and the end!"*

Gene King was known for his promptness, and he demanded the same of all whom associated and conducted business with him. It was no surprise that when the clock reflected 6:55 P.M., the King saw his dinner date making her entrance through the front door of the restaurant.

Gene had not seen Lori for several months, but something was different about her. Gene's narcissistic personality would not allow him to think Robert James had affected her life in any positive manner, thus, his thoughts were focused elsewhere.

"A picture of health," Gene thought.

"Lori, my dear, you look wonderful. The world must be treating you well."

"Just living right and eating healthy," Lori replied.

"And apparently exercising as well?"

"Just long walks, Gene. Nothing too strenuous right now."

"Well, whatever the case, definitely keep it up."

As with most places the King frequented, there was no wait for the dinner table. The hostess led them to a candlelit table in a secluded area of the restaurant where privacy was expected.

Time seemed to stand still for Lori. Her motive for this meeting was simple. Spend as little time as possible with Gene, get some evidence and get the hell away.

The evening was filled with casual conversation until Gene got to the point of asking about the arrest. The inevitable was finally here. Gene wanted to know details. "How long she was in jail? How much did it cost her to bond out? Who was her attorney? When was her court date?" These questions were rather pretentious because Lori had already, and correctly, assumed that Gene knew the answers.

"Just appease him, collect the evidence and get the hell out," Lori kept repeating silently to herself.

"Excuse me, Lori; the men's room is calling my name."

He was finally gone, and Lori knew this might be the only opportunity she had to act. Scanning the table rapidly, she came upon her target, a cloth napkin. At numerous times throughout the meal, Gene was observed wiping his mouth with the cloth and even coughing into it once. This was exactly what the doctor ordered, DNA everywhere!

In one swift motion, Lori removed Gene's cloth napkin from the table, folded it and stuck it into her purse.

"Waitress, could we have a clean set of napkins please," Lori asked.

The waitress immediately removed two clean napkins from her apron and placed them at each place setting.

"Will there be anything else, ma'am," she asked.

"No, you have been of great service. Thank you."

A few minutes later Gene returned to the table. Always attentive to his surroundings, Gene immediately noticed that his old napkin had been replaced by a clean one. With this restaurant also being known for its outstanding service, he did not think anything out of the norm occurred.

"Great service," Gene exclaimed, as he pointed to his napkin.

"The best," Lori acknowledged.

"But only the best for the King, right?" For the first time that evening, Lori's face was filled with a smile.

Gene gazed at his date and her continual smile, followed by small chatter. Lori was radiant and healthy looking, despite a few pounds she had put on. At this point Gene knew he was going to be faced with another dilemma. This would be one of a moral issue, which was a rarity for him.

Lori could not be another Jessica, Bradley or the two Belizean women in Springdale. Without a doubt in Gene's mind, Lori's situation became complicated. This decision required additional planning.

Insignificant conversation filled the remainder of the evening. It was obvious that each was ready for the conclusion of the dinner date. Both knew there was work to be done, but their agendas differed considerably.

The time Lori had been waiting for had finally arrived. Dinner was over, and it was finally time to leave the presence of the monster that killed Bradley Dean.

"I will walk you to your car," Gene said as they exited the restaurant.

"That you so much, Gene, I really enjoyed the dinner and seeing you again."

"It was my pleasure, dear," Gene replied. *"But there is one more item I need to discuss with you."*

At that time, Gene reached into his jacket pocket and produced a five-by-seven photograph for her to view.

228

Lori's facial color faded to pale and her breathing paused, as she caught the image on the picture.

"Yes, my dear, your buddy: Federal Investigator Robert James!"

CHAPTER 57

Robert sat in his office as time slowly passed. Nine o'clock, ten, ten forty-five, eleven, midnight.

"Maybe my pager batteries are low," he thought.

Robert then picked up the phone and dialed his pager number. Several beeps and a number appeared on the pager in a matter of seconds.

"And I know the phone works," Robert was now talking aloud.

It is ten minutes after 1:00 and still not a word from Lori. Robert knew he had thrown his lamb to the wolf.

CHAPTER 58

Running on only a few hours of sleep, Robert welcomed the sunrise. The other members of the team would awaken, and things would begin to happen.

At 7:45 a.m., Robert's home phone rang. It was Special Agent Michaels responding to his page.

"We have a situation boss. We need to get the guys in a soon as possible," Robert advised.

"Gene King?"

"Yes sir, Gene King."

"Robert, I am in route to the office. I will put this new cell phone to work and will start calling the team while on my way in."

"See you there, Boss Man," Robert concluded.

Since he had been up most of the night, Robert had already showered and shaved; he was out the door in minutes.

Shortly before nine, the entire JDLST team was assembled in the conference room. Robert briefed SA Michaels of the events, beginning from the time he received the video to Lori's disappearance. Special Agent Michaels knew Lori was a vital element to this investigation and would be needed to testify later in court. Her demise could greatly hamper any past work on the Gene King case.

The two men joined the other team members in the conference room.

"Men, it's game time," SA Michaels began. *"Robert is going to begin briefing you, and afterwards I will be making assignments. It's going to be a long day, gentlemen."*

Without saying a word, Robert walked to the small cabinet in the conference room which housed the television and VCR. He quickly inserted the tape that contained Bradley Dean's testimony concerning the King.

"Guys, take out your crayons and Big-Chief pad; this is some good stuff."

Without any further ado, Robert began the tape. All of the investigators in the room had knowledge of Bradley Dean's death, and some were currently participating in the investigation. To see a dead man talking on TV caused feelings of eeriness in each person's stomach. They had all seen the pictures of Bradley's lifeless and abused corpse, a sight much different from what was before them now.

For the next thirty minutes, silence filled the room. This was a room occupied by some of law enforcement's finest, who had experienced many different aspects of the good, bad and ugly of life. None of these men could recall working someone who led a life so dark and filled with crime, as Gene King. Now, each knew the days, weeks and months that were spent working this demon was a worthy endeavor. To rid society of Gene King would make the world a safer place.

After the video, Robert gave the investigators the opportunity to ask questions; there were none. Each man knew it was time to dethrone the King.

"We have one more item of concern," Robert added. *"My informant, Lori Sims, is missing. I had her meet with Gene last night to gather evidence regarding the Dean murder, and I have not heard from her. I have no doubt that Gene is holding my informant against her will, and if this is the case, her life is definitely in jeopardy."*

Special Agent Michaels began to make the assignments.

"Robert, find your typewriter and get the paperwork started. We now have enough evidence to put this guy away for life. Once we have a federal warrant for Gene's arrest, we can really get this ball rolling."

"Got it, boss!"

"The rest of you guys hit the streets. We need to locate Gene and put a lid on him. Once we have that clown in custody, the chances are we can find Lori. Now get to work."

In a matter of minutes after Special Agent Michaels gave his directive, the office was practically clear. The lone tapping of a typewriter could be heard coming from Investigator James' office.

Within a few hours, Robert completed the arrest warrant for Gene King and had it before a federal judge in Dallas.

"Very interesting, Investigator James," the judge remarked. *"How does a five-million-dollar bond sound to you?"*

"Is there any way we can no-bond him, Your Honor? Gene is a multi-millionaire with international connections. If he has the opportunity to bond out, I have concerns he will flee the country, and to a non-extradition country."

"I usually don't do this young man, but in this case, I believe Mr. King deserves this judgment. You have it, then. No bond for Gene King."

As soon as Robert exited the courthouse, he immediately communicated to his boss and colleagues that an arrest warrant was secured. The search for Gene King could be put in full gear. Local, state and federal law enforcement agencies could be notified. If he had any encounters with a law enforcement official, Gene would immediately be arrested, which may possibly save Lori's life.

The day seemed to drag. There was no word from Lori and the other investigators were coming up blank. By 11:30 P.M., Agent Michaels called everyone into the office. After a short de-briefing, each investigator was sent home.

"Tomorrow is a new day, Robert, and Gene will be ours."

"Boss, we've got to find Lori before that monster kills her!"

"I know, Son, I know. Robert, go home and try to get some rest."

Special Agent Michaels left their dark headquarters, knowing that Robert's office would probably remain lit for hours to come.

Just fifteen miles to the west of Robert's office was DFW Airport. In a plush hotel room located on airport property, were Gene and Lori. Lori sat in silence; horrified to move or speak. Gene was three feet from her, nestled up to the table where they both sat. In four small, neat rows were thin-white lines of cocaine. With a miniature straw in hand, Gene methodically positioned it in front of each row and one by one, sucked the power into his nostrils. Going back for seconds, he was assured not to leave any residue behind. It would be obvious to anyone he encountered that Gene had just anointed his nostrils with cocaine. The white crust under each was the tale-tale sign.

With bloodshot eyes, the King turned toward his captive and spent a few seconds just staring at her.

"Well, well, well; my dear, Lori!" Gene said in a loud boasting voice. *"I have come to a decision. Tomorrow, you and I are boarding a jet and heading south. How does Belize sound to you?"*

Lori refused to reply.

"This is how I see it. Right now, I cannot do to you what I really want to, you little bitch, so we are going to take a trip together. If you try anything stupid, here is what will happen. Regarding that little cop-boyfriend of yours, my boys know where he works and what he looks like. Upon my orders, or if I'm incarcerated, he is a dead man. Tomorrow, you and I will be boarding a commercial jet to Belize. If you attempt to alert law enforcement, I will take this silver metal pen here and ram it deep into your stomach. The wound will not be extensive enough to cause you to die, but there will be a death involved."

Gene paused, awaiting a reply from Lori but still, there was none.

"And, Lori, I have a reputation to maintain, but being a baby killer is not one that I want."

234

Lori's eyes opened wide with amazement, but she remained silent. It was obvious that Gene knew, but she did not want to give him the satisfaction of acknowledging his comments. To engage in a debate would be fruitless. Lori knew better. Too many times in the past she observed one of Gene's little "disciplinary sessions", with one of his disobedient flock members. While he verbally and physically abused the recipient, the more they begged for mercy, the more intensive the punishment became. Like a predator in the wild, begging only empowered him, therefore, resulting in an elevation of punishment. For self-preservation, Lori continued her stance of silence.

"You're going to be a mommy, aren't you, Ms. Lori?"

Lori still refused to speak, but nodded her head in an affirmative manner.

"Once we arrive in Belize, we will stay long enough for you to have that little child. Being the nice person that I am, I promise to find a good home for Cop-Junior. Then, you will have to answer to The King, BITCH!"

The pregnant mother remained silent.

CHAPTER 59

It was another short night for, Robert, and there was still no word from Lori. Gene King was a killer and Lori has compromised his operation. Robert's hopes for Lori's survival were beginning to diminish.

Shortly after dawn, Robert was back at the office. In less than an hour, the night owls of the JDLST team were all present and working away, except for Blake Waterman. They all knew time was most essential in this case. The passing of each hour moved Gene King closer to becoming a fugitive and most likely in a non-extradition country. With his money and connections, Gene would be gone forever. As for Lori, no one wished to think about what she might be going through.

"Everyone in the conference room ASAP," SA Michaels yelled out.

Coming from a man who was the poster boy for 'cool, calm and collected', each investigator easily identified the urgency coming from their boss.

"Yesterday evening, Mike Bales embarked on a little road trip to Florida. Once there, he and the Coast Guard began tracking Gene's ship. Apparently, the vessel left its safe- haven in international waters and is now rounding the tip of the Florida Keys. That floating den of iniquity is now under the jurisdiction of the United States. Mike also hooked up with some DEA and ATF Agents in Miami, who advised they too have been monitoring the activities on Gene's ship. To make things a little more interesting, there are apparently two U.S. Senators on board right now."

"Any word, Boss, about Lori or Gene being on the ship," Robert asked.

"Nothing yet, but we think that after the senators finish their game and are put ashore, the boat will head to Belize. We can only hope that your boy and Lori are on board," SA Michaels replied.

Robert slightly moved his head to imply that he acknowledged SA Michael's comments. Robert was afraid that if he spoke his voice would reflect his pessimistic thoughts.

"Here's the plan, guys. We have a company jet ready for us at Dallas Love Field. Get your raid gear and let's get down to the detective cars ASAP. You are authorized Code-3. We need to get to the airport quickly. Men, we're going to Florida."

Oh, hell, I have to fly! Robert thought after hearing the orders from his boss.

As Robert quickly grabbed his raid gear, he came to peace with the fact that this was a better time than any to put his fear of flying behind him.

"Lori, this one is for you."

Robert noticed his pager was going off. A number followed by 1976. It was Chad. He was probably in town looking for a few weeks of partying in the Big-D.

"Sorry, pal, not right now." Chad's page went unanswered.

As Robert drove to the airport, the usual thrill of running Code-3 was absent. This young investigator was totally consumed with thoughts and concerns for the welfare of his informant. Even the unyielding drivers on the roadway did not seem to bother him this time.

A row of Mercury sedans with lights flashing and sirens screaming entered the property of Dallas Love Field Airport. The lead car, being driven by Special Agent Michaels, veered off to a remote hanger that stood about one-fourth of a mile from the main terminal. There were no markings on the hanger. Inside, two helicopters and three small jets sat; none that revealed even a speck of dust on the shells.

237

One jet sat with doors open and a fueling truck with hoses attached. Obviously, this was their flying limo. A man dressed in slacks and a polo shirt appeared in the doorway, with a head set in place.

"Get your asses in here, boys," the pilot said in a light hearted but demanding way. *"We have a ten-minute window to blast off before things start getting busy."*

Robert looked around, noting that several members were missing. Mike Bales, of course, was in Florida. After scanning the plane one more time, Robert noticed another member was absent.

"Where in the hell is Blake Waterman? I just saw him right before we left. I wonder if he is afraid to fly, too? Robert silently thought."

"Strap it in boys," the pilot ordered. *"I understand you guys need to get to Florida ASAP, so I will be pushing this bird a little along the way."*

Robert sat in silence, clinging to the seat as the jet taxied toward the runway.

Due to the lack of doors that normally separated the cockpit from the passenger cabin, all aboard could hear the captain and his co-pilot communicating to the control tower.

"Federal Air 30 to Dallas Love, requesting priority clearance to take off."

"Dallas Love to Federal 30, you're clear. Proceed to runway 3."

"10-4, affirmative Dallas Love."

In a moments time, Federal Air 30 was airborne and expediting its cargo south toward Florida.

Robert spoke very little during the trip. With eyes closed, he was trying to convince the others he was sleeping, which was certainly not the case. Robert was petrified, but he knew it would be over soon.

Ninety minutes later, Special Agent Michaels stood up and began briefing his men.

"Once we hit the runway in Miami, DEA will be there to pick us up. Robert, you should be happy to hear that the remaining trip will be made in helicopters. That is the only way we can expedite our way to the Keys."

Oh, boy. The fun never ends," Robert thought.

"Once we get to the Keys, the Coast Guard will have a couple of their interceptor boats there waiting for us. We will split up into teams. Some of us will remain in the choppers and the others will go by water. The choppers and boats are used for drug interdiction, so all will be armed with enough firepower to take out anything we might be confronted with."

"Are there any questions," Michaels asked.

Silence filled the room.

The roar from the jet's engines began to soften. Robert sat in the last row of seats in the aircraft, which was close to the three engines that propelled it. After a while, the constant noise pacified the nervous flyer. Robert noticed each noise and movement since taking off. Even though this was Robert's first flight, he did have knowledge about flying and the little bumps and noises that one might encounter along the way. This information came from the numerous friends and family members who tried to convince Robert to fly over the past years. Even his father, who is pilot, could not get him aboard a plane.

Robert felt the jet descending. This, along with the engines being powered-back, led him to believe a landing was soon to come.

"Should I look out the window now?"

Almost simultaneous to Robert's thoughts, the pilot made his announcement.

239

"We will be landing in about five minutes, men. You people need to buckle up. You never know where I will be putting this bird down," he said in a joking manner.

It was now or never. Robert then reached over to his window and slowly opened the blind. In almost a childish manner, he moved close enough to look outside.

His glance revealed the City of Miami in a way that had previously been unimaginable.

"Damn, it's beautiful! Maybe I can get used to this flying gig after all."

As soon as their jet touched down in Miami, the group was off to the waiting choppers. On board were DEA Agents, along with Coast Guard personnel. A few minutes later the choppers were in the air and southbound.

Only a short time passed before the group touched down at the Coast Guard facility in Key West. The trip was so fast that Robert's fingers did not have the chance to go numb from clenching his fists.

It was now game time!

CHAPTER 60

The night sky captured the outline of two Coast Guard interceptor boats moving rapidly through the waters off the shores of the Florida Keys. Hovering overhead and supplying a stealth-like support were two Stingray Interdiction Helicopters. All four vessels were armed with weaponry that was capable of sinking any combative craft that they might encounter, short of a submarine or military destroyer. Aboard all four of the crafts were teams of federal agents, armed with nine-millimeter sub-machines guns, an assortment of assault rifles, along with their forty-five caliber, semi-auto pistols. A ship the size of Gene Kings would take a large group of officers to secure. The men aboard each craft knew what kind of trials may be in store for them once entry is made on the ship.

Robert James sat in one of the Coast Guard boats, his mind racing in many directions. An investigation that had taken years to complete was finally coming to head. The body count now totaled at least six. Over a dozen of Gene's drug operations have been raided. Property and cash were confiscated and many of his operatives were arrested. Now, it is time for the "king fish" to be caught.

"And, please, God, let me find Lori safe and unharmed," Robert softly pleaded as his stared into the night sky.

Conducting a search or arrest warrant on the ocean waters is always a risky venture, due to the element of surprise being practically impossible. The darkness of the night aided the federal officers, but as the boat and helicopters approached, they would probably be detected.

As the boats approached Gene's ship, a forty-six-foot speedboat was also coming in from the south. About the time the boat reached its destination, they apparently spotted the incoming Coast Guard vessels.

The boat quickly pulled away from Gene's ship and took off to the south with engines roaring.

"Air Unit 3 to all units, we will be in pursuit of the runner."

Despite reaching speeds of approximately ninety-knots, the boats twin motors were no match for the pursuing Stingray Helicopter. The chopper was soon directly above the fleeing boat, with a large flare light illuminating the craft and its occupants.

"We are United States Federal Agents; stop your boat immediately!" the voice over the load speaker rank out.

There was no response as the boat's skipper continued his attempts to elude his pursuer.

"We are United States Federal Agents. Stop your boat or we will use deadly force against you."

The powerful order was once again given. The boat continued south, refusing to heed to their verbal warnings.

When the voice commands could not accomplish the task, two shots from the helicopter's sixty-two-millimeter guns did. Though warning shots were fired, the fleeing boat skipper knew the next rounds would not miss. The boat's engines soon became silent, as it coasted to a halt.

A Coast Guard support vessel soon arrived at the scene to relieve the chopper, so the chopper could proceed to Gene's ship.

"Air Unit 3, we will take it from here," the Coast Guard Captain advised over his radio.

With these words, the chopper made an about-face and sped back toward Gene's ship.

Coast Guard officials swiftly boarded the once fleeing boat and took the crew and occupants into custody. In most cases, this type of scenario would produce a large cargo of illegal drugs from Central American, most likely cocaine. This was not the case tonight. Besides the crew, six young women were on board, later discovered to all be from the country of Belize.

"Human trafficking," the Captain told the others over the radio. *"These guys are running women from Belize."*

These words caused more pieces of the puzzle to fall in place.

"Take them into custody. I need their testimony," Robert replied to he Coast Guard Captain.

"10-4, we will hold them for you, along with the boat."

"A nice little forfeiture," Robert said aloud. The others agreed.

The choppers and Coast Guard vessels finally reached the destination. The helo-pad was large enough to land both choppers; upon doing so, federal agents poured from them like ants from a mound.

The four teams invaded the ship's interior. Robert was assigned to a team that would search the lower left section of the ship. Through several doors and down flights of stairs, Robert and five other agents went. They were dressed in black fatigues with the reflective words "Police-Federal Agents" embossed on their shirts. There would be no mistake as to the identity of these late-night callers.

Robert's team continued storming the rooms in their assigned areas. The first two men making entry would begin a left-to-right sweep of the room. Once the area was cleared, the others would begin to search closets and under furniture to assure no one was hiding. Safety and security was the first concern, then would come the time-consuming process of collecting all possible evidence.

Ahead was another door. Until now, Robert and his team members had yet to encounter anyone. This was soon to change.

As two of the team members entered the next room, loud commands rang out.

"Federal Officers, put your hands in the air!"

Obviously, a human encounter occurred.

"Get in here, guys, ASAP!" one voice rang out in an excited manner.

Robert and the other men then entered the room. Initially, one would have thought they were in the medical bay of a naval ship. This room had the appearance of a hospital operating room. Clean floors, surgical equipment and bright lights. What Robert saw next would make anyone stop in his or her tracks!

A young woman was lying on a steel hospital bed, conscious but under a local sedative. Her stomach had been cut open just a short distance below her navel, stretching from one pelvic bone to the other. A man was standing in front of her, still holding a large bag with an unknown substance in it. The exterior of the container had the consistency of a breast implant, and the entire size of the object was about twice that of a basketball. When the officers entered the room, the male was about to insert the synthetic sack into the stomach of the woman. The man immediately identified himself as Dr. Bob Perez, most likely to prevent himself from being shot.

It all made sense Robert. The pregnant women from Belize; were being used as drug mules. With the help of Dr. Perez, each female would take on the appearance that she was pregnant. This would only be after Dr. Perez implanted each one with a synthetic bag containing illegal drugs.

"Sew her up right now," Robert shouted to Dr. Perez. **"And you better pray that you do it right, or I will shoot your ass right where you stand!"**

There was no need for Robert to repeat the demand to Dr. Perez, who immediately began to reverse the surgical procedure on the woman.

"We have two more over here," another agent shouted out while securing an attached room. He soon revealed two other young Central American women, who were apparently awaiting the same procedure.

Robert removed a knife from his belt and took possession of the large implant that Dr. Perez had been holding when the team made their entry. He made a small cut, which allowed him to inspect the substance that was contained in the synthetic sack. Small pills; thousands of them.

"Formula-X men, we have Formula-X here," Robert shouted aloud.

Dr. Perez soon completed sewing up his patient, at which time Robert took custody of him. A short interview ensued with the doctor describing to the investigator how Gene was using women from Belize to smuggle drugs, mostly cocaine and Formula-X, into the United States and other countries.

The doctor continued by outlining how the procedure worked. He would first make an incision that was semi-invasive. The synthetic sack filled with the drugs would then be implanted between the woman's skin and muscles, giving her the appearance of being pregnant. Once this procedure was completed, the doctor would escort the female to her destination. He would then remove the implant and surrender the drugs to the buyer. Within a few days, the female was feeling fine and on the road to a full recovery.

Robert and the others stood in awe.

"Un-friggin-believable," one agent replied.

"And how long have you and Gene been doing this, Dr. Perez," Robert asked.

"Way too long, officer, way too long."

"Let's take these guys and head to the main deck," the team leader advised.

With an injured woman on their hands, the journey up the stairs and onto the main deck was slow and laborious. Finally, the six officers, three women and their prisoner (the doctor) arrived. By this time, the entire ship had been searched. At first count, it appeared that the agents had about fifteen in custody. Contraband, illegal drugs and cash were plentiful.

Robert began scanning the crowd. Once, twice, three times, but there was no Lori or Gene King.

"Special Agent Michaels," Robert had caught the attention of his boss. *"What about Lori and Gene?"*

"Neither are here, Robert; I'm sorry."

"Let's get the injured women on one of those choppers and get them to a hospital," SA Michaels ordered.

"Teams one and two, escort the prisoners to the Coast Guard vessel below and let's take them ashore for questioning," Michaels continued with his orders. *"And the rest of you guys start processing this evidence."*

Obviously, a long night was in store for the investigators. Despite the success of the raid, Robert was disappointed with one portion of the results. No one had any idea where Lori and Gene were. At this point, Robert was beginning to assume the worst for his informant.

CHAPTER 61

For Gene King, the hours of the night seemed to pass quickly, which was not the case for Lori Sims.

Despite being in an euphoric state of mind, Gene had enough sense left that he knew the continued use of cocaine was necessary to allow him to flee the country in an expeditious manner. If he quit using coke now, his body's natural metabolism would take over, causing him to slip into a slumber that would last at least twelve hours, and Lori would escape and alert the authorities. The cocaine would keep his sleep-deprived body in over-drive gear, therefore, allowing the completion of the mission. He would rest once they arrived in Belize.

From across the table, Lori was a spectator to a drug-crazed man. The "King Gene" that she once knew, no longer existed. Obviously, her once former lover and boss had been reduced to a junkie. The man, who in the past lived by the motto of not mixing business with pleasure, had taken a wrong turn. Lori knew Gene's world was crashing down around him and she too would probably be one of his victims.

Two more lines of coke were just sucked into Gene's nostrils. He became so involved in satisfying his lust for the powder, that Gene did not notice that Lori fell asleep in her chair. Once he did, she was allowed to continue to sleep, only because Gene was self-absorbed in his pleasures and did not want to be interrupted.

The sun was beginning to shine its rays through the thin, morning clouds to the east.

"Let's go, let's go!" Gene shouted to his sleeping captive.

Lori suddenly awoke to the sight of a wild-eyed maniac. There was no guessing how much cocaine Gene had ingested while she was sleeping.

"The first flight to Belize leaves DFW in about an hour. We need to make that flight, Lori."

Gene then held up a metal writing pen and dangled it in front of the pregnant woman.

"Remember, nothing stupid, Mommy!" Lori completely understood.

The two exited the hotel and boarded one of the transit trains bound for Terminal-3, their destination.

The ride took about a minute. As the train was slowing to a stop, Gene observed three police officers standing close by. With about an ounce of cocaine in his system, his paranoia level was extremely elevated. A change of plans ensued.

"Just keep your seat. Our plans just changed," Gene ordered to Lori.

"We are going to get a rental car and take a drive."

Lori did not know how to translate this, but she asked no questions. She observed Gene reach into his travel bag and remove an object wrapped in a small towel. Lori knew he retrieved a small pistol, which was protocol for any venture outside his home. When flying, Gene carried the weapon to the terminal, where it would be dumped into a trash can before entering the building. The cost of a disposal weapon was not a concern for this wealthy criminal. His peace of mind was worth the expense. This weapon would remain on Gene, and he purposely revealed its existence to Lori.

Being in the presence of an armed, dope-crazed, paranoid, drug dealer was not a cozy feeling. At this moment, Lori knew her life was in grave danger.

CHAPTER 62

After the agents were approximately an hour into the evidence gathering process, Robert was approached by Special Agent Michaels. The classic sober look on his boss had now evolved into a smile, as he looked at his young investigator.

"What's up, Boss Man," Robert asked.

"I just got a phone call from Investigator Waterman. He is in Cedar Park, Texas, and has some company with him."

"Robert; Gene King is in custody."

Robert went blank.

As he began to speak, Special Agent Michaels interrupted Robert.

"And Lori is fine, son. Not a scratch on her."

Robert turned his head and walked away. His eyes were swelling, and water was beginning to trickle from each corner. SA Michaels was not naive to what was occurring. His investigator was overcome with emotion. The biggest case of his life had come to a climax. One of a magnitude fit for the big-screen. The damsel in distress had been rescued. Special Agent Michaels knew if Lori became another of Gene's victims, Robert would hold himself responsible. That huge burden was lifted.

With his back toward his boss, Robert asked SA Michaels for the details.

"Well, Son, let me tell you a story. I am sure you noticed that Investigator Waterman was not on the plane with us when we left Dallas. Apparently, you were in too big of a hurry to hear that we had a visitor at the front desk who needed to speak to an agent ASAP. While you and the rest of the crew were rushing out the back door, Blake contacted the visitor. It turned out that the caller was a United States Intelligence Officer."

"Ever heard of Chad Cooper," Agent Michaels said smiling.

"Yes, sir, I do believe I have."

"Well I would hope so, because he certainly told Blake some interesting stories about you."

"That bastard," Robert said as both men broke out laughing.

"Please, continue, sir."

"Apparently during his last visit down here, you and Chad were discussing Gene King."

"Yes, sir, we were, and actually he gave me some excellent information about him."

"After your meeting, Chad went to the trouble of flagging Gene's air travel out of the country. A few weeks ago, Gene booked a flight to Thailand, where Chad happened to be on assignment. I am sure it was by total coincidence, but your buddy found Gene at a local strip joint and engaged in conversation with him. After Gene had some stiff drinks and inhaled a few Thai sticks, he and Chad formed a bond."

"Don't stop there," Robert laughed. *"I can picture that BS artist at work."*

"Gene was in Thailand for several reasons-to conduct a large jewelry transaction. After a few drinks, Gene needed to relieve himself, so he wandered to the men's room, leaving a briefcase loaded with jewels at the table with Chad. By chance, Chad had a new tracking device he was dying to try out in his pocket. It was a microchip transmitter, about

half the size and thickness of a dime. While Gene was in the restroom, Chad was able to insert the tracking device into his briefcase. Those intelligence guys get all the good toys."

"Go on, Boss, go on," Robert pleaded.

"Chad was on leave in the U.S. and tried paging you after he arrived. Your buddy wanted to let you know what he had done to Gene. When you did not respond, he came to the office right about the time you were storming out the back door. After identifying himself to Investigator Waterman, Blake informed Chad what was occurring. This is when your friend told Blake that he could be of service to this investigation, but it would take several hours before he could return with the necessary equipment. Chad left the office. Apparently, his words to Blake appeared to contain enough validity that it convinced him to remain behind."

"About the same time, we were boarding this ship, Chad arrived at the office with some type of high-tech device that enabled him to track down Gene. Investigator Waterman then rounded up a posse and went to Cedar Park, where he found Lori and Gene in a hotel room."

"Apparently Mr. King crashed, due to a three-day cocaine binge he had been on. The SWAT officers were able to take him into custody without a shot fired. According to Blake, Gene was so out of it that he did not even wake up when the cops broke the door down."

"And Lori," Robert asked.

"Your informant was shaken up a little bit, but just fine. She is with Blake right now and they are in route back to Dallas. A couple of U.S. Marshals have Mr. King and they will babysit Gene until he is behind bars. Let's wrap things up and head home. We can turn this crime scene over to the Florida DEA boys and let them handle it from their end."

Robert nodded as his boss walked away.

Investigator James approached the Florida DEA agents and discussed the case and evidence handling. Without a doubt, the ship and all its possessions would be seized by the government and sold at auction. Gene King donated a few million to the operational budget of the feds.

"One last thing," Robert said to one of the DEA agents while they were parting. "The two girls from Belize that were in the surgery room; I need them to testify at Gene's trial. Can you put the ladies into a protection program and keep tabs on them until Mr. King goes to court," Robert asked.

"We certainly can; consider it done."

"By the way, a very commendable job, Robert. Great work!"

A wave of the hand and a smile was the only response Robert could muster. His adrenaline rush had subsided, and the day was finally taking its toll. Robert was ready for the plane ride home, but that would have to wait until tomorrow. Some clean sheets in a cool hotel room were foremost on his mind.

As Robert left the Coast Guard vessel, one of the crewmembers volunteered to take him to a local hotel. The ride went quickly, perhaps because he was dozing some while in route.

The room was clean and cool, just what was needed for a great night's sleep.

As Robert laid his head on the pillow, a smile covered his face. The voices that normally were begging for help had finally gone away. Their murders had been vindicated. Still bearing that smile of contentment, Robert faded into a deep sleep.

CHAPTER 63

The next day, Investigator Robert James returned to his office at the JDLST Headquarters in Texas. His first order of business was to contact Lori Sims. No longer was the word 'informant' synonymous to her name. To Robert, Lori had become much more. A professional woman who had taken a wrong turn in life, but who had the intelligence and fortitude to alleviate and leave behind the few wrong choices she had made.

"A person is not judged as much by the mistakes made, as by the way they recover from them."

This was an old saying that kept going through Robert's mind while thinking about Lori Sims.

On a personal note, this woman remained true to their secret. Robert never stopped thinking or worrying about the night with Lori, when he committed the one 'Cardinal Sin' a cop can make while working an informant. Lori remained true to their vow of confidentiality.

Lori Sims also won her right to freedom. Going above and beyond what was demanded of her from the Federal Prosecutor's Office. She was the Achilles tendon that was a key factor in toppling Gene King's empire. Most importantly, Lori almost paid the ultimate price during her last assignment. Robert could not deny that God exists, having witnessed Lori's rescue from one of the devil's own.

To Robert James, Lori evolved from the status of an informant to a friend, a confidant, and a person deserving utmost respect.

When Robert entered the JDSLT office, the first person he saw was Blake Waterman.

"Just the person I wanted to see, my hero," Robert said to his colleague.

For the next few minutes, the men engaged in a conversation about the apprehension of Gene King and the events that transpired to his capture.

"How is Lori, Blake?"

"She is fine, but maybe a little shaken-up. Someone was certainly watching over that lady, Robert."

With a nod of agreement, Robert began to excuse himself, telling his associate he needed to contact Lori and pay her a visit.

"Robert, I know you want to see her, but Lori is no longer here."

"The U.S. Marshall's Office immediately placed her into a witness protection program and whisked her away to some unknown location. I don't even know where she is, Robert. Lori wanted to see you, too, but that was not possible. The next time either of us will be able to speak with Ms. Sims will be at Gene's trial."

Robert understood, but these were not the words he wanted to hear. The young investigator just realized that for months, Lori had been the leading woman in his life. Robert just recognized that since meeting her, he had not even been on one single date. Something out of the norm, or maybe it was Lori that was out of the norm.

"And what about Chad Cooper, is he still around?"

"He's gone too, Robert. The last words he mentioned were something about too many women and too little time. He seemed to think that you would understand," Blake responded.

"Chad will be Chad."

Robert shook his head and laughed as he walked away.

CHAPTER 64

The chase was over. Gene King was in custody and it was time for the part of the job most law enforcement officers despise, the paperwork.

Multiple cases had to be put together. The charges involved organized crime, racketeering, human trafficking and manufacturing illegal drugs. In addition, there were the murders of Jessica and the two Belizean women in Springdale. In addition, thanks to DNA testing and a dead man's testimony, Gene will be prosecuted for Bradley Dean's death. Yes, Mr. King would visit the federal country club for the remainder of his life.

Once the criminal cases were ready for prosecution, civil forfeitures would have to be prepared. Gene's houses, properties, cars, boats, helicopters and financial assets would all be seized by the government and liquidated. Federal and state law allows law enforcement agencies to seize any tangible items derived from illegal moneys. Robert was going to do just that.

Investigator Robert James was faced with several weeks of paperwork. He worked no other cases until everything was prepared. For the next few weeks, the office of Investigator James would echo the ring of his typewriter.

There would be pauses though, when Robert would sit back, engaged in thoughts of his accomplishments and wonder about his ex-informant, Lori Sims.

CHAPTER 65

Only three months passed, and Gene King was headed to trial. Gene's attorney filed a Speedy Trial Motion, which is a law some attorneys use in hopes the cops and prosecutors have not fully completed their court preparations in cases of such magnitude. They were wrong though. Investigator James and the Federal Prosecutor's Office were ready.

Robert could not sit still. In an hour, the trial of Gene King would begin. Despite being the largest criminal case in his career, there was another reason he was so tense. In a few minutes, he and Lori Sims would be reunited.

Investigator James instructed the court bailiff to bring the star witness to him as soon as she arrived. Robert reserved a small conference room for this occasion. He wanted a few minutes alone with his Lori before they joined the other officers and witnesses in the conference room.

The wait was not long. Robert popped the cap to his diet cola and had a few sips of the cherished beverage, when the door opened. Two large men, U.S. Marshals, made entry.

"Are you Investigator Robert James," one asked.

"Yes. I am."

"We are Federal Marshals. May we see your ID and badge please," the same man demanded.

Robert quickly complied with his request, knowing what was to follow.

"We have a special package for you, sir. We will be waiting outside the door when your meeting is completed."

This was the moment for which Robert had been waiting months for. As the men moved aside, Lori Sims came into sight. Initially, not a word was spoken. As their eyes met, Lori broke into a slight gait and embraced her knight in shining armor.

They realized that watchful eyes were still present, and Lori pulled back and focused on Robert's face.

"I have someone I want you to meet, Robert," Lori said as she walked back toward the door.

At this moment, a third Marshal handed Lori a bundle wrapped in several small blankets-it was a baby!

"Please, close the door and give us a few moments of privacy," Lori ordered her three escorts.

The men complied with her orders.

"This is not the way I wanted this introduction to occur, but Robert; I want you to meet your daughter."

Lori handed the little bundle to her new father, stood back and awaited his reaction. Robert stood motionless a few minutes and a look of excitement erupted across his face.

"You like?"

Robert still could not speak, but Lori got her answer as she watched Robert's eyes cloud with tears.

"Ms. Sims," a Marshall said to Lori as he burst into the room. *"The Federal Prosecutor wants you in his office, ASAP."*

"Robert, we will talk about this more after trial, but do you think you can handle fatherhood," Lori asked.

Robert looked up and gave Lori an affirmative nod, as she and the child left the room.

As if a miracle occurred, the Federal Prosecutor entered the room of awaiting law enforcement officers and announced the trial was over. After Lori and the two young ladies from Belize testified, Gene's attorney asked for a recess and a meeting with the prosecutor. It did not take much to reach a plea-bargain agreement.

Gene King agreed to an offer of life imprisonment in a federal institution, along with forfeiting all his assets to the government. This alleviates Gene's chances of receiving a guilty verdict, along with an accompanying death sentence, which was a very strong possibility. The prosecutor accepted the agreement.

There was just one additional, but odd, request that Gene's attorney had made. Gene wanted to meet Investigator Robert James. Without hesitation, Robert agreed.

As the investigator entered the courtroom, he and Gene's eyes met immediately. Both knew who the other was without an introduction. Robert approached Mr. King.

"I just wanted to meet the man who dethroned the King," Gene said while extending a hand to Robert.

Robert looked at Gene, but refused to accept his gesture of a handshake.

"No hard feelings on my end, Investigator James. You were doing your job, and you did it well. I must tell you, though, if I had not started doing that nose candy, I would have never been caught. I was big, too big for an investigator from Springdale, Missouri."

"Have you ever read the Bible, Mr. King," Robert asked.

"Yes, I have."

"Then, I might recommend that in all of the spare time that you will now have, you might re-visit the story about David and Goliath."

Gene boiled with anger as the victorious investigator turned his back to him and left the courtroom.

As Robert entered the hallway, Special Agent Michaels and the two women from Belize were waiting for him.

"Investigator James, these two women would like a word with you."

With surprise, both spoke English fluently, and began by explaining to Robert how they were sisters, and their father had sold them both to Gene King. They had no choice but to carry through with their mule run; otherwise, Gene would probably have killed them both.

The conversation was filled with many thanks for rescuing them before the surgeries, but the women were also concerned about their return to Belize. If they returned, their lives would be in jeopardy for testifying against Gene. Even though he was now in jail, Gene's tentacles ran long and strong in Central American.

"Excuse me, please," Robert said as he stepped away from the women and approached Special Agent Michaels.

"Did you hear that, Boss Man? What can we do to help these women?"

"Well, Robert, they don't qualify for the Witness Protection Program, but, we did seize a ton of cash from Mr. King."

"Go on, Sir. You have my full attention here."

"Well, they do fall within our guidelines to financially reimburse an informant for their work. Would one-hundred-thousand dollars each work for them, Robert?"

"You bet, Boss."

"Then, the ladies are now your responsibility, so get them out of here," SA Michaels directed his investigator.

Before leaving, Robert had one more item he needed to tend to, Ms. Lori and his daughter. There was no doubt in Robert's mind that this baby was his. The sign and indicators of Lori being pregnant was defined in his mind, plus, without the words being said, Robert felt assured that Lori was in love with him.

Robert approached a U.S. Marshal he recognized as being one of Lori's bodyguards.

259

"*I need to see, Lori,*" Robert professionally demanded.

"*Sorry, Investigator James, but we have already taken her away.*"

Before Robert could respond, the Marshal handed him a business card with an address on the back. It was a local restaurant in North Arlington.

"*Be there at 7:00 sharp. We won't have much time, so please try to be prompt.*"

Robert took the card and walked back to the awaiting ladies.

CHAPTER 66

"Ladies, we need to go for a ride," Robert said as he pointed toward his car.

Robert proceeded to take the sisters to the evidence room and appropriated two-hundred-thousand-dollars of the money they seized from Gene King. Paying informants a percentage of a cash seizure is allowed under federal guidelines.

With a gym bag full of cash, Robert drove the women to one of the city's most luxurious hotels in downtown Dallas and turned off the car motor.

As they left, the women stood in anticipation as Robert opened the truck and recovered the gym bag. He handed the bag and contents to its new owners.

"Ladies, welcome to America, your new home. Here is my business card. Around the first of next week you need to stop by my office, and I will have IDs and passports with your new identities awaiting you."

The women acknowledged his orders, but they were somewhat oblivious. Both women were mesmerized by the Dallas skyline.

"Once again, welcome to America!"

Robert smiled at the sisters as he entered his car and drove away.

A glace in his rearview mirror reflected the two women standing in amazement, looking like children on their first trip to Disney Land. They were absorbing their newly found home; they were now free women.

Robert looked at his watch. It was almost 6:30 P.M. and he was still twenty miles away. With 7:00 P.M. imbedded in his mind, he raced down Interstate-30 to ensure his prompt arrival.

It was 6:55 when Robert pulled into the driveway of the restaurant. While trying to find a place to park, he noticed two men exiting a Ford Crown Victoria, with windows tinted. It was obvious who these men were, U.S. Marshals.

Robert parked next to the officers, and recognized them from their earlier courthouse meeting.

"Is Lori in there," Robert asked as he peered into their car.

"No, Investigator James, she isn't. Our orders were as soon as the trial concluded that we transport Lori to her new home. She has been relocated under the Witness Protection Program, and we are not allowed to divulge her location, not even to another law enforcement officer."

Robert's face immediately reflected his disappointment, as he stood silent.

"But we do have a package for you, Investigator James."

At that time, one of the marshals reached into the car and pulled out an infant's car seat, which contained a small child.

"Lori's gift to you, Robert; and here is some accompanying paperwork. It is time for us to go, sir. It was a pleasure meeting you."

The marshal extended his hand and shook Robert's, who was standing in silence, with baby in hand.

As their car drove off, Robert took his daughter and placed the infant into the car next to him. A large envelope was given to him, which was stuffed with paperwork. Robert slowly opened it and noticed a smaller sealed envelope among the assortment of legal documents. The envelope reflected the words 'To Robert James – Personal'. The enveloped contained a short letter.

Dear Robert,

This must be short, and I apologize for not being able to tell you these words in person. Last year when I was arrested in the lab, I thought that to be the worse night of my life. Instead, it soon became the turning point in my life. I was traveling down the wrong path and I knew it; I just had no way to break the chains of Gene King. I was caught up in his spider-web, to say. Then you came along and offered me a way out. Initially I was scared, knowing that my life was in jeopardy, but I knew this was my only way of getting out.

During the months we were working together, I must admit that I fell for you, Robert. That night in the hotel room in Dallas, I was not having sex with you; I was making love. Robert James, I have fallen in love with you.

A few weeks later, I realized that I was pregnant. I wanted to tell you, but I did not want to derail your efforts of dethroning Gene. In addition, I knew that if this came out, it could be the end of your career. The Gene King case and many innocent victims needed the talents of one of American's best cops — which is you, Mr. James. As much as I wanted to, I could not be selfish.

Living on the run in a witness protection program is not the life I want for my child. I have enclosed all the legal documents that you need to show that you are the father. These include the DNA tests results, along with paperwork reflecting I have surrendered my rights as a parent. Robert, I want my child to grow up with her father in America and not with a mother on the run on foreign soil.

Someday, Mr. James, we will be reunited. Until then, I want you to know that I love you. Please find a way to convince our child that her mother loves her, too.

Until then, Robert;

Lori

Robert reached down and grabbed his cell phone. His mind was overflowing with thoughts to the point that he could barely recall his boss's phone number.

"Boss Man, this is, Robert. Would you object to me taking a few weeks off? I am hoping to make it back to Missouri to do a little deer hunting."

"Not two weeks; but how about four? You have a ton of comp time that you need to take. Enjoy your vacation, and Robert — one hell of a job, Son!"

"Thanks, Boss, see you next month."

263

CHAPTER 67

The next morning, Robert was packed and in route to Missouri, with an infant daughter by his side. Being a young, single father with no parenting experience was a scary thought, which is why a visit with his father was much needed. Dad managed to raise his kids alone, so perhaps there were some pointers he could pass along.

Highway-75 through South Oklahoma at twilight revealed a spectacle of radiant lights reflecting from the few clouds that were floating above. They seemed to line his route back home.

Robert could not keep his eyes off his daughter. Being a cop, Robert knew that the child seat should be in back, but he wanted his prized possession next to him.

At this point in Robert's life, all was well. Thoughts about his new daughter, and Lori, brought a chin-to-chin smile to his face.

"And Gene King, Investigator Robert James kicked your ass!"

Another smile broke across Robert's face, as he looked at the new cell-phone lying on the seat next to him.

"Should I?"

The cell-phone keys began singing ten digital-tones. 214-999-3222.

"Agent Michaels, may I help you?"

"Boss Man, this is Robert; I have a question."

"Oh God, should I sit down, Robert?"

264

"No sir, it's not that bad. Well, hum, there is one thing about this job that bothers me, Boss."

"You have my full attention; continue."

"I am having a hard time with this 'Investigator James' title."

"And what might you be suggesting then, Investigator?"

At this moment, Agent Michaels knew Robert's next sentence before it was spoken.

"Robert, let me guess. You miss the title of "Detective", don't you?"

"Yes, sir, I do."

"Well, you arrogant little ass. You come into my unit, crack a huge case and expect favors?"

Robert was silent, being unable to translate the boss's response.

"See you next month, Detective Robert Lee James," Agent Michaels replied in a light-hearted tone. Without another word, they disconnect the call.

Yes, Detective James!

The highway had few cars, making the drive easy. Robert noticed a pickup truck that had been behind him for some time, but finally passed. The truck became a nuisance, with its four-wheel drive and lift kit, making its headlights invade Robert's vehicle. Finally, it was gone.

"What an idiot!" Robert remarked, as he noticed a vehicle traveling southbound toward him with high beams blaring.

Robert then flashed his headlights on and off several times, in an attempt to get the on-coming vehicle to dim his. No luck.

The truck began to slow as it approached Robert's pickup.

"What the hell!"

There was a man leaning out the window, with a shotgun extended.

The muzzle flash was almost blinding, as the gunpowder exploded, propelling buckshot into Robert's vehicle. The gunshot hit its mark. The fleeing shooter could see Robert's vehicle coasting to the shoulder of the road and coming to rest in a ditch. This was apparently a successful mission for the assailant.

The ringing in Robert's ears erased the night's silence. Fortunately, there was not a sound from the baby, who remained in a deep slumber next to her father.

There was no blood and no injuries, just a crippled vehicle resulting for the incident. An unsuccessful attempt at Robert James' life occurred.

"You should have killed me, asshole! You made a huge mistake; you almost hurt my child!"

Robert shouted as he watched the suspect vehicle speed away.

"Someday, you and I will meet again, and I will be sending you BACK TO HELL!"

About the Author

Author Ronald (Ron) Long was born and raised in the Ozark Hills of Southern Missouri. After graduating from high school, Ron attended college at Central Missouri State University (CMSU) where he obtained a Bachelor of Science Degree in Criminal Justice Administration and later entered the CMSU Master's program.

In his second year of college, Ron diverted his goal of attending law school to that of focusing on a law enforcement career. After graduating from CMSU, he accepted a full-time position with the St. Robert, Missouri Police Department, where the author's exhilarating law enforcement career began. Two years later, Ron moved to Texas where he spent 26 years of combined service with the Arlington Police Department, the Tarrant County Sheriff's Office (Ft. Worth) and the Travis County Sheriff's Office (Austin). While in Texas, Ron was also very active in the insurance fraud arena and served as a senior investigator with Texas Farm Bureau.

The author's law enforcement career consisted of a variety of jobs: working patrol, a general assignment's detective, along with a tenure as an undercover investigator in the Vice, Narcotics and

Organized Crime Unit. Ron's duties also encompassed an array of supervisory assignments, ranging from a Field Training Officer to the rank of Major.

After a rewarding career in Texas, Ron returned to his home state of Missouri, where he was elected the Pulaski County Sheriff. The author recently retired from law enforcement on January 01, 2017, at which time he returned to Texas with his family and is now enjoying his new career as a full-time author and educator.

During his 37-year tenure in the criminal justice profession, Ron received numerous individual awards relating to law enforcement and insurance fraud, along with serving as a member and elected officer to a multitude of professional organizations and governmental boards. In 2016, the author had the privilege of being a Merit recipient of the American Police Hall of Fame.

Ronald Long has also written articles for numerous professional publications and media outlets, along with authoring the following two crime novels:

- ***Drugs Without the Sugar – America's Addiction*** *(Non-fiction, drug education)*
- ***The Devil's Elbow Project*** *(crime novel)*